Jo Brand is a stand-up comic with many TV and radio shows to her name. She is married with two children and lives in South London.

Praise for Jo Brand:

'What the hell, pass me one of life's cream cakes – that new book by Jo Brand will do'   *Guardian*

'A lovely amusing walk down memory lane'   *Daily Echo*

'Anyone growing up in the seventies will relate to this tale of teenage friendships, parent trouble, boyfriends, sexual fumblings and punk. At the same time wonderfully funny and sad, it has a twist that will keep you riveted to the last page. A great book to read on holiday . . . or anywhere else for that matter!'

Nottingham Evening Post

'Funny, but very poignant'   *Lancashire Evening Post*

'Wickedly funny . . . Some of the situations she describes will stick in the mind forever . . . the fragility and strength of relationships, whether it be between family or friends, is beautifully explored'   *Eastern Daily Press*

'Slickly funny tale of subtle one liners . . . Told with Brand's own special drollness'   *Big Issue in the North*

'The queen of stand-up comedy is back with this hilarious novel'

Coventry Evening Telegraph

'Rude, crude and crammed with brilliant one liners'

'This no-holds barred, no langua
bad tale of our times packs as m
and is guaranteed to leave you

Northern Echo

Also by Jo Brand

Sorting Out Billy

It's Different for Girls

Jo Brand

review

First published in 2005 in Great Britain by HEADLINE REVIEW
An imprint of HEADLINE BOOK PUBLISHING

First published in paperback in 2006 by HEADLINE REVIEW

A HEADLINE REVIEW paperback

4

Cataloguing in Publication Data is available from the British Library

ISBN 978 0 7553 2230 5

Typeset in Caslon 540 Regular
by Palimpsest Book Production Limited,
Polmont, Stirlingshire

Printed and bound in Great Britain by
CPI Mackays, Chatham ME5 8TD
Headline's policy is to use papers that are natural, renewable and
recyclable products and made from wood grown in sustainable forests.
The logging and manufacturing processes are expected to conform to the
environmental regulations of the country of origin.

Headline Book Publishing
A division of Hodder Headline
338 Euston Road
London NW1 3BH

www.reviewbooks.co.uk
www.hodderheadline.com

To Matt and Bill, who are not Alan and Clive.

I would like to thank Vivienne Clore, Martin Fletcher, Lucy Ramsey, Catherine Cobain and everyone else that was helpful in the torturous production of this book. No more time to be eloquent – so sorry.

Prologue

December, 1979

A pair of outsize pink knickers blew lazily along Hastings pier like a stout flamingo trying to take off. As they came to rest by his wellingtons, Vince looked down and spotted some other party debris – crumpled mistletoe and a lonely, wrinkled condom.

'Bloody brilliant night,' he thought to himself and smiled.

'Oi, pig, what are you smiling at?' said one of his fellow anglers. The grin stayed on Vince's face, for it was not an insult. Vince Pigg knew his name sounded like a farmyard animal in a children's book, but he'd had plenty of years to get used to it.

It was Sunday morning and as he breathed in the smells of ozone and chip fat, despite his hangover, he was glad to be free for the day. As he stood on this rickety finger of iron pushing itself towards France, he was overcome by a sense of freedom; today was a day in which he had no responsibilities apart from throwing out his fishing line and eating his sandwiches.

Hastings at six-thirty in the morning looked so full of promise, with the half-light constructing a magical seaside town crowded with interesting architecture, clean pavements and the nostalgic shapes of fishing huts and castle. Of course, advancing daylight revealed a rather different story – a shabby façade, victim of many years of neglect and abuse. The East Sussex resort clung to the sea's edge like an old man in need of a good wash.

Flanked on one side by the bigger, more fashionable Brighton, and on the other by Rye – a quaint medieval town which seduced tourists into handing over their money as they trailed through its puzzle of rambling streets and 'olde' hostelries – Hastings decayed on. Its picturesque Old Town was the area of choice for visitors and drinkers, whilst its new town hid a series of social problems that would have trounced the East End of London in a Social Problems competition. Even the town's fame was misplaced, as the Battle of Hastings didn't actually take place there. William the Conqueror had landed further up the coast at Pevensey and had fought the *soi disant* Battle of Hastings at Battle. Therefore 1066 was really all about the Battle of Battle. Perhaps someone had said to William, 'Don't go to Hastings, the beaches are shit.'

As Vince cast his fishing line out onto the waves, he was aware that the sea beneath him sounded a bit different from its usual watery echo; only someone like himself, who had stood in this position for twenty years, would have noticed. There was a quiet, rhythmic slapping that didn't belong, although it was quite difficult to hear with all the bustle going on around, seagulls calling and Vince's transistor radio broadcasting *Farming Today*, his favourite programme. For a milkman, he was quite interested in milk.

Vince lowered himself to the ground and lay on his stomach peering through the planks of wood down towards the great ornate legs of the pier to see what he could see.

What he could see was a man's corpse gently knocking against one of the iron struts beneath him.

Chapter 1

7 Years Earlier

Saturday night's revelry had thrown up its normal catch of hungover citizens. Walking down George Street in the Old Town on a Sunday morning, there was usually at least one body left over from the night before, slumped in a doorway or on a bench. The Aquarius Nightclub – a dump which dispensed vodka and limes or light and bitters to anyone with a few quid in their pocket, was usually responsible.

On this beautiful August morning there were three bodies – two fishermen called Colin and Les, who did this most weekends, and a student from Eastbourne called Jerry who lay smiling contentedly, his memory of the night before completely wiped. As Vince Pigg wandered down the street towards the paper shop, he coolly assessed the consciousness level of each snoozing body, resisting the temptation to give each layabout a good kick up the arse to get them going.

Vince was usually really glad to get out of the house on a Sunday morning to go fishing and leave his family snoring in their beds. They were his adopted family – wife Terry, whom he had rescued from a violent and destructive marriage when the girls were four, three and one and a half, and now they – Jennifer, Kim and Susan – were in their teens and driving him insane. He feared metamorphosing into a dirty old man. He just couldn't seem to prevent phrases like 'burgeoning womanhood' floating into his head and wished bromide was available in the chemist's at the bottom of their road.

Vince bought a packet of twenty Number Six cigarettes, a *News of the World* and a can of Coke and headed down towards the seafront for a sit-down and a read before he had to get back to the Pigg household. Today, however, there could be no fishing.

The family were not, in fact, all snoring in their beds. Susan, the youngest, had been awake for ages. It was her thirteenth birthday – 15 August 1972. She was thinking about being called Susan Pigg and how much of a trial it had been so far. Ironically, it was her real dad who should have been called 'Pigg' because that's what he was, given that Wanker or Bastard weren't popular as surnames. And it was Vince who should have had the neutral name. Then again, she thought, serial killers usually had normal names until they were rechristened 'The Panther' or 'The Wolf'.

Her old surname used to be Evans which, unlike Pigg, was not a name to be comically bandied about in the play-ground. Susan had thought of reverting to it, but realising how much it would upset her mum, she put up with all the snorting and references to troughs and pork scratchings. What's more, Vince didn't knock her mum about and he gave her housekeeping money – a concept alien to Susan's real father Malcolm Evans, who could not have lived with himself unless he had spent any cash at the bookies or pissed it away in the pub.

Susan's first thirteen years had not exactly gone smoothly, her mother's marriage to Vince being the most traumatic thing that had ever happened to her. She had been eighteen months old when her dad left, and Vince hadn't married Terry until two years later, by which time Susan was right in the middle of toddlerhood. It had been a very grumpy day. Susan hadn't wanted to wear her bridesmaid's dress, and had deliberately covered it in tomato sauce. Then, seeing the ring left momentarily unattended on the hall table by Vince, she had dropped it into the cat's litter tray and sat back and watched the household go bananas. She was questioned several times about her involvement in the disappearance of this most essential of accessories for a wedding, but after half an hour genuinely could not remember what she had done with it.

Eventually, a substitute was found and the wedding went ahead, with most of the major players looking very surly. Susan put the finishing touches to everyone's temper at the reception when she pulled the tablecloth off the top table, bringing the wedding cake and other vol-au-venty delights cascading to the floor and giving Vince a reason to dislike her pretty much for the rest of her life. This destructive tendency never left Susan who, despite being both pretty and fairly bright, when given some big advantages, always saw to it that she pressed the FUCK IT UP button each time.

Other traumas in Susan's short life included being held under the water in the local swimming pool by a boy with a personality disorder and being bullied by a teacher at primary school – a sour-faced woman who had taken against her elfin face and carefree manner.

Apart from these incidents, the girl had arrived at her teenage years relatively unscathed.

Susan had planned a fantastic birthday for herself in her head but doubted it would happen. Vince, of course, had temporarily forgotten but Terry hadn't, although she had deliberately not reminded Vince of it today, because after ten years or so together, one of her few pleasures was winding him up.

Although Vince didn't actually know it yet, Terry had promised Susan she could have a small party on her own while she and Vince went out.

He'll go fucking mad, she thought to herself with relish, savouring the image in her head and considering when and how she would tell him. Vince was houseproud and borderline obsessional, and his brain would torture him all night as he conjured up images of coleslaw and cheesy footballs being trodden into carpets, pubescent couples snogging each other's faces off on his and Terry's bed, and his precious home-made beer being discovered in the garage and drunk or sprayed over the wallpaper he had so painstakingly stuck up in the lounge a year ago to the very day. Yes, it was the wallpaper's birthday as well, but only Vince remembered that.

'Ow!' The birthday girl was seized upon by her two sisters. 'Piss off,' she objected as they started the well-worn birthday ritual of dragging her very slowly out of bed by her feet,

'Piss off' didn't work so she tried hitting out wildly and caught Jenny in the chest.

'Christ, you silly cow!' shouted Jenny. 'I'll get breast cancer now.'

No one was really sure where the idea came from that a thump in the chest caused breast cancer, but it was certainly a widely-held belief among Jenny's teen-magazine-devouring friends.

'Come on,' said Kim. 'It's your birthday. Get up, do birthday things. Here you are.' She tossed a badly-wrapped present onto the bed. Kim was a fan of the Sweet and wished she'd got inside their dressing-room at the local nightclub where, it was rumoured, Karen Timson in Jenny's class had given the lead singer a blow job while he did his accounts.

Susan flew at it like a hyena and tore it apart. Some glittery nail varnish fell out onto the bed.

Terry put her head round the door. 'Happy birthday, love,' she said.

'Cheers, Mum,' said Susan.

'Come on – I've made you some breakfast,' said Terry. 'Are you coming down? Your dad'll be back with the paper in a minute.'

Susan resented the 'your dad'. Her real dad, whom none of them had seen since they left eleven years ago, was still her proper dad, despite everything.

Vince himself was a milkman who tolerated with good cheer the expectations of a general public who categorised him as barely able to control his libido when faced with a housewife clad in a Brentford's Nylons nightie. However, Vince was far too embarrassed to tell anyone that he had never actually once been propositioned on his rounds – a first, surely, in the twilight world of *doubles entendres* and nudge-nudge that milkmen share with vicars and nuns.

Susan went down and ate bacon and eggs, a rare treat and a change from the usual cereal and toast. Jenny, who was a Ryvita away from an eating disorder, looked on in barely disguised horror as what she assessed to be well over fifteen hundred calories slid down her little sister's throat. Susan was glad when Jenny left the room to go to the toilet so she could enjoy eating for once. Looking round the shabby room, with its crappy Vince wallpaper, she wished some people would magically turn up and redecorate it for her birthday.

Just then, Vince appeared at the door. 'Hello,' he said. 'What's going on here?'

'It's Susan's birthday,' said Terry, gloating.

'I know. Happy Birthday, love,' said Vince, barely missing a beat, kissing the girl and leaving the faint smell of fags, toothpaste, hair cream and Old Spice aftershave on her.

'Thanks,' Susan said, as ever studiously avoiding calling him Dad. It made life difficult, as it meant she could never directly address Vince and had to get his attention by other methods, like coughing or trying to catch his eye. She didn't like to call him by his Christian name either because she hated it. Only once had she been in a situation where she required him sharpish, on holiday in Devon when, as a nine year old, she had started to wobble and fall backwards off a five-bar gate. She needed a hand to pull her back, and Vince was nearest. Even in that split second, she could not bring herself to address him as 'Dad' but 'Vince' – which got her into trouble immediately afterwards, as only middle-class parents and hippies allowed their children to call them by their first names.

Susan often fantasised that her real dad was now a good man who, having fucked up his wife's and daughters' lives, had repented and gone abroad to work as a missionary. She hadn't quite managed to justify in her head why, after this Damascene conversion, he hadn't come back immediately to England to throw himself at their feet and beg their forgiveness, but maybe the authorities had prevented him leaving whichever South American country he was in because they needed him so badly and were worried he might never come back.

The sad facts were that he had ended up running a miserable pub in Hull with a woman called Tracey, more to fulfil their own drinking needs than anyone else's. Various half-hearted attempts by the brewery to shut it down had so far been unsuccessful, and Mal Evans and his girlfriend sank a little lower each day.

'So, Mum,' said Susan, as she sat at the breakfast table, 'is it all right for my party tonight?'

'What party?' asked Vince, turning from the telly.

'I said she could have a little party tonight,' Terry told him, affecting an air of nonchalance.

'What!' shouted Vince at a decibel level well above what Mr and Mrs Sanford, the elderly neighbours, could tolerate.

'You heard,' said Terry. 'Come on, misery guts, let her have a party.'

'They'll wreck the bloody place,' said Vince.

'Oh, come on, spoilsport,' said his wife. 'It'll be fine. You'll keep an eye, won't you, Jenny?' she asked her eldest.

'Course,' promised Jenny, who was thinking about taking her new bloke, Paul, into the garden shed and offering him rather more of herself than he'd been offered before.

'Course,' she said again. 'Don't worry, Dad.'

This was a tactical 'Dad' guaranteed to make Vince feel part of the family, and it had the required effect.

'Oh, all right then,' he said, 'but you must be finished by ten at the latest.'

This brought a chorus of protest.

'No point having a party if it's going to stop at ten,' said Susan sulkily.

'You're thirteen years old, for Chrissakes,' Vince snapped.

'Mum told us eleven,' said Kim, always pushing.

Terry hadn't said anything of the sort, but she supported this statement and it was agreed that she and Vince would go out for a meal, then a drink, and be back at eleven o'clock.

The rest of the day was spent in Sunday mode until at six o'clock Susan decided it was time to get ready for the party. She had invited a few friends from school who would do their best to rustle up some boys who could hold their drink and not collapse in an acnefied giggling heap as soon as a girl looked at them.

Susan had told Terry and Vince she would wear the dress they had bought her for her birthday, even though she hated it. Obviously Terry had nodded towards Vince's taste in the purchase of this dress, which would have looked much better on a ten year old. Or even a poodle. How on earth was she supposed to attract Marc Bolan lookalike Steve wearing *that*, she wondered gloomily.

Susan pretended as much enthusiasm as she could manage but her parents knew she didn't like it.

'But you'll wear it tonight just for me, won't you, sweetheart?' said Vince in a manner that both Terry and Susan thought came across as ever so slightly pervy, although Vince had intended it to sound manly and loving.

Terry and Vince set off out at about 7.30 p.m. They were going to a local Italian and had given the girls the telephone number, should they need it.

As soon as the car had disappeared round the corner, Susan ran up to her bedroom and ripped off Bo Peep's standby party dress which, apart from anything else, would have suffocated her on this muggy August night. She began to wind a piece of gorgeous Moroccan silk round herself.

'Kim!' she shouted. 'Give us a hand with pinning this, will you?'

'You're not wearing that, are you?' said Kim in a horrified voice, which disguised the fact that Susan looked amazing in it and several years older than she was.

Unfortunately, the Pigg girls' make-up routine was not the most professional, nor the most experienced. Jenny, who had plucked her eyebrows defiantly into a single line some weeks before ('You'll regret it when you're twenty-five and Denis Healey eyebrows are in,' said Terry), looked like a constantly surprised Joan Collins. Kim had overdone the ivory foundation and looked as though she had recently died, and Susan's eyelids bore the weight of so much glittery eye-shadow she looked like she'd had a stroke.

Various children began to arrive; the parents who stood on the doorstep expectantly waiting to see if a responsible adult was around dropped them off the earliest. Jenny was wheeled out for this purpose, having donned a grey school cardigan to cover the lack of true clothing over her chest area and some NHS glasses. The parents were impressed.

'Don't worry,' she would say soothingly, as three or four sets of slightly worried couples handed over their offspring who were about to be filled up with as much cheap alcohol as they could tolerate without dying. 'I have a direct line to my parents who will be home at nine thirty,' she told them reassuringly.

In all, roughly thirty kids had been invited but with the benefit of hearsay, by nine o'clock this number had swelled to fifty. Thankfully, Hastings's finest greasers were occupied elsewhere, although a couple of older teenage boys had sneaked in to check out the talent.

Any parent in any century who wonders whether they should give their teenage children a free rein in their house without them in it, knows what the ghastly truth is, and they should *never*, under *any* circumstances, indulge their offspring in this way. But parents like to hope and every opportunity taken by a parent is an opportunity trashed, as each child will set about laying waste to the trust and respect of his or her mum and dad.

And so it was with Susan, Jennifer and Kim. Although they didn't start the evening wanting to make their parents cry, that was the end result. It all started so well, too.

The parents were all gone by eight o'clock, although Alison Moor's parents lingered in the car outside in the road for half an hour to check whether the boy they suspected was penetrating their daughter at regular intervals had turned up at the party to do it again. Satisfied that he wasn't there, they drove home for a cup of tea for three-quarters of an hour until they went to pick her up again, little knowing that at that very moment their dearest daughter was lying on Terry and Vince's bed with her legs high in the air, laughing her head off underneath the very offender himself.

At first, the children had gathered nervously downstairs, girls in one room and boys in another, giggling and eyeing each other up even though they all knew each other very well. But with the benefit of alcohol, the great socialiser, things soon became more relaxed. The groups merged and the antics of the pre-adults began to spiral out of control in direct relation to the amount they had drunk.

Jennifer, because of her low weight and low tolerance for alcohol, normally managed to get virtually unconscious on a couple of glasses of wine. She didn't do that often though, because there were ninety calories in a glass of wine. However, she had decided to give herself a bit of a treat and sat as seductively on the arm of the settee as she could, chatting to a young man called Tel Townley who was desperately trying to work out whether she would snap in half if he lay on top of her. He didn't realise he was being played off against her new boyfriend, Paul, who was quietly fuming in the corner and planning violence should snogging start to occur.

Susan was upstairs in her room with her three best friends. She knew this was a contradiction because in theory you should really only have one best friend, a trusty companion who stuck to you like an amiable leech and tolerated all your flaws until you expired in their arms at the age of ninety, because your husband never made it past seventy-three. Susan really wanted a best friend, but the trio with whom she spent most of her time were like a best friend collectively but not individually. Each one had an element of best friend-ness but not the entire package.

For example, Marie was kind and tolerant, but she was also quiet and slightly dull, not someone Susan could imagine swimming naked with in the moonlight when they were pissed.

Bev was a really good laugh and up for anything, but unfortunately she was someone who would crap on you from a great height if she thought it would imrpove her own situation, and therefore Susan felt very insecure with her. She knew that once they all started going out with boys, she wouldn't be able to trust Bev one little bit.

Annette was fiercely loyal and supportive of Susan, and had been there for most of the difficult moments in her relatively young life. But she charged her a high price for this, being given to cursory wrist-slashing on occasions and much high-expressed emotion.

So Susan was still looking and rather absentmindedly jogging along with what she'd got before finding what she really wanted. It wouldn't be long, she knew, before they were all competing for boyfriends. Personally, she wasn't ready to go through that door just yet and had been holding off, much to the relief of her parents. Terry and Vince constantly looked for telltale signs of sexual activity in their youngest daughter and would have been so much happier if they had known that Susan was doing her best to delay the whole process.

Some very loud Tamla Motown struck the walls downstairs.

'Come on,' said Susan to the three of them. 'Let's go down and see what's happening and have a dance.'

Downstairs was starting to look like a party, with a few bodies strewn around, a slightly smoky atmosphere and a bit of dancing going on.

Jennifer had got fed up with flirting with the boring one and had taken Paul out to the garden shed where, earlier in the day, she had strategically placed a small bottle of vodka and some ribbed condoms. Paul saw the packet of Durex as soon as they got into the shed and got very hopeful, but he shouldn't have done. Jennifer was like her mum in that she really enjoyed winding people up, and she hadn't decided yet whether she was actually going to do it with Paul or not.

Kim was in the kitchen leading a breakaway group of intellectuals who, despite the fact that they were only fourteen and a half, felt vastly superior to the children with whom they were having to spend their party. They were smoking Gauloises, which they all hated, and wished they could have a Number Six. Kim had discovered an extraordinary thing to do with cigarettes for asthmatics. She had made a pot of tea with six cigarettes, which the group were just about to try.

In the shed Paul realised he had come rather earlier than expected – in fact, even before he and Jennifer had touched each other – and he wondered desperately how he could get away to sort himself out and how long it would be before he was ready to have another bash.

Jennifer, who was building up to stroking his trouser zip area, had absolutely no idea this had happened, despite his constipated expression, and was quite surprised when Paul said he had to pop back to the house.

'What for?' she asked petulantly.

He didn't know why he said it but he did and couldn't believe it as the words came out of his mouth.

'Feeling a bit peckish.'

Jennifer glowered at him. It wasn't the best thing to say to someone with an eating disorder who spent her entire life being hungry.

'Hungry!' she finally exploded, driving Paul even further down the road of unavoidable untruths from which we all rarely return unsullied, when he announced, 'It's my diabetes.'

Meanwhile, Terry and Vince were having an uncomfortable evening out together. It had been so long since they'd actually been on their own without the distractions of domestic turnover that Terry realised they had very little to say to each other. Vince, on the other hand, felt he had an awful lot to say to Terry concerning the performance of Brighton and Hove Albion Football Club, his job and how difficult it was becoming for him, the fact that they needed a new lawnmower, his inability these days to maintain an erection and the fact that he had a lump in his testicle, but he was absolutely convinced that she didn't want to hear any of it so he kept his mouth resolutely shut.

Take the lumpy testicle. It was so momentous and yet so potentially trivial, it was impossible to know how to pitch any mention of it. Does one, thought Vince, do a throwaway, light-hearted, 'bit of a bollock problem,' or try and mention it in a more serious manner and run the risk of being laughed at. He felt the same about his GP. She was an attractive woman in her thirties. He could feel himself reddening just thinking about explaining his problem to her. He had decided, however, tonight, that he must do something about it. At least mention it or it would disappear forever into the sealed cave that was Vince's personal problems, never to be discussed again until he was on his deathbed.

They had prawn cocktail for starters and Vince was forming the testicle sentence carefully in his head because Terry's sharp-tongued responses in the past hadn't made it easy for him.

'Love,' he said. 'I've got something to tell you.'

Alarm bells immediately began to ring in Terry's head. Oh fuck, she thought. He's going to talk about something excruciatingly dull to do with work and I'm trapped here in a restaurant with no escape.

'Come on,' she said lightly, 'talking bollocks is strictly forbidden.'

Vince wondered if she could read his thoughts or had somehow managed to see through the bathroom wall as he fumbled about trying to convince himself there was nothing there.

Vince blushed and at that point the waiter arrived and took away their plates and the moment was lost. Terry looked at her watch and said, 'I wonder what the kids are up to now.'

What they were up to was multifarious, but entirely built upon a foundation of Babycham and bottles of ready mixed Snowball, one sniff of which is enough to make a normal person violently sick.

Jennifer was waiting patiently in the shed for her paramour to return from the house having fed himself. Paul was cowering in the toilet wondering how long before there was a resurgence of sexual interest in his now dormant genitalia. Kim's small group of intellectuals had imbibed the tea made of cigarettes for asthmatics and were looking incredulously at each other as their perceptions began to shift and mutate. One of the group, Clare Fox, said, 'I think I can fly,' and rather than being told she was a bloody idiot who was just a bit stoned, the rest of the group nodded sagely at her.

'Let's go to my bedroom,' said Kim, and they all dutifully trooped up to give it a go.

Susan was dancing wildly in the front room with a big group of friends and laughing the laugh of The Foolish One Who Has Mixed Her Drinks. Dressed in her silk wraparound sarong she looked out of her time as all the others were Laura Ashley or loons-clad with scruffy T-shirts. There was one girl in the group, Donna Payne, who couldn't bear to see people having fun and there was something about the glowiness of Susan's smile that really got to her. She stumbled towards her and, during a particularly active song, while Susan was leaping up and down trying to pretend she could dance, Donna pulled at the dress and it slid right off, leaving Susan in the middle of the party wearing only her pants.

Susan screamed and a couple of quick-thinking friends backed her into the curtains, giving her something to wrap round herself. Donna came up to apologise and one of Susan's sidekicks, the ever-resentful Annette, let a fist fly and it caught Donna, knocking her out cold.

'Jesus, call an ambulance!' said someone, pulling back

the curtains as if the mere act of mentioning an ambulance might conjure it up in the street. This happened at exactly the same time as Clare Fox jumped from the bedroom window and landed with a splatting noise on the crazy paving outside.

Five minutes later, Terry and Vince arrived home to see the blue flashing lights of police and ambulance vehicles. Terry, having forgotten her keys, rang the doorbell whilst simultaneously screaming through the letterbox, 'What the fuck is going on?' The door opened to reveal Paul, who said something like, 'I don't feel so well,' and vomited on Terry's shoes.

Chapter 2

Retribution was swift and terrible, fuelled by Vince's complete emotional collapse when he saw the state of the house. He reckoned it would take about three weeks to put the damage right.

Susan recorded it in her diary thus:

> *Mum and Vince went absolutely mental because of my party and we're all being punished. I don't care as it was a good laugh, but I wish Donna had jumped out the window and not Clare. And bloody Steve never turned up.*

The mess was multi-layered. Alcohol had soaked into the carpet and chairs and curtains in a couple of rooms; cigarettes had been stubbed out on the living-room and bedroom carpets, shoved down sinks and in plant pots, and a fag end was even found flattened in Terry's Mills & Boon novel on her bedside table. Vince found some cheese footballs in his underpants drawer, crisps in the bed – and some little bugger had got the fondue set out, put cheese and chocolate into it and spilled the contents on the kitchen floor. Susan couldn't tell the difference between this and the vomit on the doorstep and would have told Vince, had he not looked so tragic and potentially violent.

Jennifer suffered the brunt of the wrath as she had been the responsible adult, 'in inverted commas' as Vince later said to Terry. A tiny bit of Vince felt rather sorry for Jennifer, who had probably been unable to control the shenanigans at the party. Too much had been loaded onto her bony young shoulders.

Still, someone had to suffer and Jennifer's pocket money (she preferred to call it her allowance because it made her sound like a wealthy heiress whose mother, the Countess, had died tragically young) was stopped for six months. Nor was she allowed out with her friends for a month. Kim suffered a similar fate and Susan was also punished but as the youngest slightly more leniently, which irritated the older two and drove the wedge a little further in.

As for Donna Payne, she had come round pretty quickly and only acted up for the benefit of the young ambulanceman who looked at her with such concern. She stayed a night in hospital under observation and made everything she could of it, leaving the nursing staff very happy to wave her goodbye in the charge of her over-perfumed mother.

Clare Fox broke both her legs and had to stay in hospital for somewhat longer, but as many of the parents said, nodding ominously at each other over coffee, it could have been so much worse. They all resolved to prevent their own teenage children from having any sort of birthday celebration at home alone.

The sisters didn't have too long to wait to return to school for the new term in September with the delicious prospect of endlessly regurgitating the events of the party in huddled groups. Susan hoped this would improve her kudos at school, as up to that point she had suffered from pretty low status, with many other girls who had better-off parents or good-looking brothers rather higher up the popularity table than she was. Lots of people disliked Donna Payne, who went to a private school down the road, so Susan had increased her notoriety and popularity in that sense, and Annette's clumsily delivered punch had been reinvented through a series of Chinese whispers into as skilful and well-timed an uppercut as any Muhammad Ali would deliver. Donna hadn't been invited to the party either, so her whack was considered justifiable punishment for gatecrashing.

The two weeks before school started again had seemed endless as the three sisters were marshalled each day to clear up the mess of the party and clean the house from top to bottom. Actually the party debris was disposed of in a couple of days but Terry, giggling gleefully to herself and on the odd occasion with Vince when sparks of their early relationship fleetingly returned, used the girls to spring-clean the house even though it was late August. The house had never been springcleaned so there was a lot of work to do, and although Jennifer, Kim and Susan felt like grumbling, they knew they were guilty as hell so they kept quiet.

On the Thursday before school, Susan had been given the job of clearing out the cupboard under the stairs and she found an unidentifiable crusty mess on Vince's car coat and sensibly kept her mouth shut about it rather than taking the coat out into the hall and saying to her mother, 'What do you think this is, Mum?' She and her friends knew enough to be aware that the gummy by-products of sex ended up in the most surprising places. A girl in her class had kept them spellbound one breaktime by describing how her older sister had 'tossed someone off' on the end of the pier and ended up covered in white stuff and all over her new top and some in her handbag too.

Susan had asked what this girl's sister had actually got out of the experience and everyone had turned to her incredulously and laughed.

Susan was ambivalent about the fumblings and scuf-flings she knew were heading her way. She wondered if Vince had ever come on any of her mum's clothes and then queasily tried to put that image out of her head. She scrubbed listlessly at his coat with a cloth and then shoved it to the back of the cupboard, hoping it wouldn't occur to him to wear it. As she hung the coat up she put her hand in the pocket because she could not help herself being nosy about the private lives of her parents, even though the knowledge gained was often too horrible to contemplate. She felt something flat, smooth and square. Bringing it out, she beheld with some horror a packet of ribbed condoms.

Imagining them doing it was bad enough, but actually finding out they were still at it was flesh-creepingly unsettling. Or perhaps Vince was using them for someone else? Surely not! Who'd have sex with Vince unless they had to? Her poor mum. She was so pretty too, in a flattened and blowsy sort of way.

Susan delved deeper into the cupboard in search of the comfort of her fast-disappearing childhood. On the floor in front of her was evidence of recent bad fashion decisions. Clumpy pairs of platform shoes used for the odd teeter out and back before they turned an ankle or ruined a desperate run for the bus, lay strewn in a big heap. Jennifer had bought a very high pair, and then started going out with someone who was very short. Terry's silver platform boots had been worn once and never again because a bloke with no teeth and a greasy quiff had said she looked like a fat giraffe on heat.

Susan went several years further back in the cupboard and found some toys that she and Jennifer and Kim had loved, but now would barely recognise. They were mostly ancient Sindys, all with missing legs and red and yellow eyes, the victims of someone with monopede mania and a penchant for colouring in.

There was a yoghurt-maker Vince had bought Terry one Christmas. This had been used once and the product pronounced 'bloody disgusting' because the family were only used to the highly sweetened version you could get in the shops. 'Perhaps Nanna might like it,' Terry had said, knowing full well that Nanna would have no idea what it was and would probably try and sterilise her teeth in it. Beside it nestled an Afghan coat that smelled like an Afghan hound that needed to be put down.

'How much longer are you going to be?' shouted Terry in a rather irritated fashion. 'Hurry up, I've got to go to work soon so you're all going to Nanna's.' This was the familial equivalent of borstal. Because of the fallout from the party, Terry, who worked at Boots two afternoons a week and all day Saturday, now did not trust the girls to be left on their own for the few hours she was at work and therefore insisted they go to her mother's small bungalow for the required period. This curtailment of their freedom was frustrating in so many ways and not because once their mother was out they wanted to invite drug dealers, pimps and willing hyper-sexed young boys into the house in order to be impregnated by them, but because, in a quiet way they enjoyed the time when their mum wasn't there, watching rubbish telly like *Crossroads*, trying out her make-up and helping themselves to what they wanted in the kitchen and making the odd phone call to friends.

Instead they had to sit in Nanna's front room, which smelled of cat pee and air freshener, and listlessly read her selection of boring magazines about what it's like to be an old woman. There was *Woman and Home* and something called the *People's Friend*, which contained possibly the most anodyne, tedious stories and articles ever written. Susan fantasised about going on a spree with a machine gun round their offices and doing the world a favour. Nanna also got the *Reader's Digest* magazine and the *Watchtower*, and there was not a sniff of sex or violence to be had in either – which, if you were a teenager, made them utterly pointless to read.

Nanna fussed round them, constantly trying to get them to eat a piece of her fruitcake which was useful only as a missile for flicking at the tomcat that came in and sprayed the room with his maleness, or tormenting Jennifer with its calorie content.

'Back to school Monday then?' asked Nanna, who often neglected to wash – not because of creeping memory deficit but because she simply couldn't be bothered. Poor Nanna had new teeth which didn't fit very well so the sentence came out as 'Plack ter saul marnder?'

'Yes, Nan,' said Susan who, despite poor Nan's excess chin hair, her own special aroma and terrible cooking skills, still loved her very much, as opposed to her slightly more emotionally hardbitten sisters who tolerated her. Whether they had suffered more because of their difficult early lives with their father or they just happened not to have such nice personalities was debatable, but it was Susan who listened patiently to the old lady and smiled while Kim and Jennifer affected bored expressions and stared sulkily at the telly.

Nanna only had a black and white TV too, which seemed so old-fashioned in this day and age, and she only watched things like *House Party* in which a group of menopausal housewives talked about how to make a bed properly or drain an abscess.

It was hell on earth at Nanna's. One hour there seemed

like a day, so by the end of the week Kim and Jennifer were well and truly demoralised and determined never to get themselves into a situation where they were punished like this again. Susan herself was determined to help Nanna sort her teeth out and get her a boyfriend, something which Jennifer and Kim thought was disgusting because the idea of old people touching each other's wrinkled flesh seemed criminal to them. Susan was convinced they probably wouldn't want to at their age and that Nanna would be happy with a bit of company. There was an old man called Sid a few doors away who seemed quite keen, and Nanna always became a bit girly when Susan suggested they get together.

The only thing that broke the monotony of going to Nanna's was the possibility of bumping into the flasher who hung around the cut-through the girls took across a piece of scrubland optimistically called a park by the local council. He had initially appeared about a year or so ago when Susan was eleven and a half, and the first time he had done it, all three of them were walking along chatting and giggling.

The man was standing there on his own, which seemed an unusual thing to do . . . no dog, or newspaper. He was quite young, very tall and the sort of skinny that verges on emaciated.

'Got the time, girls?' he said amiably.

'If you've got the money,' said Jennifer, and Kim and Susan laughed.

Kim had glanced at her watch, which had given the man

time to open his coat, display his freely swinging genitalia and close it so quickly that it seemed to all the girls that it might not have happened at all.

The three sisters broke into a run, giggling, while the flasher forlornly watched them disappear, before looking at his own watch and deciding to go back home for his tea.

At first the girls were not quite brave enough to do anything about the flasher or make any comment, but after a couple more sightings over the following months they became bolder as a trio and would shout as much abuse as they could manage over their shoulders as they ran off. The abuse wasn't very sophisticated or cutting, and tended to be along the lines of the paucity of his appendage, but it made them feel better and more importantly, it made them laugh which released the tension each one was feeling inside but left unspoken.

For some reason the sisters never told their parents about this, nor did they go to the police. Was it because the character himself – they called him 'Jumping Jack Flash' – was so pathetic and seemed so harmless, and the thought of Vince and a few mates giving him a good kicking or the police nabbing him seemed too much? Or was it because they all felt they wanted a bit of the world, however sordid, for themselves, something private? They all believed in some way that growing up meant not allowing your parents to monitor every aspect of your life, to begin having private thoughts and intimate secrets. And this was one hell of an intimate secret.

In time, Jenny and Kim began to feel uncomfortable

about Jack. His rota was impossible to fathom, which meant he always popped up when they least expected it. By now they'd become inured to the initially rather shocking glimpse of white flesh set against a dark forest of pubic hair, and it held no fear for them, just a sense of concern for other younger potential victims. They wondered if he ever covered other areas of town, or if he only did it when he was on holiday.

Jenny eventually suggested they tell Terry about it, but it was Susan who persuaded everyone to keep quiet. She didn't want to get 'Jack' into trouble. Kim and Jennifer weren't happy though and eventually, under pressure, Susan agreed they should tell an adult. In the end, Susan told Nanna about it because she thought somehow the old lady would understand. Nanna nodded sagely and said, 'Ish it errer?' which shocked Susan because she had assumed that her grandmother would have forgotten the concept of erect penises.

Nanna insisted from then on that she waited for them at the side of the scrubland, and Jack's appearances all but stopped. Then one day, not realising she was there, he gave the girls a flash as they hurried across on a wintry afternoon.

Nanna appeared from nowhere and caught him a glancing blow with a wooden spoon.

'And cloant shlum ba ler, wanker,' she called after him. He understood perfectly and decided he wouldn't come back.

And now their visits to Nanna were penis-free.

*   *   *

Over the last weekend of the summer holidays, the girls prepared themselves for a new term at school. Jennifer was going to be taking her O-levels this year and Terry and Vince were not terribly impressed that so far she had only put down Domestic Science and English as possibles. Jennifer wanted to be a model but hadn't discussed this with Vince and Terry yet as she could predict their reaction, which would involve a lot of shouting and a big 'No!' yelled very loudly at her. Doubtless, she would be laughed out of the room and sent down the road to get a job in Marks & Spencers or at the factory up on the new estate that made jam, neither of which prospect she could bear.

Susan and Kim, under a little less pressure to come up with the goods for a few years yet, were more relaxed. Kim lay in her bedroom reading *Lord of the Flies* and savouring every page, her uniform strewn about like jumble-sale items, while Susan spent a long time in front of the mirror hitching her school skirt up and wondering if she could get away with a mini. She suspected that what now appeared to be a pair of shorts rather than a skirt would not get the sartorial thumbs-up from the Headmistress, who for some strange reason didn't like the girls to look like child prostitutes.

Chapter 3

About half a mile from Susan's home in an area rather inappropriately named Bohemia, for it had nothing of the Prussian Empire about it nor was it an artists' quarter, someone else was preparing for the new term. Rachel Weston and her family had recently moved from London to their new home in Hastings. The process of shifting oneself and one's belongings from one pile of bricks to another had proved even more traumatic for the Westons than they had anticipated. Rachel was thirteen and the middle child of a family of three; she had two brothers, Alan and Clive. Her dad, Dick, told them he had recently been made redundant from his rather comfortable position as a quantity surveyor in a big London building firm, so the family had sold their house in Balham and planned a move to the coast.

Rachel didn't understand why her dad couldn't just get another job in London. At night she could hear only snatches of their rows, because her parents' attempts to have a whispered shouting match were reasonably successful. But she knew a huge disagreement about the future was going on.

When she said to her mum and dad, 'Why are we moving to Hastings?' her dad said, 'We need to be somewhere cheaper,' at the same time as her mum, Helen, said, 'I want us to live by the sea.'

Helen, had been brought up in Bexhill, a small seaside enclave which was like Hastings's elderly aunt, and she had always secretly harboured a wish to wallow in the fleshpots she had always assumed existed in Hastings. Bexhill was a demure kiss on the cheek, Hastings a big lolloping tongue down the throat.

Dick would have preferred to live in Eastbourne, which *he* always assumed had more class, and fewer 'rough characters', meaning in *Daily Telegraph*-speak working-class people who probably indulged in some sort of criminal activity and if by some stroke of fate they did not, were at the very least dirty.

Rachel and her brothers quite liked the prospect of living by the seaside, although none of them relished the 'new school' gauntlet, bringing with it the possibility of finishing the day face down in the mud to the music of taunting vocals or lying tear-stained in one's bed at night wondering how painful an overdose of aspirin would be.

The children were all going to the local comprehensive. Helen and Dick couldn't afford a private education for their children, much as Dick would have liked it, so he would have to satisfy his taste for stringent regimes with homework rotas that would defeat even the most youthful of alienated child geniuses. Helen, whose politics veered much further left of her husband's, desperately wanted the kids to do well at the comprehensive to show Dick it was possible, and for their own sakes, and also to prove to him that it wasn't just, as he thought of it, a prison-in-waiting.

All their arguments about education were ultimately futile as they couldn't afford anything other than what the state had to offer. Still, the couple liked nothing better than a good ruck.

Hastings offered so much to the teenager. There was the Old Town with its pretty, narrow streets containing a wealth of pubs out of which spilled old hippies, foreign students, fishermen, drug dealers, bored secretaries, shopworkers, doleys, plainclothes policemen and civil servants. There was the pier, like a long thin Christmas cake, groaning under the weight of big-name bands from all over the country, stuffed with amusement arcades and bars offering nooks and crannies for anything from a drunken fumble to full-blown virginity loss. And below the pier, the shingle beach stretched along the promenade, offering its salty, crunchy surface for sex, midnight swims, acid trips, winter plunges, endless man, woman and dog pissing, and a grey-green sea like cold soup. Rachel Weston couldn't wait to immerse herself in every single aspect of her new home town.

It had occurred to Rachel that recently, she was beginning to worry about the way she looked – something that had never been of much importance before. In her middle-class household, being the child of a well-educated mother who had been only too happy to welcome in the first vestiges of women's liberation, she had had an upbringing fairly free of the usual female standards about appearance. Sindy dolls had been banned and as she had two brothers this hadn't really been a problem, as she was far too busy being chased round by her siblings who used to tie her to trees and generally batter her when they felt like it, to play with dolls. The boys were obsessed with sport and consequently so was she, and they had forced her, as Manchester United fans, to support West Ham and gave her a thump every time the Hammers lost – which was often.

Rachel had had a crush for years on Bobby Moore, whose blond hair and cleanshaven good looks carried with them the promise of unthreatening, unsticky coupling. As she moved towards her teenage years though, Moore wore off.

Dick and Helen Weston were beginning to reach the end of their tolerance for one another, and it seemed likely that they wouldn't stay together for very much longer. They were bored and irritated by each other. Dick didn't like sex and Helen did, and they settled into a pattern of Dick avoiding Helen at bedtime and Helen wondering how much to pressure him without being too clingy.

This imbalance was disguised by the arrival of the children because then Dick had the excuse of tiredness to cover his turning over in bed every night. Helen concentrated on her children and began secretly reading feminist books from America about satisfying yourself. American women seemed to be masturbating in a variety of venues with unfettered abandon and Helen marvelled that they ever got any hoovering done. She just could not see self-contained, somewhat prudish English housewives ever managing to even have a little fiddle about down there, let alone fling their legs open in the midst of a group of their peers and reach a climax with a sound that was very like a herd of psychotic elephants trumpeting.

Helen did get a vibrator for a while and she and it spent some happy times together. But she was always on edge, terrified that one of the kids, or even worse, Dick, would find it, so she could never truly relax. Also, one night it turned itself on in her bedside cabinet and she leaped, heart pounding, to turn it off before Dick woke up and got involved as he inevitably did with anything electrical.

To the children, who were not party to every intimate communication between their mum and dad, mostly everything seemed fine with the odd blip when arguments happened or there were frosty silences which sometimes lasted a couple of days. Only Rachel who, curse of her gender, was slightly more attuned to these things, had the vaguest idea that things were not quite right and occasionally poked about in her mum and dad's chest of drawers to see if she could find any clue that things were either good or bad. One day she found some contraceptive jelly, which she beheld with horror. Undignified images kept occupying her head and she cringed at the thought of these two lost in a cartoonish coupling. Had she only looked more closely at the label on the contraceptive jelly, she would have discovered it was three years out of date.

* * *

Moving day had involved the sort of chaos that tends only to be created by people who are in the manic stage of a bi-polar illness. The sale had been completed the day before and Helen had travelled down to Hastings in the car to take a few essentials with her, clean the place and put up curtains while Dick did something akin to holding the fort in Balham, which meant he ignored the children, did no packing whatsoever, watched telly and seemed depressed. Helen arrived back in the evening, looking tired and flushed, and swatted Dick's questions away as he got ready to go out as if they were irritating flies buzzing round her head. The next morning everyone overslept and consequently got up in a foul mood because there was no time to get properly organised.

Helen had tried her best to pack everything in a systematic way but had ended up just shoving armfuls of different objects into some rather weedy-looking cardboard boxes she had got from a supermarket up the road. Dick had been out with some guys from work the night before to say goodbye, and was feeling rather sorry for himself.

Thus, their house was covered in a big dark blanket of grumpiness. The removal men were late and displayed the sort of apathy and clumsiness that one tends mainly to associate with serious dope smokers. Boxes were dropped, that chinked ominously. Helen just closed her eyes and gritted her teeth, hoping they would get through the day without violence being committed.

Rachel, Alan and Clive, in the true spirit of teenage children, contributed an enormous amount to the atmosphere of barely suppressed tension, and rather than sit quietly in the house playing Scrabble as their parents had instructed them to, they ran around like mad things, shouting and screaming. The plan was to start the removal men going and then to head off in the car to Hastings and meet them there to supervise the unloading of all their belongings. This was a perfectly good plan, and everything would have happened with the minimum of fuss had it not been for one thing. Helen could not find the car keys. She assumed that, in the panic of the night before when she finished her frenzied packing, they had somehow been thrown into one of the boxes.

'Dick!' she shouted to her husband who was sitting doing the *Telegraph* crossword in the midst of a pile of boxes.

'What?' he asked grumpily, signifying by his answer that he was not to be called upon to do anything that day.

'Have you seen the car keys?' said Helen desperately, trying to keep the tremor out of her voice.

'No!' shouted back Dick. 'You had them last.'

Not wanting to face a critique of her packing or car-key storage, his wife stomped into the kitchen and began ripping open boxes and pouring the contents onto the floor until a mountain of pointless junk which they had accumulated over the years, including things like a Ronco Buttoneer, salad servers in the shape of a woman, a donkey that dispensed cigarettes from its bum, a plastic picnic set, a small coffin with a skeleton in it they had bought in Alicante, old boxes of cereal and many more useless artefacts lay staring up at her and she could hear them all saying, 'Look, no keys!'

She wondered whether they'd fallen down the back of one of the chairs and instructed the removal men to pull everything out. No luck. She then tipped all the rubbish out of the dustbin and went through that with her bare hands because she'd packed the rubber gloves several centuries ago.

Dick, meanwhile, sat glued to twenty-one across.

Helen, by this time, was dangerous. The children seemed oblivious to the fact that this was a real crisis and that they might have to travel on the train or get a lift with the removal men and find the keys at the other end. Helen saw Clive open the back door into the garden.

'What the hell do you think you're doing!' she screamed at the top of her voice.

Clive turned to her, shocked. He had very rarely seen his mum in such a state of advanced hysteria.

'Going into the garden,' he said guiltily, as if going into the garden was akin to stringing up and torturing his pet hamster.

'But I told you to keep the back door shut, didn't I?' said Helen, who even in the midst of this crisis could not resist turning into a teacher.

'Don't know,' said Clive, biting his lip, his eyes filling with tears.

'Oh shit!' howled Helen as the cat's bum disappeared out of the back door attached to the cat.

Clive hadn't seen it.

'What, Mum?' he said, knowing that it must be very serious for her to swear.

But Helen was already out in the back garden and sprinting as fast as she could towards the cat who, once he had made his escape, was strolling nonchalantly down to the bottom of the garden for a wee. She knew it was now or never. She wasn't coming back for that flea-ridden bundle of contradictions.

Diving in the manner of a rugby player, she landed awkwardly right on top of the cat, who let out a strangled scream. The soft squelch that had occurred as Helen's ten stone met the cat's seven pounds nearly made her throw up. She lay on top of it not wanting to look and praying that somehow it would start to meow and try to claw its way from under her. It didn't.

'Oh Jesus Christ,' said Helen. The cat belonged to Rachel who'd had it since she was seven and had loved it without reservation.

Dick stirred from his coma and strolled through the kitchen which had become a sea of rubbish and looked through the back door to see Helen getting up off what appeared to be a ragged fur stole. He went out.

'What's going on?' he said.

Helen pointed at the cat and mouthed, 'Dead,' and, 'We can't tell Rachel.'

Dick had no idea what the second bit was about and thought she had said, 'Weak heart, tell Rachel.'

He opened his mouth to shout for his daughter to come and managed to get the first syllable out. Helen clamped a clammy hand over it.

'What the fuck are you doing?' she hissed, her face

contorted into that of an unrecognisable sadistic head-mistress.

'Don't swear at me, you fucking bad-tempered cow,' said Dick, head pounding and mouth dry.

'The fucking cat's dead, you stupid bastard,' said Helen through gritted teeth. 'Rachel mustn't know I fell on it.'

Dick started to laugh.

Helen, at the height of her hysteria, could not tolerate this and punched him in the stomach and as they tussled, throwing insults at each other over a dead cat, they realised Clive was standing there. A look of panic crossed Helen's face as the plan she had been forming in her head to lie to Rachel had been seriously set back by the appearance into the plot of an eleven-year-old child who was absolutely hopeless at keeping secrets.

'Look, love,' she said, the tone of her voice changing to soothing and loving, 'don't tell Rachel, darling, please . . . It'll really upset her.'

Clive couldn't understand the connection between these two statements, as 'really upsetting Rachel' was pretty much his raison d'être, and therefore telling her seemed the first thing he should do.

His mother knew this and wondered whether to use bribery or threaten horrible punishment. She decided to go down the bribery road and said, conspiratorially, 'I'll get you a new bike if you keep quiet.'

'Really, Mum?' Clive was very impressed by this offer. 'OK,' he said and being an innocent, forgot that he could probably demand a lot more than this.

Dick heard Rachel and Alan flinging themselves down the stairs. 'Quick,' he hissed at Helen. 'Hide it.'

The only place available that was big enough and near enough was under the grill of the barbecue they'd bought last summer. Helen shoved the cat under it and stood in front to discourage closer inspection.

Alan and Rachel appeared in the garden to see an awkward family tableau that, if they had thought about it long enough, would have demonstrated to them something was wrong.

'Are we taking the barbecue, Mum?' said Rachel. 'I think we should because—'

Helen cut across her with a slightly weird rendition of the word, 'No.'

'But . . .' she started.

'No buts,' said Helen. 'Just do as you're told.'

'Can I have a chopper, Mum?' said Clive.

'Don't be bloody ridiculous,' said Helen, forgetting the non-swearing in front of the kids rule. 'They're dangerous and besides, there's nothing to chop.'

'No, a Raleigh chopper,' said Clive. 'You know.'

'Yes, yes,' said Helen dismissively.

'Well, if he's getting a bike, I want something big too,' said Rachel.

'And me,' said Alan.

'Shut up,' said Helen in such a threatening way that even Dick's mouth closed in fear. 'Right,' she went on. 'I can't find the car keys so we'll have to travel down with the removal men or get the train.'

'What about Fluff?' said Rachel. Helen felt herself begin to redden.

'Oh, don't worry,' she said, mustering all her acting skills. 'He can come in his basket on the train. By the way, where is Fluff?' She looked round and began calling, 'Fluff! Fluff! Where are you?' and realised that Clive and Dick were looking at her as if she was Torquemada.

The removal men refused to have more than two people in the van with them so Dick and Alan were volunteered to join them in the mobile manly smell carrier decorated with the odd picture of a woman with huge bosoms, which Alan thought was very exciting. Rachel wanted to stay behind to look for Fluff and Clive was quite happy to torture his mother with reproachful looks just in case she had forgotten she had promised him a bike.

It was good in the van. Radio One was blaring out the summer hits and everyone sang along, even Dick who was slightly snobby about pop music and preferred a bit of light opera which always made Alan and Clive want to blow up the radiogram with their junior scientist sets.

Helen, Rachel and Clive, having got the train, arrived in a cab fifteen minutes before the removal van in their new road to see two fire engines, a crowd of people and a smoking ruin where their house should be.

Chapter 4

Susan was slightly peeved that talk of the new girl's house burning down had overshadowed her birthday-party post mortem, although she need not have worried as the two topics jockeyed for position all day amongst her class.

For Rachel and her brothers it couldn't have been a better introduction to what they had all assumed would be quite a tough school full of bullies who dribbled long gobbets of spit into your face as they sat on top of you or poked your tender bits with a stick. To be the object of curiosity and sympathy rather than uncontrolled teenage resentment was a pleasant surprise. Rachel thought that most of the girls in her class looked at least two years older, with the exception of Patricia Wyngold, who looked about forty, and Susan (surely it couldn't be Pig?) – the one who had just had her thirteenth birthday and just looked her age.

The two found themselves chatting with each other during a break and although wary of this extremely pretty girl (having an extremely pretty friend means hours of sitting alone in discos, staring at the floor whilst said friend is wooed by a series of young men whom very average-looking self could not hope to bag), Rachel found herself saying far more than she normally would to someone she had just met.

'So where are you living now?' said Susan, aware that Rachel's accent was somewhat posher than hers. 'In a hotel, I suppose?'

'Christ, no,' said Rachel, who interjected the surname of Jesus at frequent intervals into her conversation mainly to wind up her parents. 'No, we've got some shitty, rented flat up the arse end of St Leonards.'

Susan herself lived up the arse end of St Leonards, but let the comment go because she knew Rachel was only trying to impress everyone with her aggressive-pursed-lip-new-girl-don't-give-a-shit approach. If we become friends, thought Susan, she'll remember that comment when she first comes to my house.

'So how did your house burn down?' she asked.

'Don't know really,' shrugged Rachel. 'The police think it was either kids mucking about or squatters.' Then, rather indiscreetly for her, she said, 'But my dad reckons it was Barry Nesbitt.'

She had heard the phrase, 'I wouldn't put it past that fucking Barry Nesbitt,' come through a closed door and into her eavesdropping ear during a particularly ferocious row the night after they arrived in Hastings.

'Don't be so ridiculous,' had come the reply from her mother.

'Who's Barry Nesbitt?' asked Susan.

'Some bloke my dad used to work with,' said Rachel. 'My dad really hates him.'

'What does your mum think?' Susan wanted to know.

'Oh, she told my dad not to be ridiculous,' said Susan, feeling slightly uncomfortable that she was saying too much too soon.

'I wish someone had burned our bloody house down,' said Susan. 'Then I wouldn't have had to do so much cleaning.'

'Oh yeah,' said Rachel, brightening up. 'That party sounded fab. Pity I missed it by a week.'

'Don't worry,' Susan said airily. 'It's my sister Kim's birthday in two months, we'll have another one.' Although she knew the likelihood of being allowed another party was somewhere down the list from a proposal of marriage from Marc Bolan.

'So, have you got a boyfriend?' said Rachel, wishing she didn't sound quite so much like a market researcher.

'No,' said Susan, 'and I don't want one neither. My sisters are bloody stupid about boys, the pair of them. Gets on my nerves. Jennifer's after this right fucking wally called Paul. He's like a dog on heat.' They both giggled, even though neither really knew what a dog on heat was like, apart from the leg-mounting bit. 'And Kim is obsessed with make-up and clothes – that's all she goes on about, even though her and her friends try and pretend they're intellectuals who read and that. What about you, you got a boyfriend?'

'Well, there was someone in London,' said Rachel.

'Going steady?'

'Sort of . . . not really.'

'What do you mean?' asked Susan.

'We wanted our freedom, you know,' Rachel said lamely.

'So how long were you going out with him for?' said Susan, rather pedantically.

'Actually, I didn't go out with him,' Rachel admitted. 'I just liked him.'

'And did he like you?'

'Don't know, hard to tell.'

'I suppose it is hard to tell, especially when they're with their friends,' said Susan.

'Yeah,' said Rachel. 'To be honest, I've never had a proper boyfriend. I feel a bit embarrassed about it. Everyone seems so grown-up at this school.'

'Don't worry,' said Susan, 'it's not like we're eighteen or anything. We don't have to if we don't want to, we can just have a laugh. All these silly cows here with their make-up and their "getting engaged when we're sixteen" rubbish. It's bollocks. I've never had a boyfriend and I'm proud of it.'

Rachel felt cheered by this. Over the past couple of years she had felt the pressure mounting to start doing all that being-interested-in-boys stuff and the behaviour of her brothers hadn't exactly encouraged her. Why get closer to someone who might pull you off the settee, sit on top of you and then fart as loudly as possible in your face with the social abandon of a caged gorilla? And with such hilarity, too! No, she was quite happy to stave that off for a few years. It was for those stupid girls who believed all that rubbish in *Jackie* about boys being 'dreamboats'. In the real world they were irritating little bastards whose bodily fluids sloshed around everywhere and they weren't even embarrassed about it.

Both girls parted from this first encounter feeling that something quite unusual had happened and that a friendship might begin.

Rachel walked home believing herself to be fleeter of foot, not quite so plain and chunky, and much more interesting than she usually was. But all too soon, the slippery eel of self-esteem that is always alert on the seabed of most women's perception of themselves began to strike for the surface.

'What are you staring at, Ugly?' said a voice and Rachel, who hadn't actually been staring, looked up to see a skinny hard-faced girl with a concertina-like mouth and a smile that could barbecue rivals. It was Lesley Keerman.

Now Rachel wasn't ugly at all in the traditional pantomime Ugly Sister make-you-bring-up-your-tea sort of way. She wasn't beautiful either. She just had a nice face that would probably manage to launch a couple of fishing boats and a pedalo, as opposed to Susan who could have come pretty near a thousand ships.

But the rules state that unless your parents have fostered in you either a monstrous ego or supreme self-confidence from a very early age, and if you are just plain, you must pitch your tent in the field of self-deprecation and this is what Rachel had done. She would spend ages looking at herself in the mirror, not in a vain way but marvelling that there was very little that could be done to salvage what was a very average set of features. True beauty, she had read somewhere, is all to do with the perfect symmetry of the face. So she must be pretty lopsided.

Like many girls and women, Rachel froze when attention was focused on her, and she never had the right retort ready for any threatening occasion. If only she could combine insult with putdown. But she wasn't a fucking comedian, so why should she? The girl, who was probably about fifteen, stepped sideways and blocked Rachel's progress down the pavement. Rachel thought that such an expression of mixed envy, hate and resentment made *her* ugly, but could not rephrase it to sound snappy and sarcastic, so she just mumbled, 'Leave me alone,' and tried to stumble past with her face down.

However, this bastardess wanted a bit more of a reaction than that. She caught up with Rachel and walking beside her began a running commentary on her shortcomings.

'Your ankles look like an old lady's,' intoned Lesley. 'Your legs are shapeless, your stomach sticks out too much, you've got no tits, your hair's mousy and your face is just like the fucking moon.' She cackled and continued on, looking behind her and not seeing a big dollop of dogshit approaching her right foot.

Squelch.

Rachel, whose eyes had begun to fill up with tears, started

to laugh. Lesley was not amused and looked at Rachel as if she wanted to hit her. Rachel thought it was probably best to run and Lesley turned to run after her, but she slipped on the aforementioned dogshit and sat down in the road.

'You stupid cow, I'll get you!' she shouted from her sitting position.

Rachel shivered slightly and thought she must be better prepared, especially if Lesley had a gang. She resolved to discuss it with Susan and work out a plan, should she ever get cornered.

Lesley sat there thinking, Pathetic little cow with her fucking first day at a new school, face all open and wondering and saying, 'Please like me.' Hope you're going to make friends and have a good time, do you? Well, you fucking ain't. I'll see to that.

Rachel, who'd not really come across a bully before, wondered as most nice people do, 'What have *I* ever done to her to make her hate me so much? All I ever do is try and be friendly to people and this is what I bloody get. She doesn't even know me. Have I got a sign on my head that says *kick me* or something?' It didn't occur to Rachel to think, It's not about me, it's about her – because the impact of Lesley's appraisal had made her so angry.

However, as she walked home thinking about it, she became a little more sympathetic towards Lesley and wondered if perhaps she had a horrible homelife or had been hit by her dad or something worse. Perhaps she'd been bullied herself. Rachel thought that next time she saw her, she should try being nice to Lesley and see what happened.

All of this socialworkeresque ruminating could have been avoided if Rachel had only had access to a CV of Lesley Keerman, which would have told her the following.

Only child, from a nice home. Mother a nurse, father an occupational therapist, both pleasant people who had lavished care and attention on Lesley from the second she popped out to the present day, although over the years they had witnessed with growing unease the development of a weaselly, petulant, disobedient child whose language, behaviour and looks they did not recognise as having sprung from their joint loins. The more they tried to help and understand, the worse she became. In fact, Lesley's mum Sandra wondered if there'd been a mix-up at the hospital and someone had swapped their beautiful daughter for a little runt from a family of local criminals.

Sandra and her husband Ken had withdrawn back into each other and kept a measured distance from Lesley, trying their best to be fair and generous and recoiling occasionally from her when she used very bad language or implied to them that she was entertaining boys sexually in the park. Ultimately, it was just too much for the couple to admit they could have produced someone like Lesley and that nurture had played such a small part in her upbringing. They needed to sit down and chat with each other and agree that she was a horrible, unlikeable person and there probably wasn't much they could do, then relax and forget about it. But she was their daughter and they couldn't, and so they both carried around her badness like a guilty secret and kept her out of the way of people they liked as much as they could.

Rachel didn't feel like going home yet so she headed down to the beach instead and plonked herself on the shingle, looking out to sea and wondering how badly poor Lesley must have been treated to end up such a cow.

'All right, love?' says a voice behind her and down sits Laurence Hidalgo, a local 'eccentric' and suspected 'perv'. Reasons to be suspected of pervery in Hastings though, amount to mentioning in the newsagent that you like poetry and not smelling of fish six days out of seven.

'Yes, I'm fine,' says Rachel, assuming that because Laurence looks like a perv, he is one, but unable to step outside the good manners Helen has drummed into her, and get up and leave. Instead, she shifts uncomfortably across the shingle and gets herself into a position where a big sharp stone sticks into her bottom, but not wanting to remove it just in case any suggestion of her hand wandering anywhere near her own bottom inflames this strange man to some sort of sexual action, she tolerates it.

'You can tell me all about it, you know,' says Laurence, causing Rachel to do a very unconvincing, 'Oh, is that the time!' glance at her watch and try and stand gracefully up on the shingle and go. Now, even more mortified, she realises halfway across the beach that her skirt is tucked into her pants and Laurence's eyes are following her bum as it leaves his line of vision (although, short of deliberately staring in the other direction, he doesn't have much choice). Laurence, who's a nice bloke, rather lonely, not a pervert but with a distinct lack of social skills, wonders where he went wrong and decides to make more of an effort to find out. Perhaps he'll write to the problem page in the *News of the World*, although he's not sure his problem is vulgar enough, or maybe he'll talk to his brother who has no problem fitting in.

As Rachel steps from the shingle onto the safety of the gummy pavement, she hears a very familiar voice and sees her extremely angry mother coming towards her.

Chapter 5

For some reason, Rachel found it difficult to incriminate someone else while her mother was closely questioning her about why she was so late home. She didn't want to relate the bullying incident because she knew that Helen would sail straight round to Lesley's house and flay the skin off her within seconds. Unless the situation got more serious, there was no point getting her involved. As for Laurence Hidalgo – what on earth was her mother implying? That within one week of being in Hastings she had met and started having an affair with a man who looked like an extra in a porno remake of *Oliver Twist*?

'Mum,' she protested, 'he approached *me*.'

Helen knew this really. It was just that when she had seen a grown-up man talking to her only daughter, a protective hysteria had taken hold of her.

Eventually they both calmed down and headed home. On the bus they chatted about their respective days. Helen was pleased that Rachel had had a reasonable day at school, as she had worried about her daughter having problems or being bullied. Rachel hadn't even mentioned Fluff yet, which was a good sign.

They were in the flat within ten minutes. It smelled musty and slightly of urine even though Helen had scrubbed the toilet for what seemed like hours and then sprayed copious amounts of bleach-based products around the room. Clive and Alan were watching cartoons on the telly. Dick was out. Although he wasn't working and hadn't started to set himself up in business yet as he had promised, he spent most of the day out in an attempt to convince himself and the family that he was doing something useful.

'How long do we have to stay here, Mum?' Rachel asked.

'Well, when the insurance comes through after the investigations are finished, we should find a house in, oh, six months probably,' said Helen.

'Oh, the humiliation,' said Rachel.

Helen snapped at her and launched into a parental tirade of untruths. 'Look, Dad's doing his best' (he wasn't), 'he wants us to stick together as a family' (he didn't) 'which is why he won't take a job in London and just come down at weekends' (he'd have loved to) 'and wants you to settle in and make friends.' (At the moment, Dick Weston was so self-pitying about his life he couldn't have cared less how the children were getting on.)

Rachel started to find this intimacy with her mother a bit stressful even though she knew it only scratched the surface of what was really going on. She was fearful that

Helen might need some more support and drag her down emotional roads she didn't want to travel. So she did something that she was eventually to become very good at; she closed down this particular area of discussion and changed the subject to something safe and boring.

'Do you know where my sports kit is, Mum?'

'Well, of course I do,' said Helen. 'Why?'

'We've got PE tomorrow,' said Rachel.

Rachel wasn't the sportiest girl in the school but she did enjoy sport, providing the competitive element was absent. And it is common for wheezing no-hopers to be told that it is the taking part that is important rather than the winning.

And so the following morning, Rachel found herself with her class on a blustery, somewhat chilly sports field, mottled legs unwilling to get going, no enthusiasm for running anywhere at all except inside, and wondering as the new girl what torture she was going to be put through for the entertainment of her peers.

Miss Cromwell, the sports mistress, had decided Rachel should run the 200 metres so she could get an idea of the girl's fitness level. But rather than put her into the race with Gemma, Sheila and Liz, the three slug impersonators, she had chosen to race Rachel against the three fastest girls in the class.

Rachel, who was nervous and therefore desperately in need of a pee, thought she was not going to be able to control her bladder. As she walked towards the starting line, she realised why there had been a stifled giggle when Miss Cromwell had asked her to run in the outside lane. She was up against the three Olympians, who could not have been more intimidating had they had flames coming out of their noses. Rachel knew she was going to be seriously shown up.

Susan stood beside her. 'You're going to fucking die,' she said humorously. 'Good luck.'

Miss Cromwell stood at the side as Rachel and the other three lined up.

'Ready, steady, go!' The race began. The three Olympians took off like true professionals, leaving Rachel to come up out of the blocks like a fat baby seal. The Olympians had powered away and so Rachel, who very happily would have feigned injury or simply just walked off, felt obliged, given this was a new school, to go the distance. After about fifty yards she was convinced that her lungs were bleeding and didn't want to cough in case she stained the ground red. She was vaguely aware of some sniggering going on behind her and got a brief flash of the entirely unsympathetic face of Miss Cromwell as she ran along trying to encourage her by shouting abuse at her.

The Olympians' time was around twenty-eight seconds. Rachel took forty, and as she came wheezing towards the line to see a mixture of sympathy and Schadenfreude on the faces of her classmates she knew she was set for a year of pisstaking.

Susan was philosophical.

'You did your best,' she shrugged, 'and you honestly didn't look as much of a knobhead as you probably thought you did.'

'Cheers,' said Rachel, not convinced but appreciating her almost straight face. 'I was dying for a wee, I nearly pissed myself in the home straight.'

'We all did piss ourselves,' said Susan, breaking into a laugh. 'I'm sorry,' she said, 'but you looked so funny trundling along on your own at the back in such a bad mood.' And she began to laugh until the tears ran down her face.

Someone else taking the piss, thought Rachel. But there was a difference between Susan's laughter and the others'. It wasn't cruel, it was good-natured and funny and Rachel found herself infected by it. She began to chuckle too.

'I'll get those bloody carthorses that beat me,' she said.

'If you can catch them,' said Susan, and the pair of them sat down and laughed even harder.

Chapter 6

Some people tell you their whole life story, including when they last had sex, within ten minutes of meeting you, but for others becoming more open is a painful process. Susan came from a family in which intimate secrets were bandied around like chocolate digestives at a WI meeting and therefore it was no big deal to her to tell Rachel that she had not yet lost her virginity. She had been very close once when a mechanic called Tom who was eighteen had got over-excited and covered her with sperm before shame-facedly leaving whichever appalling local band they were watching on the pier; and she related this to her new friend with a rueful, yet comic tone. Rachel was surprised that Susan was allowed out on her own, let alone getting into a situation where she could be sprayed with high-speed ejaculate. Didn't her mum mind? 'What, Tom coming all over me?' laughed Susan, who had actually found the incident quite traumatic.

Although Terry didn't seem to be worried about her daughter abroad amongst all these villainous packages of testosterone, this was because she'd forced herself not to be, for fear of being permanently overwhelmed by a crippling anxiety about who her daughters were with and what they were doing with them. So she'd just decided to trust them, and believe that they could look after themselves – and this enabled her to get on with her life with Vince without being hamstrung by fear.

Rachel's mum, by contrast, was well and truly crippled by her anxiety. Having only one daughter, she fantasised nightly about the terrible fate that might befall her, and had she been able to, would have tracked Rachel constantly, ready at any moment to appear and protect her from harm. This happened even in the case of slights by shopkeepers or mildly sardonic comments from teachers, and Rachel had learned to keep these to herself, unless a major incident occurred.

Rachel found it very hard to tell Susan anything private about herself as she had learned, given that she had two brothers, to become self-sufficient emotionally, and it was not her habit with relatively new friends to divulge her innermost thoughts. She had had little experience with boys or men and was frightened, didn't know how to talk about it, envied Susan's easy manner about it all and hoped she would be able to relax and have the sort of carefree friendship with much laughing in it.

Each had visited the other's house and tried to gauge the reaction of the respective parents. Of course, when

Rachel first went round to Susan's, the remark she had made when they had first met about where she and her family lived came back to her like a slap in the face.

'Yes, here we are at the shithole,' said Susan cheerfully, trying to lighten things and help her out, having seen the expression on her face. As Rachel tried to somehow explain herself, Susan interrupted her.

'Look, it's all right,' she said. 'I know you didn't really mean it.'

'Thanks,' said Rachel before being catapulted into the living space of the Family Pigg, a place of such chaos it genuinely shocked her.

Jennifer and Kim and their mum had taken over the front room and were involved in the sort of beautifying routine that Rachel would not have conducted in front of her mother, let alone before a guest she had never met before.

Both girls had white moustaches of hair remover cream which instinctively made Rachel put her hand up to cover her upper-lip area in case it was scrutinised and found wanting. Terry had curlers on under a very unattractive puce-coloured chiffon cap. She was plucking her eyebrows, sprawling in a very short baby-doll nightie with depilatory cream smeared all over the front of her legs. As Susan entered, she took the fag out of her mouth and waved a greeting.

'Hiya, is this your new little friend?' she said to Susan.

'She's not little,' said Susan crossly, 'and we are not fucking five years old, Mum.'

Rachel nearly fainted at the sound of the 'F' word uttered in front of an adult. She had just about managed to cope with it being sprinkled into Susan's conversation, but to use it at your own mother! Was her stepdad going to beat her so she fell over onto the really horrible brown and yellow carpet?

Suddenly, Rachel was aware of a glum-looking male face buried in the middle of this all-female tableau. It was Vince, trying to read his paper and being used as a table for everyone's beauty products.

'Don't swear at her like that,' he said to Susan and looked to Terry to offer some sort of rebuke but Terry was too interested in *Coronation Street*.

Rachel, whose family never watched ITV, was fascinated and wondered how she could persuade her mum to let them watch this as it looked brilliant.

'Shall we go up to my bedroom?' said Susan. Rachel would have loved to have stayed in the warm, bickery, tele-visual heat of the Piggs' front room but she agreed, wondering what the bedroom would offer as a new experi-ence.

'Do you want a coffee?' asked Susan.

'Please,' said Rachel, starting to rather resent the formality of her own homelife as against this glorious mayhem of make-up and pluckery.

In her bedroom, Susan put on *The Magician's Birthday* by Uriah Heap, an enigma of headachingly loud proportions with its tales of dwarves and elves, which sat incongruously amongst the Donny Osmond and David Cassidy singles.

They talked about periods and stuff like that. Rachel was unsure whether to tell Susan that she'd had absolutely no idea what her period was when it started and had immediately thought she was dying of some terminal illness. She did tell her because she wanted to share confidences with her.

Susan was aghast. 'Why didn't your fucking mum tell you?' she said. Yes, why didn't my fucking mum tell me? thought Rachel.

'Dunno,' she said. 'Perhaps she was too embarrassed.'

'What's there to be embarrassed about?' said Susan. 'We all have periods, even Vince . . . well, he certainly seems to have PMT.'

The idea of Vince down the chemist trying to make up his mind between SuperTampax or Boot's own-brand sanitary towels filled them with the giggles again and within seconds they were collapsed over the bed.

When Susan came over to Rachel's home, despite the fact that it was in the same area as hers, the gap between their lives seemed cavernous. There was a quietness about the Westons' flat that suggested not much fun was had there, thought Susan, as she surveyed the neatness and the rows of educational books which were completely missing from her life and home. Rachel's parents seemed a bit distant, and despite their politeness, Susan could sense they were probably calculating how soon they could break up the friendship and find their daughter a more suitable companion whose father's earnings were in the same salary bracket as Dick's. She got the impression that anyone who earned a wage of under ten thousand a year was not welcome, despite the fact that Rachel's dad didn't seem to be working himself.

They all sat round in an awkward way in the front room. Helen had turned the telly off in a gesture of sociability because visitors were coming but it only served to accentuate the apprehensive silence between all parties. When Rachel finally said, after what seemed like years, 'Shall we go to my room?' Susan was so relieved she shot out of the door like a rocket.

Alan and Clive displayed totally opposing reactions to Susan. At the age of eleven, to Clive girls were silly braying imbeciles who only ever spouted rubbish and should be reduced to tears whenever possible. Alan, on the other hand, now fourteen, had metamorphosed into a bumbling red-faced tongue-tied buffoon who seemed to physically change at the mere mention of girls. When he had first seen Susan he couldn't even look at her, he was so embarrassed, and she, aware of her sexual power, had laughed at his awkwardness and teased him about his shambling gait.

'Can I see your bedroom?' she'd asked as he tried to escape, occasioning an expression so shocked she might have requested a quick look at his unsavoury nylon Y-fronts. His and Clive's bedroom was a mass of different kinds of stickiness and smells that could not be tamed even with regular cleaning of the space itself and its two occupants.

'Another time,' he mumbled, fleeing.

'He fancies you,' said Rachel, with a mixture of delight and repulsion.

Susan felt a bit cowed by Dick and Helen, who seemed so uptight compared to Terry. She wasn't sure she liked them. Still, in the very early days of testing a friendship, no one ever breaks it off for the reason that one's friend's parents are awful, because in the teenage years, parents grow increasingly peripheral and thankfully are not present for bus-shelter groping sessions, vodka swigging on the bandstand in the park and hitch-hiking lifts from lascivious lorry drivers at ten o'clock at night.

For Rachel, however, there were other hurdles to get over.

Rachel had assumed discretion would be the order of the day with any secrets she discussed with Susan, though why she had done this is anybody's guess, as even the most amateur of psychologists could have told her that Susan would be riding round town in an open-top bus with a loud-hailer at the merest hint of a new confidence. For Susan it was natural to discuss everything with her family, and she couldn't understand Rachel's seething anger when she came back to Susan's house after school to be greeted by Terry with the words, 'How are your mum's piles?'

Rachel was mortified. In fact, the only reason she'd been aware that her mum had haemorrhoids was when she'd overheard snatches of conversation on the phone to Grandma and found a scary-looking leaflet in the bin in the bathroom.

'For fuck's sake,' she said later to Susan, the first time she had ever used the 'F' word so Susan knew she was angry.

'What's the big deal?' asked her friend.

'The big deal is, it's private. I suppose you've all had a good laugh, have you?' sobbed Rachel. 'Told anyone at school? Told the papers, have you?' And with this she flung herself blindly down the stairs and left the house, ignoring the entreaties behind her.

It took Susan a lot of apologising and a lot of promising before things got back to normal. An uneasy truce in which Susan promised to be tighter-lipped and Rachel said she'd try to be more open was arrived at, though it was a while before Rachel felt she could trust Susan with a really big confidence.

Other friends were an issue too. All too predictably, as Susan and Rachel got closer, Marie, Susan's quiet and dull friend, could be spotted sitting morosely in a corner looking bereft, while Annette the loyal and supportive one seemed permanently overwhelmed by anger and the desire to cut herself. Meanwhile Bev, usually a good laugh, grew closer to Susan's acknowledged enemies and used information about her to embarrass her when she felt like it.

There were constant disagreements between Rachel and Susan about attachments to different pop stars and how each presented themselves to the world. One afternoon in Susan's bedroom Rachel found herself looking at a David Cassidy poster.

'Mmm, lovely, isn't he?' said Susan.

'He's not my cup of tea,' Rachel told her.

Susan felt strangely miffed, as if someone had been horrible about a member of her family. She thought, Well, he wouldn't touch *you* with a bargepole, and then felt terrible about even thinking it. She actually said, 'Well, who do you like then?'

Rachel had begun a hippy phase in her life. 'I like Bowie and Dylan,' she said, thinking she was sounding grown-up.

'Bob Dylan's a horrible smelly old hippy who can't sing,' said Susan, raising the level of debate. 'At least David looks like he's had a wash,' adding, 'but really it's talent that counts.'

'And David Cassidy's got talent, has he?' scoffed Rachel. 'All he does is look pretty and sings all right. He doesn't actually write any of the songs.'

'Yes, he does,' said Susan, not knowing whether he did or not but prepared to defend him against this unfair attack.

'Oh, don't be ridiculous,' said Rachel. 'Course he doesn't.'

Susan changed tack. 'Well, at least he looks like a bloke. David Bowie looks like a girl.'

'Well, David Cassidy looks like Laurence Hidalgo,' sniggered Rachel.

'No, he doesn't.' Susan was getting riled. 'That's rubbish. Anyway, David Bowie looks like your dad in a dress.'

This was the ultimate insult. Without thinking, Rachel jumped up on the bed and with a felt tip she'd been holding, because they'd been drawing ideas for trouser suits on a pad, she drew a moustache on David Cassidy.

'Ooh look, it's Vince,' she said, referring to Vince's recent and rather poor attempts to foster a Peter Wyngarde moustache.

'You've ruined my fucking poster,' said Susan.

Rachel came down to earth. 'Oh, I'm really sorry. I'll get you another one,' she promised.

Susan didn't really mind. 'And I'm getting *you* a bra,' she said.

'I don't bloody want one,' Rachel told her.

'Your tits'll go all saggy and you won't get a husband,' said Susan.

'Good,' said Rachel, ''cause I don't bloody want one.'

A pillow hit her in the face.

Quite a few days were spent skiving off school at Demarco's café down on the seafront, just enough for it not to become noticeable. When they got bored in Demarco's, the girls would wander round Debenhams looking at make-up and handbags and trying to pretend they were meant to be strolling round the shops in their school uniforms in the middle of the day.

Then an incident occurred as the friendship reached its critical three-month stage which nearly finished things off. Rachel had mentioned Fluff many times to Susan, who could not have cared less about pets. Her motto was, 'If you don't get on with them, get rid of them.' She listened sympathetically but it stretched her patience on some days when Rachel was moping about how difficult life was without Fluff. It seemed that the cat had just disappeared, and despite several phone calls to a neighbour back in London with instructions to look out for him, there had been no sightings. Rachel had asked Helen if they could go back up to the old house and look for Fluff but Helen didn't feel she could cope with such a charade and managed to put Rachel off by being extremely irritable with her. Her daughter had noticed that she seemed distracted and bad-tempered much of the time and wondered if the menopause was on its way. (Or perhaps her piles were bad.) It didn't occur to Rachel to think that at thirty-five this was pretty unlikely.

Susan had always felt that humans were much more important than animals, and couldn't understand why you would want to spend your life emotionally shackled to a ball of hair that smelled horrible at both ends.

One afternoon round at the Westons', while Rachel had popped to the shop to get some crisps, Alan was hiding in his bedroom, sexually aroused by the mere presence of a girl and Susan was flicking through *Bunty* rather superciliously in Rachel's bedroom, it being far too young for her, but Helen wouldn't let Rachel have *Jackie*.

'Ow!' Something hit her on the cheek. 'What the hell was that?'

Clive's grinning face appeared round the door. 'It was me!' he exclaimed, waving his catapult. An ancient half-chewed boiled sweet plopped onto the carpet.

Susan was across the room in half a second and had him down on the floor, sitting on his tummy and holding his nostrils together with thumb and forefinger.

'What did you say?' she said. 'Say it again, why don't you.'

Clive, not a master of the concept of sarcasm, did just that. Susan pinched his nose a bit harder.

'I'll call my bum,' he said. 'Let me go. Bum! Bum!' He started to shout for Helen.

Susan clamped her other hand over his mouth, quite enjoying being in control of this little squirt.

'Beg, you little creep,' she said.

He managed to pull his face away a bit. 'Let me go,' he panted. 'I'll tell you a really big secret.'

'Come on then,' she said.

'It's about Mum killing Fluff . . .' he began.

Some weeks later, Susan and Rachel were arguing with one another in the park about Lesley the Bully, who had made a couple more appearance as Rachel was on her way home on her own. Susan was dispensing advice.

'Don't let the little cow get away with it,' she said.

'Easier said than done,' grunted Rachel.

'No, it's not. Just tell her to piss off! Stand up to her, for God's sake.'

'Oh, it's all right for you,' said Rachel. 'You've got your scary mum and sisters to look after you.'

'You've got your mum too,' said Susan unwisely, 'and we all know what she can be like when she gets going.'

'What do you mean?' demanded Rachel.

'Well, you told me she can be a right old cow.'

'I never said that,' said Rachel.

'You might not have actually said those words,' said Susan, 'but some of the things you told me she'd done . . .'

Rachel found herself in the weird position of having to defend her mum from her best friend. She had become inexplicably angry, really quickly too.

'Just shut up!' she shouted. 'At least she doesn't look

like a prostitute.' Even before the words had escaped her lips she knew she had said a really appalling thing. Susan looked horrified. Was it the content, Rachel wondered, or the fact that it sounded like a really bad line from *Crossroads*? She started to say she was sorry but Susan's face by this point was about two inches away from Rachel's.

'At least she didn't kill my fucking cat and cover it up,' said Susan.

The earth stopped rolling for a couple of seconds.

'What?' said Rachel, thinking, Now we're in a scene from *Doctor Who*.

Susan's mind whirred furiously. Within a split second she had to decide whether to pretend she had said it for a joke or brazen it out. Brazening won.

'You heard,' she said.

'How?' said Rachel, feeling tears start to push at the edge of her eyes.

'Ask your mum,' said Susan and left.

Chapter 7

Helen Weston was reading the paper in the living room when she heard the front door slam, followed by Rachel's bedroom door.

'Rachel!' she called. No answer. 'Rachel!' she repeated. 'Come here.' No answer again. It was very unlike her daughter to be this disobedient and Helen wondered if teenagedom had come upon her all in a rush and she was making up for lost time by having a day of being really appallingly difficult. In the end, she went to Rachel's room and, sensing the mood, did something she'd never done before: she knocked on the door.

'Go away,' came Rachel's voice.

Now Helen began to worry. What could possibly have happened in the pantheon of teenage crises to cause Rachel to behave in this way? Could it be a boy, a bully, or an argument with Susan? She opened the door and rather irritably, despite wanting to sound sympathetic, said, 'What on earth is the matter?'

Rachel turned towards the wall and put her little transistor radio up to its full volume.

Helen marched across and clicked it off. 'What the hell is the matter with you?' she snapped.

'You killed my cat.'

The words almost made Helen sink to the floor in a Jane Austen-type swoon. Through her head at the same time ran several trains of thought, which were:

Oh shit, she's found out.

Thank Christ she's found out.

At least I don't have to do everything that Clive says any more.

'How did you find out?' she said falteringly.

'Clive told Susan,' said Rachel.

I'll kill the little bastard, Helen thought to herself, then said aloud: 'I'm sorry, I truly am. I wanted to tell you, but I didn't want to hurt you and by the time I let the lie go on it was too late to turn back.'

'How did you do it?' said Rachel, not knowing if she really wanted to hear.

'Are you sure you want to know?' Helen asked, unsure if she could tell her.

'I'm not a kid any more,' said Rachel.

'All right.' And Helen explained in as tactful a way as she could what had happened in case Rachel questioned Clive about it afterwards.

'But how could Fluff get under you and be crushed?' her daughter wanted to know.

'Well, I suppose I did sort of fall,' Helen said apologetically.

Rachel wanted to laugh at the image of her mother squashing her cat and killing him, and wondered if this was some weird grief reaction or was it genuinely funny.

'I want to be left alone now,' she said.

'All right,' said Helen. 'Are you coming out for tea in a minute?'

'Don't know,' said Rachel.

'OK,' said Helen. 'See you in a bit, hopefully.'

'Mum!' called Rachel as Helen got to the door.

Oh, she's going to forgive me, thought Helen. She turned. 'Yes?'

'If Susan phones, I don't want to talk to her.'

'OK.' Helen felt depressed again. She kicked Clive's Raleigh Chopper as she passed it in the hall.

Susan did phone. Many times. But Rachel was determined and did not cave in. Susan's old friends Marie, Bev and Annette were like vultures hovering over Rachel's corpse and cleaning the body down to the bone. At home Rachel was grumpy and unforgiving with everyone. She was monosyllabic with her brothers and terse and distant with Dick and Helen.

'What shall we do?' said Helen to Dick one night in bed after this had gone on for two weeks.

'Oh, I expect she'll snap out of it,' said Dick, ever the amateur psychologist.

'But what if she doesn't?' said Helen. 'She'll ruin Christmas.'

Dick felt like saying, 'Well, it's all your own fault for not telling her at the time,' but he bit his lip and kept quiet. One bloody miserable female in the house was quite enough for him.

Clive and Alan in the manner of young boys were not particularly helpful in encouraging Rachel through each stage of the grieving process. In fact, they were positively disrespectful and between them managed quite a lot of miaowing when Rachel was approaching which just made her rage at them, much to their delight.

Things were no better at school. Rachel studiously avoided any contact with Susan, who said to anyone who would listen, 'Now I know what it's like being a leper.'

She didn't, of course. Terry said to her, 'Look, a leper would give his right arm merely to be ignored by someone at school,' and didn't realise exactly what she had said.

Things were getting critical. It looked as though the growing friendship between Susan and Rachel had failed its first real big test. Susan had given up phoning Rachel, who never returned her calls, and Rachel found herself rather disappointed. She wished Susan would try harder. Of course she didn't discuss this with anyone because she knew they would urge her to reconcile with Susan and then they could really enjoy the season of good will. Rachel sat in her room listening to Neil Young and Bob Dylan. She played *Harvest* over and over and felt hard done by. She lay on the bed staring at the ceiling with which she was now intimate and thought, I could trace the contours of the damp very accurately.

It was unlikely she would ever be called upon to do this.

Why didn't anyone recognise the full tragedy of her losing Fluff like that? She knew everyone was laughing about it. It just wasn't fair. All the girls at school had seen a change in her from the relaxed friendly girl of the first few weeks of term to the sullen, dull-eyed sulker of the present day. Eventually Helen could bear it no longer and ended up phoning Terry on a night she knew Susan wouldn't be around

'What are we going to do?' said Helen. 'Can't we find some way to get them back together? She's a nightmare to live with.'

'My Susan's not best happy either,' said Terry. 'Why don't you and your hubby come over for a spot of dinner and we'll hatch a plan.'

The thought of Dick as her 'hubby' made Helen feel physically ill, but anything which livened the atmosphere at home and sorted Rachel out was worth a try, so she agreed.

Dick and Helen told the boys and Rachel they were going to the pictures. Helen made a bit of an effort, put on a long skirt and a shawl, tied her hair back with a velvet ribbon and donned a nice choker that Dick had given her for her birthday and a chain belt.

When they arrived at Terry and Vince's place, Helen gave a little shiver. It was very near their own temporary place and Helen thanked her lucky stars that she and Dick were not living there permanently.

Vince ushered them into the living room which was very orange with a lot of dark wood in evidence.

'We're having fondue. Is that OK?' said Terry. 'Got bought a set for my birthday by Vince and I've been dying to try it out for ages.'

Vince confided in Helen and Dick while Terry was in the toilet that in fact he'd 'got it off Green Shield stamps' and Helen marvelled at the number he'd had to collect here, there and everywhere to be able to get a fondue set. Normally you collected fifteen books and found yourself with a light bulb or a Parker Pen set, something you could buy in the shops for about a pound. A fondue set must have required hundreds of books.

They all sat round the table and a bottle of wine was opened that, surmised Helen, would be worth one Green Shield stamp. You could have cleaned an oven with it and still had some left over to take off three layers of an elephant's hide. Still, they grinned and bore it, twirling their long forks with bits of bread. Terry wasn't sure what sort of bread you were meant to use so she'd got Wonderloaf and cut it into easy-to-spear squares. Some bread fell into the fondue and Vince tried to get it out with his fingers while Terry gave him the most evil look.

Eventually the sparse conversation came round to Susan and Rachel. By this time Terry and Helen had made up their minds about each other and Dick and Vince had done the same.

Terry thought Helen was all right but stuck-up and a bit patronising. Helen thought Terry was nice enough but just too animated and rather cruel to Vince. Dick thought Vince was a bit of a wanker who was far too obedient to his missus and Vince thought Dick was a bit of a wanker who was far too obedient to his missus too.

Having traced the history of the row and Vince having had a good laugh over the Fluff incident which he had not fully appreciated before, much to the embarrassment of his wife and the seething resentment of Helen, they then tackled the topic of who was to blame.

'Well, obviously Susan is. However angry she was with Rachel, she should never have told her what Clive had told her,' said Terry.

'Obviously,' echoed Helen.

'Obviously,' said Dick and Vince together.

'But on the other hand, Rachel must have made her really angry to do that because Susan would really have to be under pressure to be so nasty,' said Terry.

'So are you implying it was Rachel's fault that it got so out of hand?' demanded Helen.

They were all under the influence of the shit red wine at this point but didn't realise it.

'I think she's got to take some responsibility,' said Terry.

'The way I read it,' said Helen, 'is that Susan and Rachel were having a row. Rachel was probably getting the better of Susan verbally because she's a very quick girl and Susan felt pushed into a corner and blurted out that secret to be nasty.'

'Oi, hang on a minute,' said Vince. 'You were the one who tried to bribe an eleven-year-old boy to keep quiet, for Chrissakes. Susan's only thirteen: how long do you think that was going to last?'

'Are you saying you can't trust her in those circumstances?' said Helen, furiously pinching Dick's leg under the table in an attempt to elicit some support or alternatively any sign that would demonstrate he was still alive. Dick's head lolled slightly and he sat bolt upright when he was pinched.

'She's thirteen years old,' said Vince.

'So you keep saying,' said Dick, even though Vince had only said it twice, and then couldn't follow it up with anything meaningful before he slipped back into a semi-coma.

Helen said, 'Look, we all know now that Susan can't keep her mouth shut about anything and I can see who she gets it from.'

'You don't mean old Big Gob next to me,' said Vince, trying to interject a joke and bring the temperature down a bit.

'Fuck off, Vince,' said Terry, 'and you can leave now too, you snooty cow,' she told Helen, 'implying my girl's got no control over her mouth.'

'Yes, we're going,' said Helen, 'and what a hugely successful and mature discussion this has been.'

'Oh piss off,' said Terry, picking up a handful of fondue and slinging it in Helen's general direction.

It landed on Helen's face.

'It tasted appalling the first time round, I don't want any more,' said Helen and ducked as Terry aimed again.

Before long, the Piggs' living room-cum-diner was covered in fondue and Wonderloaf, and many bridges had been burned.

It took some time to filter through to Susan and Rachel that their parents weren't talking to one another. As they weren't communicating either it was difficult to piece together the bits of the story and Rachel, who heard Helen talking about it to Dick, began to realise that an 'incident' had occurred. When she asked Helen what she was talking about, her mum went red and mumbled something about falling out with someone she didn't need to know about.

Then Rachel bumped into Kim at the bus stop; Kim was being very civilised about the problem with Susan and still chatted quite happily about everything. 'Your mum and dad were round ours the other night,' she said, and Rachel felt herself gripped by a cold hand.

'Why?' she enquired, trying to keep the tremor out of her voice.

'Well, I'm not sure but I think it was about you,' said Kim.

'Why?' repeated Rachel.

''Cause they know that Susan and you are really unhappy, and they were trying to sort things out.'

'Did it go well?' asked Rachel.

Kim, rather undiplomatically at this point, emotional control not being a strong family trait, began to laugh. 'Sorry,' she said, looking at Rachel. 'It was nothing really.'

'What happened?' said Rachel. 'Oh, come on, Kim – tell me, please.'

Kim by this point was almost crying with laughter. 'They only threw fucking fondue at each other,' she managed over her shoulder.

Rachel's instinct was to phone Susan and have a good laugh about it, but instead she went home, into her bedroom, put on 'School's Out' by Alice Cooper and screamed along to the words at the top of her voice until one of the neighbours rang the doorbell.

Chapter 8

Christmas, the season of good will, was upon the good burghers of Hastings and the town looked like it had really cheered up.

Rachel decided that not having a best friend at Christmas was worse than not having a boyfriend so she phoned Susan and tried to sound really casual.

'Yes?' said Susan, slightly aggressively.

'Can you meet me in town?' said Rachel. 'At Demarco's?'

'I'm a bit busy,' said Susan, trying not to sound bothered, yet not completely unfriendly either.

'Oh, sorry,' said Rachel. 'Forget it then.'

'No, it's all right,' said Susan. 'See you in half an hour.'

Once they sat down, it was easy.

'I'm really sorry for being such a cow,' said Rachel.

'It wasn't your fault. I'm sorry too,' said Susan. 'My big mouth. I'm really sorry and I promise I won't do it again, ever.'

They hugged each other and then the conversation got round to their parents. Susan had all the details ready for Rachel, who was half-appalled, half-touched that Helen and Dick had thought her happiness was important enough to go round to Terry and Vince's for.

'Oh well,' sighed Susan. 'I don't suppose it matters, them falling out. I don't think they were ever going to be the best of friends.'

The two set off to explore the Christmas shops, a pleasure Rachel had been hoping she could share with Susan. Christmas was Rachel's favourite time of year. For her, it was like the final chapter of *Little Women* – the family reunited and expressing their love for one another, knitted together with good Christian values and a few memorable days filled with bonhomie, mutual respect and joy.

Susan, on the other hand, found that she was surrounded by most types of excess at Christmas and couldn't wait for it to spiral down the great pan of past experience.

Vince always turned the garden into one of those lovably awful Santa's grottos with fake snow, reindeer and other Christmas garbage whilst Terry ensured that the inside of the house looked as hideous as the outside. Jennifer generally got more and more agitated as The Great Big Eating Festival approached and Kim and her friends became unbearably charitable towards the elderly which, considering they were complete cows the rest of the year, was very difficult to live with.

And Terry insisted on buying Christmas food that no one liked. On Christmas Eve little piles of dates would appear on the table that would be sufficient to open the bowels of a small but constipated European country. Amongst the dates could also be found proper Turkish Delight, in other words solid mucus covered with icing sugar, which everyone hated, as opposed to the bars by Frys which were lovely but not authentic. Although Terry knew no one liked what she bought, as she chucked it all away unopened on Boxing Day, somewhere in her rapidly deteriorating memory she visualised a-just-after-the-war-type Christmas that she had only ever seen in a Timex advert and annually tried to recreate it.

Anything that made a mess made Vince nervous and he approached Christmas as a superannuated three-day chore involving more paper, more rubbish and much more washing-up than all the lesser festivals of the year put together.

Round at Rachel's house Helen and Dick were slightly more laidback about Christmas, although Helen also had her sentimental Christmas leanings and would dust off her childhood decorations and hang them on the tree. Dick thought this was sad but never said so.

Alan and Clive were permanently disappointed by Christmas. They never got what they wanted. It was either the cheap version or something completely different so they didn't even bother to ask any more . . . just hoped their presents wouldn't be too crap. Helen also insisted they go to midnight mass, the only light relief for the boys at that particular ceremony being a competition to count the number of old people who slept or farted during the carols.

The other problem for all girls of a certain age during Christmas – one that preoccupied Susan and Rachel enormously over the run-up and all the way through to the New Year – was the question of snogging. It was down to mistletoe and the custom on New Year's Eve of having to kiss beneath it. If you were under the age of fifty and your lips had not acquired that gathered-up look round the edges that is particularly favoured by smokers, it was virtually compulsory. This excited some and terrified others.

Susan had decided that this was going to be the year she got a decent squelcher.

'Don't you think we're still a bit young?' said Rachel, who would quite happily have been hit in the face with a cricket bat rather than be kissed.

'Come on, you frigid old moo,' said Susan. 'That's not the right attitude. Think about who you'd like to do it with and then we'll try and work out a plan to pin them down.'

There then ensued a very long discussion on potential candidates. For Susan, interaction with the opposite sex had always been an effortless experience, due to her delightful little heart-shaped face and friendly manner, and so there was a comprehensive list which was whittled down to three. They were: John Pearson, a boy in Jennifer's class who was lanky, dark, silent, brooding and very kissable. He and Susan had never talked but a little flutter happened inside her every time she saw him, and his full red lips looked like a rubber mattress waiting to be bounced on. He was going to the Christmas Eve disco on the pier. This information had been reliably verified by both of Susan's sisters.

Roy Barnett. He worked as a gardener at the local park and was the only one there under ninety who looked vaguely sentient. He was friendly and a laugh. The fact that he was twenty-two might have to be kept from Terry and Vince, they decided.

Mr Grover. The Sociology teacher at school. Married, gorgeous and available, judging by the constant rumours of his forays into infidelity. This dangerous course of action hugely appealed to Susan, who felt only a teacher could bestow a kiss with the right amount of wickedness, sophistication and guilt-tinged spirit.

Rachel couldn't think of anyone.

Susan chivvied her along cheerily and said they would come up with someone in time. She then tried to tackle the problem of how Rachel was going to make it out to the pier disco on Christmas Eve. This had to be very carefully considered. If she asked her mum and Helen said, 'No,' then she had blown her chances of lying about it. Rachel really did want her mum to say yes. She didn't like deceiving her parents, but going out was an unknown quantity and she suspected they would not be too happy about her swanning round on the pier at a mere thirteen years of age. Rachel decided after consultation with Susan not to even bother to ask. She would say she was going to a 'do' at Susan's house. She wanted to tell her mum it was a family do to make it sound less threatening, but she knew because of Susan's family it sounded worse, so she left that out.

Rachel and Susan then had to decide whether to let Terry in on the secret in case Helen phoned her or Vince to check the details of the evening and find out what time Rachel would be home. The decision was made that they would bring Terry in on their deception, especially given her current feelings about Helen and Dick, and it also meant that they felt slightly more secure because an adult had taken some responsibility even though it was only Terry. Terry, of course, didn't tell Vince because she knew he would try and talk her out of it, so by the time Christmas Eve came around, more than a few people were being deceived.

Rachel was a very unconvincing liar so she kept her mouth shut about the evening rather than happily chat away about the details and embellish the proceedings like the happy neighbourhood psychopath would. Susan had promised to lend Rachel something to wear and so she left the flat about seven o'clock looking remarkably like a thirteen year old with no make-up on, a clean pair of jeans and a demure white top.

'Have a lovely time,' shouted Helen from the bathroom. 'Dad'll pick you up at eleven.'

Rachel immediately felt bad because she could tell Helen didn't suspect anything and eleven was far too early.

'Don't get pregnant,' whispered Alan as she passed him in the hall.

'Piss off, Fuckface,' said Rachel.

'Miaow,' said Alan and mimed a big fat tummy.

Round at Terry and Vince's it was all excitement. Kim and Jennifer were going to the disco on the pier as well and Terry and Vince were going to a dinner and dance in

Eastbourne, which, for Terry and Vince, was very sophisticated. Jennifer was wearing a sparkly boob tube and some velvet bellbottoms which made her look like a flared stick of rock, Kim had on a 1920s dress bought from a local charity shop, and Susan wore a long skirt and a halter-neck top and looked lovely. She had got a similar set of clothes for Rachel, whose smallish chest area wasn't best suited to a halter-neck top and she immediately felt self-conscious as she put it on because she never got her shoulders out, let alone what felt to her like a vast expanse of chest as well.

'You look lovely,' said Susan unconvincingly and Terry and Jen and Kim nodded so furiously in agreement it was a wonder they didn't get a whiplash injury. Susan then made Rachel up, treating her rather like a child having a lesson.

By the end of it Rachel had so much make-up on, her face felt heavier and the pores in her skin were struggling to breathe. She looked in the mirror and saw a twenty-five-year-old midget staring back at her.

'Are you sure?'

'Well, we need the make-up or they'll never let us in,' said Susan. 'Come on, it'll be a right laugh.'

Rachel's misgivings multiplied. But she swallowed the proffered half a cup of Babycham with a grin and they headed outside to get into the taxi.

It was cold and frosty and their excited chat as they made their way towards the pier entrance formed a halo of mist around their heads. They got over the first hurdle, paid their money and went through not realising that the woman on the till didn't give a toss how old they were and had been instructed just to get their money. 'Jailbait,' she muttered as they passed her, giggling.

When they got onto the pier they headed straight for the bar and Jennifer was employed to get the drinks, as she was the oldest. The bar was beautiful with fake snow everywhere, an enormous Christmas tree and the bar staff all kitted out in elves' costumes and smiling broadly as most of them were already half-pissed.

'Vodka and lime, please,' said Susan as if it was the most natural thing in the world to be ordering a drink. Jennifer looked at Rachel. 'What do you want?'

'I'll have the same, please,' she said because she didn't know the name of any other drink combinations.

'Oh look,' said Kim, nudging Susan. 'There's Lee Greenwood.'

Lee Greenwood was the lead singer of local band Smoke, whose stock-in-trade was cover versions of recent hits, but they had a rather elevated opinion of themselves and believed they performed them rather better than many of the originals.

Kim had been quite keen on Lee Greenwood for some time and was angling for the opportunity to get him in a dark corner and cover him in kisses. Lee, though, had a very attached girlfriend called Sara, pronounced Sahara without the Ha, and she could see through walls. If anyone looked in the slightest bit likely to move in on Lee she turned into a revenge machine. Tonight, however, she was at home nursing a very red nose and crackly throat.

The atmosphere on the pier was thrilling, consisting as it did of two parts laughter and one part danger. A huge blanket of unfettered anticipation lay over everybody at the beginning of the night and as always was more enjoyable than the actual outcome of the evening, for most of the girls particularly. All those about to set foot on the sex/love road were tingling with excitement, so much more satisfying than the oft-played-out stark reality of lying on a wet dark beach, knickers round ankles, full of vodka and lime with the satisfied man-boy making off across the shingle to rendezvous with mates or collapse into his unmade bed.

No one wanted an evening spent flattened against the wall watching everyone else have the most fascinating, wonderful time, as opportunity after opportunity passed them by until they felt they needed a sign round their neck and a small bell to ring.

No one wanted to be the one whose date never showed and left them standing like a lemon next to the ticket kiosk, or who turned up with their boyfriend only to sit on the sidelines all night while he and his mates leered at huge bosoms, made 'wanker' signs at each other and had pissing competitions with fag ends in the urinals.

The pier was the perfect place for romantic melodrama. Its ballroom with a stage at one end looked like it hadn't changed since the 1950s, the mirror ball and decadent overblown furnishings lending it the air of a shabby knocking-shop. Its magic dwelled in the fact that it stood on big legs that went down into the sea. Sounds were muted and echoey, and the light was diffused by the ever-moving sea.

Jennifer, Kim, Susan and Rachel hung together for a bit and spent the first hour or so on a circuit which took in the toilets, bar and dance floor. Outside was for later when you had someone to hang on to and share the ozone-filled, sharp night air.

Rachel was nervous and found that the soothing burn of vodka on her throat was a real confidence-booster, so for the first hour she concentrated on pouring enough down her to stop her internal wobble and increase her boldness.

Jennifer, Kim and Susan were all accomplished dancers who had achieved nirvana in Rachel's book . . . they didn't look like twats when they were bobbing about. This was all Rachel aspired to and she did the sort of awkward swaying that bad dancers do in the vain hope that should anyone pass their eye over her, they would hardly notice she was moving let alone trying to dance.

John Pearson and Roy Barnett were both around and so Susan as usual found herself wishing that Mr Grover were there. Mr Grover was actually having sex with an underage girl on the settee at her house while her parents were out at a carol service and this would be appearing in the local papers before too long.

Someone who looked like a small weightlifter seemed to have taken a fancy to Rachel and gradually she became aware that she was being circled.

'I think that bloke's after me,' she said to Susan, losing for a moment the idea that this was an apparently enjoyable flirty night out rather than an ordeal during which you were stalked by a series of threatening-looking gorillas. 'Please don't leave me on my own,' she panicked, but obviously the Pigg girls didn't know Rachel well enough yet for, one by one, either through friends or their bladders, they all drifted away, leaving Rachel staring at the floor, cursing them and praying they would come back soon before the weightlifter pounced.

'Hello, love,' he shouted above the noise of 'Ballroom Blitz' by the Sweet which Rachel had started swaying to but had given up on when she realised the tempo was way beyond her capabilities.

'Hello,' she replied.

'Can I get you a drink, darling?' said the small one.

'No, thanks,' said Rachel. 'I'm fine.'

'What about a dance then?' he said, manoeuvring an arm behind her and making her flesh crawl slightly.

'No.' She moved away.

'Fuck you then,' he said and stalked off.

Rachel felt tears prick her eyes. Being talked to like this wasn't something she was used to. Still, she supposed she'd better *get* used to it if she wasn't going to gratefully collapse into the arms of the first bloke who came along.

Alcohol began its inevitable intervention into the path of events, shifting the sensible controlled behaviour of the participants off on a course of disinhibition and abandonment of civilised daytime manners.

Having bopped so far to a series of unrelated chart songs, Rachel began to panic as she realised the disc jockey was entering his first period of 'slowies'. John Pearson had beaten Roy Barnett to it and he and Susan were locked together in a tableau of teen romance whilst Kim and Jennifer seemed to be dancing with Dull-But-Acceptable blokes from the middle range of what was on offer.

It was at this point, very early on in her dating career, that it began to dawn on Rachel that she was always going to end up with the slightly less good-looking/odd/not so bright/badly dressed/spotty/halitosis-ridden/friend while for Susan nights on the pull were always, always going to be peopled with good-looking, attentive, high-status young men.

Rachel decided to go to the loo and thought that by the time she returned, one of the Pigg sisters might be back from their smooching and waiting at their allotted rendezvous.

The toilets on the pier weren't the most comfortable place to sit and reflect on life's vicissitudes. Obviously the Women's were not as bad as the Men's. Legend told that almost every virus or infection from the Middle Ages had at some time or another swirled along the urinals of that hallowed institution. However, the women's toilets were not the sylvan glade of sweetness one might have imagined. The smell was a watered-down version of the male equivalent but still not easy on the nose. Several doors had been kicked in; others had bolts that were hanging on for grim death. Some were blocked, many had unidentified pools of brackish liquid lying on the floor in front of them and the chance of a bit of toilet paper was about as likely as John Pearson suddenly appearing at the door, picking Rachel up and carrying her in his arms to the White Rock Pavilion for a luxury piss in a nice clean toilet surrounded by unsoggy carpet.

All the girls in the toilet were making do with whatever scrappy bit of tissue they had and a straggly queue had formed of every imaginable style and form of teenage cult. In front of Rachel were three skinhead girls in their Tonic suits and monkey boots. Next to them was a hippy in a Laura Ashley skirt, no shoes no bra and a loon T-shirt, and behind her was a pair of greaser girls in dark leather, one with a bicycle chain over her shoulder looking a bit drunk and frankly a bit frightening.

Rachel was terrified. It wasn't often that she was in these situations, and a wave of guilt and nausea swept over her at the thought of how her parents would react if they could see her now.

Caught in her reverie, Rachel hadn't noticed that the room was emptying, apart from the girls in black leather. She went into a cubicle and sat gingerly on the edge of the toilet with the seat up, and because the catch had broken and it was too far to lean across and hold the door she had one foot up, holding it shut with her toes. Someone pushed against it.

'I'm here,' she called out, hating herself for sounding so small and pathetic.

'Fucking good for you,' said a harsh voice, and lots of people laughed. Rachel found a scrap of Izal toilet paper as effective as using a thin sheet of metal for all the absorbency it offered. She flushed the toilet which actually worked and exited to come face to face with a group of rather intimidating-looking seventeen- or eighteen-year-old girls, an odd but endearing mixture of shapes and sizes. However, they were not there to look sweet. They stood in a row blocking her path.

Rachel supposed that if they were blokes, they would already have kicked the crap out of her.

'What do you want?' she said.

'What do you want?' mimicked one of them and they all laughed. She seemed to be the leader. She was tall and slightly paunchy and in her leathers looked like a podgy bat.

Rachel thought that the longer she was in there, the more likely it was that fat Bat Woman would do her some serious damage.

Like Kim last year, they were reading *Lord of the Flies* at school. Rachel had a vision of Piggy tumbling into the sea and wondered if she was to be slung off the pier. She decided to go for broke and ran, head down, shouting, 'Get the fuck out of my way!' and holding up a clenched fist. She looked ridiculous, but it worked.

The sea of black leather was so surprised it parted, and once Rachel was past them she felt she was running for her life. Within seconds she had been reabsorbed into the comforting warmth and darkness that lay round the edge of the ballroom. With relief she saw that Susan had divested herself of John Pearson and was looking around for her.

'Oh God, I nearly got beaten up by some greasers in the

toilet,' she shouted above the noise of Mud's 'Lonely This Christmas'.

'Never mind,' shouted back Susan, to whom this seemed a banal occurrence. 'The band's coming on in a minute.'

'Where's John?' Rachel rather hoped he had pissed off home and she and Susan could have a laugh.

'He's gone to get me a drink, he's lovely.'

The music stopped and a sense of chattery anticipation swept through the room as the band appeared onstage.

Lee Greenwood was looking resplendent in a Father Christmas outfit and the rest of the band were dressed up as Santa's pixies. They started with a couple of very well-known Rolling Stones numbers, 'Get Off My Cloud' and a particularly poor version of 'Ruby Tuesday'. Fortunately, by that point no one cared. They were all drunk and only vaguely recognised what was being played.

Smoke then went straight into 'High Ho Silver Lining' much to the delight of the crowd who sang like manic rugby players. Then they did something very foolish. They tried to sneak in one of their own slightly avant garde numbers called 'Slapper' and the crowd turned. There was a lot of booing and throwing stuff and they were forced halfway through the song to reroute to 'Route Sixty-six', after which equilibrium was immediately restored.

Rachel looked at her watch. It was ten fifteen. As her dad was picking her up at Susan's she really had to be back by five to eleven and ready to appear casually from round the side of the house saying, 'Oh, I just saw the car pull up.'

She tapped Susan on the shoulder. 'We should be going in ten minutes,' she said. Susan had agreed to be part of the deception but caught in the Christmas haze of drink, smouldering looks, a squeeze from John Pearson and the excitement of the evening she suddenly became all reluctant.

'OK!' she shouted.

The band played for another ten minutes or so and then it was back to Christmas singles and smooching. Rachel turned to say something to Susan and saw that John was kissing her in a rather ferocious way. It looked feral. Roy Barnett, who had been hanging about hoping Susan would notice him, gave up and in a 'Fuck it, you'll do' sort of way asked Rachel to dance.

Rachel had missed out on the nuances of the John/Roy dichotomy and as Roy seemed like a fairly safe bet she agreed and found herself being clutched rather desperately and moved round the floor as if she was an errant chimp that had escaped from its cage and was being clung onto for grim death by its keeper and edged back towards captivity again. Rachel had had quite a bit to drink and everything started to happen in a surreal way; the surroundings went past her like an abstract painting, but with the occasional clue like Susan's face or Jennifer grinning at her over a large drink. As the record came to a climax and people began to realise that they had few opportunities left for a seasonal fumble, clinches started to happen all over the place and Roy, seemingly overcome by Christmas, the atmosphere and several pints of Directors, decided to risk giving Rachel a kiss.

Rachel had never been kissed properly before and numbered among her kissing experience, family hugs and pecks, slightly wet grandma ones, a shy boy when she was ten who did a big smacker on the side of her cheek, and Clive and Alan holding her down and letting their old dog Shandy slobber all over her face which didn't really count but maybe should have done because the experience of Roy kissing her was turning out to be not so dissimilar.

Most teenage girls who have never been kissed are prisoners of their expectations. They will have witnessed many thousands of kisses at the cinema or on TV, as well as experiencing the ones in their dreams with pop stars and their favourite male film stars. Had Roy realised how much was riding on his performance he probably wouldn't have bothered, and to say Rachel was shocked and disappointed by his kiss is a massive understatement.

Rachel couldn't believe how horrible it was, like a hot wet slug trying to force its way into her mouth and wiggle around before it bored down further and blocked her throat. It felt like an assault and Rachel would have put a stop to it if she had more confidence. But she was thirteen, didn't know if this was normal, socially acceptable or merited a prison sentence even, but she let it continue until he decided to break it off.

'Excuse me,' said Rachel, gasping for breath. She turned and ran away as fast as she could. The length of the pier flew past as she ran across the wooden slats, making a soft thumping noise with the too-high platform shoes she had borrowed from Susan. She looked round. No, Susan hadn't seen her go and followed her. What time was it? Shit, five to eleven. She had five minutes to get outside Susan's house which was a mile and a half away before her dad arrived. Becoming aware of a crunching, moaning noise, she looked round and under the legs of the pier, lit by a faint frosty moon, she could just make out a strange-looking couple. As she focused her eyes, which seemed to have been jogged out of their sockets by that kiss, she realised that Father Christmas had someone up against one of the struts of the pier and was going at it with the abandon of a terrier. It was Lee Greenwood and Jennifer with her legs clamped round his waist lost in a drunken Christmas Wonderland.

Season's Greetings, thought Rachel.

Rachel knew she would never run a mile and a half in five minutes, and the fact that she had even wasted a few seconds thinking about it made her realise how drunk she was. However, for once the gods were on her side. There were two taxis at the rank. Oh, Joyful Happy Christmas! She flung herself into one and gave the address, adding, 'Please, it's really important that I'm there in five minutes.' The cab driver felt sorry for this rather drunken girl-woman who was a bit plain, and thought she must have had a bad night so he would be nice to her. He drove as fast as he could, then at the road next to Susan's, he pulled in and turned round to Rachel and said, 'How about a little Christmas kiss?' Given her very recent experience, Rachel was not going to be kissed again for several years and she threw him a look of horror coupled with a strangled retort which was lost by her opening the door and falling out onto the road. She glanced at her watch. Two minutes past eleven. She began to run, aware that either she was too late and her dad was already there and she'd been rumbled, or that her dad was coming any minute now and would see her running like hell dressed in different clothes from the ones she had gone out in, although Christ, if it was her dad, he probably wouldn't even notice. But Rachel was in luck. She arrived outside Susan's house, still in darkness, hid round the side, dumped her clothes in the garden and struggled into her normal clothes just as she saw her dad's car pull up.

In as natural a way as possible she went across the scrubby grass to meet him and got in the car. She knew the vodka didn't smell so hoped he couldn't tell she had downed nearly half a bottle.

'Hello,' said Dick. He was wearing his horrible maroon and black striped dressing-gown, grounds for divorce on its own, and some rather tatty slippers. 'Did you have a nice time?'

'Yes, lovely, thanks,' said Rachel. 'We played some records and had a bit of a dance.'

'I'll just pop in and thank Susan's mum and dad,' said Dick, obviously having forgotten that the last time they saw each other they were trading insults. 'Besides, I'm dying for the toilet.'

Rachel's heart travelled up towards her throat again. 'Oh, don't do that,' she said. 'They've all gone to bed.'

'Are you sure?' said Dick. 'I mean, you've only just come out.'

'Yes,' said Rachel. 'They were going up just as I left.'

The joy of a dad like Dick was that he believed that sort of rubbish and he turned the car round and headed for home, holding his legs together.

Rachel fell gratefully into bed, put Radio Luxembourg on under the covers and reflected on the fact that she'd got away with it properly for the first time. She knew that if Helen had come to pick her up, she wouldn't have been fooled for a minute, so she had to make sure that she always manoeuvred her dad into that role. She could lie in the back of the car, naked, snogging two thirty-year-old blokes and her dad wouldn't even notice.

Chapter 9

Christmas, 1974

Two years later to the very day, Rachel woke up in a very bad mood, particularly because Clive had tied a piece of string round her toe and was pulling quite hard on it from the safety of behind the door.

'Fuck off, you little monster!' she shouted. Rachel had still not recovered from the indignity of being kept in on Christmas Eve when everyone else was out going mental and enjoying themselves before they had to spend the day chained to their family, bored out of their minds and receiving a series of presents that they didn't want from a group of people they didn't want to be with.

Down the street, Susan woke in an equally bad mood. Jennifer's baby Lucy, now fifteen months old and the result of some unsafe sex with Father Christmas, aka Lee Greenwood, under the pier on Christmas Eve two years ago, had woken her up. Despite the fact that Jennifer and the baby were in a different room, the house was so small and the walls so thin that even the minutest sound swirled everywhere. At least the baby seemed to have cured Jen's eating disorder and she was now a healthy nine and a half stone and trying very hard not to think of herself as enormous. Lee Greenwood was long gone and Jennifer, contrary to expectations, bore her lot with good humour, energy and very little moaning.

Rachel had settled in at school and into her new Hastings life and felt very comfortable. She and Susan were closer than ever and spent most of their time together, much to the irritation of Helen and Terry who, for very different reasons, considered them unsuitable friends. Terry felt Rachel would give Susan ideas above her station. Helen, on the other hand, thought Susan would entice Rachel to settle for a suburban existence with a dullard of a husband and some under-achieving kids. Both girls steadfastly resisted their mothers' disapproval although they did not know all the details and both mothers were sensible enough to keep their mouths shut, knowing that should they spill the beans about their antipathy, it would only strengthen the bond between them.

Despite fitting into Hastings, Susan and Rachel felt slightly strangled occasionally by its smallness. They knew everyone and there were no surprises but it was early days to do anything about that yet. Rachel had managed to have a reasonably liberated social life but not to the degree she wanted. So far, she had managed to get out roughly every couple of weeks and she and Susan had begun to spend time in the Old Town pubs with a group of people both their parents would have been horrified by. Luckily, none of them knew. Although Terry was much more liberal than Helen, to her the Old Town meant drugs and they were for middle-class people with money to burn.

'If I ever catch any of you taking any sort of drugs I'll bloody kill you, understand?'

They did.

Rachel had taken one too many risks and had been found out – and that was why she was being kept in. She and Susan had tried to get a drink in a bar called the Crypt, and one of the excessively grumpy barmen had told the two underage drinkers to get out.

Rachel hated being beaten like this so she and Susan had waited a couple of weeks, dressed themselves up in their finest mature apparel, put a wig and sunglasses on and slid into the dark of the Crypt on a Saturday lunchtime to see if they could fool 'Grumpy'.

Susan ordered the drinks and all would have been fine had Rachel not spoiled it by doing a combination of an explosive giggle and taking a sip of her drink at the same time. The drink went everywhere and her wig fell off. As they were preparing to run, Grumpy grabbed Rachel by her collar and said, 'Right, what's your name and where do you live?' Caught offguard, Rachel dutifully recited the correct details.

'You silly cow,' said Susan.

'I know,' said Rachel. 'But Grumpy will never bother to contact my parents.'

However, Grumpy was more conscientious than they both imagined and Rachel arrived home from school one afternoon the following week, having forgotten all about it, to find her mother enraged and vindictive.

'Stay in for a week over Christmas? That's really bloody mean,' wept Rachel.

'Right – that's an extra day for swearing,' said Helen. 'Get used to it.'

Rachel told Susan the bad news on the phone.

'Oh bollocks, I'll have to go to the pier on my own then,' Susan said.

'Thanks for the sympathy,' sniffed Rachel. 'What about Kim, won't she go with you?'

'No, her and Roy are going to the pictures,' said Susan. 'Bor-*ing*.'

Kim was now going out with Roy Barnett and an odd couple they made, given that Kim had always fancied herself as a bit of a brain and poor old Roy could barely manage a tabloid newspaper. Rachel often wanted to ask Kim how she could possibly bear to be anywhere near Roy and his killer tongue, but couldn't quite bring herself to do so. She would have got Susan to do it but that meant she would have had to tell her the truth about Christmas two years ago and she pretended at the time she had enjoyed it just for the sake of a bit of peace. Kim and Roy were saving to get married but on Roy's small wages (he was still working as a gardener for the council) and Kim's potential earnings (she had taken a job at the local hairdresser's as an apprentice and was being paid a pittance), they thought they would probably have to get on the council waiting list.

John Pearson had long since disappeared from Susan's life. For the past two years she had dallied with a series of keen but rather unchallenging young men, all of whom she could quite happily have dumped, but continued to see until some incident which irritated her brought the relationship to an end, usually a demand from them for full sex. Susan wasn't one of those girls who got pressured into sex for fear of losing someone. She wasn't really saving herself for marriage so much as feeling why on earth should she open herself up for someone who didn't really deserve it.

Rachel, on the other hand, had steered well clear of all that sort of thing since Roy had swooped down and skewered her with his tongue on the pier. She began to see nuns in a different light and thought that the reason the ones in the Church of England convent up the road looked so cheerful was because they never had to kiss or have sex with anyone.

Susan was constantly enquiring about Rachel's preferences and they often did quizzes in *Jackie* about their love lives and other important issues, and Rachel found herself inventing a whole new persona who fancied boys, loved clothes and make-up and just wanted to go steady with someone called Steve. She knew she would have to come clean about her virginal aspirations soon, because she needed to talk about it and the only choices were her mum or Susan. She thought at a pinch Terry might be good at listening but was worried she'd blab to the Ceefax sisters and thereby it would definitely get back to Roy.

'Are you coming out?' Helen called from the kitchen. 'I've made some breakfast.' Rachel was really hungry and would have loved the full breakfast her mum always cooked on Christmas Day, but just to spite her because she still had not forgiven her parents for grounding her, she shouted, 'No thanks, I'm not hungry,' and then sat in her bedroom and sulked because she had just ruined her own morning.

Two hours later Helen called out, 'We're opening presents!'

'I've got a headache,' replied Rachel.

'If this goes on much longer, I'm going to slap her silly face,' Helen raged to Dick who, rather than being worried or angry with Rachel's behaviour, was just bored by it.

'Can't you just ignore her?' he pleaded.

'No, I can't,' said Helen. 'She's going to ruin Christmas again and I've had enough.' She started to cry. How did it all get to this point, she thought. Sulky daughter, apathetic sons and wanker of a husband, but as usual she didn't express any of it, just wiped her eyes and got on with the turkey.

About midday, Rachel relented. She was starving, could smell dinner cooking, could feel her mum was upset and knew that she was ruining things, so she put a smile on and went out to join in.

'Sorry, Mum,' she said, hanging by the kitchen door. 'I really am.'

Helen was relieved. 'All right then, let's just try and have a nice day without any rows, shall we?' she said, thereby implying that once Christmas was over, it would be back to sulking and shouting.

Alan and Clive moved around like bit-part actors in family life. Alan was now sixteen and had entered the increasing hair/decreasing social skills phase of adolescence. Clive seemed to be on another planet. It was not that he was unpleasant, but he seemed to have nothing in common with anyone alive and was almost a scientific phenomenon, so little did he communicate anything that was worth hearing.

Everyone desperately wished for Christmas to be over, from Roy Barnett who had been forced to spend a fortune on Kim's Christmas present (he knew which ring she wanted as she took him past the shop several hundred times and pointed at it), to Mr Grumpy the barman in the Crypt who hated the extra work Christmas brought with it, the hysterical laughter of anyone under twenty-five and the fact that once again he was on his own without his wife and he had to make his own bloody dinner.

Rachel was kept in for two weeks and if she had thought about it, she would have enjoyed the lack of pressure and being able to take sanctuary from a world which seemed to be becoming increasingly competitive. As important exams loomed nearer, she realised that academic achievement was just another competitive element of a girl's life these days. If you were a female, you also competed on the level of looks, domestic achievements, childbearing ability, skill in snaring a decent bloke, clothes and an array of other seemingly trivial but important things like record collections, posters on walls, number of times you'd been kissed et cetera. There was so much pretending going on during one's teens it was a wonder anyone got to their twenties in a stable emotional state.

Because of Rachel's increasing resentment over the past couple of years she had started to move towards a group of people who dressed scruffily and didn't seem to care about material things too much and could be found most nights outside the pubs in the Old Town staring up at the stars. They were called 'hippies' and the women wore long skirts or loon jeans, beads and no bras. You could smell them coming a mile off because most of them were covered in patchouli oil. Patchouli oil is like Marmite; you either love it or it makes you want to vomit – and that was the effect it had on Helen who, whenever she stood close to Rachel, felt sick. She could barely enter her daughter's room without wishing some sort of surgical mask could be made available.

There had been many arguments about the way Rachel looked, although Helen secretly admired her choice in a world that was becoming increasingly hostile and capitalist in its outlook and threatened, Helen felt, to explode in a frenzy of spending, envy and flashiness. Terry couldn't wait for this to happen.

Dick, by contrast, barely tolerated Rachel, her music and her appearance. He had hoped for a demure daughter who might perhaps become a teacher and remain a virgin until she was twenty-one, whereupon she would marry the local vicar and set up home at the vicarage, producing lovely children and managing to be more right-wing and rampantly misanthropic than anyone else around her, despite Jesus's entreaties in the Bible.

Dick was building up to what is known in the oil industry as a gusher. All it needed was one incident with Rachel to tip him over the top and his temper would ensure things were changed forever between them.

Susan had decided to go down a non-hippy route as far as her appearance was concerned. She craved the order and rigidity and smooth lines of skinhead girl fashions, although she wasn't even aware of the implications of looking like a female representative of the British Bulldog. However, there was within her a frustrated and slightly aggressive streak, and she would have been horrified if anyone had suggested this be targeted at black people. No, she wasn't a racist. The fact was that something in Susan wanted a bloody good ruck and a bloody good ruck with a bloke too.

Once Rachel was let out again and escaped round to Demarco's to meet with Susan she came clean on the kissing blokes front. Susan was surprised but unlike so many girls of her age, non-judgemental. She asked a question which Rachel had not even considered.

'You don't think you're one of those ... lesbians, do you?'

'Don't know,' said Rachel. 'I've not even thought about it. I don't think so. I think I'm more like a eunuch. I just don't want to do anything with anybody.'

'Well, I think you haven't met the right person,' said

Susan. 'It's been two years. Shall we try a few more and see how we get on? To be honest, I'm fed up with being on my own.' (She had been on her own for precisely three weeks, having hidden from a perfectly decent bloke called Mark Beasley who had annoyed her by looking a bit like David Cassidy but being a bit like Vince.) 'Let's go to that party on Saturday and see what happens, shall we?'

They had both been invited to a party at a farmhouse out on the edge of a village in Sussex by Amanda, a girl Susan had known from primary school. Amanda was very posh and liked to show off about it by being as ostentatious with her family's wealth as possible. The party was to be held in a barn on their land and fifty guests had been invited, all of whom would be provided with sleeping bags to stay the night. Amanda's mother had guaranteed to all parents that the party would be well supervised and that she and her husband Dudley could be relied upon to do the right thing.

Rachel had had to approach the matter gingerly with Helen, given that the doghouse was her permanent place of residence lately.

'I'll just talk to Amanda's mother again and then Dad and I will decide,' Helen said. 'I'll let you know in a couple of days.'

Rachel waited in a frustrated bubble for two days and eventually Helen relented and said she could go. Rachel was surprised as her money had been on Helen forbidding the whole venture. However, her mother seemed slightly distracted and a little bit depressed. Rachel couldn't worry about that, though; she was simply pleased that she'd been allowed out.

A very long list of rules accompanied the permission. There must be no drinking, no drugs (Amanda's mum had assured Helen that there would be just weak cider and absolutely no drugs), the girls must stick together, not go off on their own into the countryside, not try and climb a tree when they were drunk – except they mustn't be drunk. The list was very long and boring.

'All right, Mum, I get the message. I'll sit in the corner and have a cup of tea,' said Rachel.

Helen laughed. 'Sorry,' she said. 'I just want you to enjoy yourselves safely.'

No such thing, thought Rachel.

Chapter 10

It was absolutely glorious to be out of the town and in the crisp and even countryside. Rachel and Susan whooped with the sheer joy of anticipation. A whole night out and about on their own having a laugh and going mental. They had walked from the nearest station and it had been pretty dark by then. Neither of them were used to the country-side so the sights and sounds were alien, causing them to feel as if they'd walked onto the set of a low-budget horror film as, gradually, the scratchings and skitterings going on in the hedgerows began to make them uneasy. Then all of a sudden the farm appeared up ahead and they could hear all sorts of noise – music, laughter and chattering – and realised that most people had already arrived.

'Hiya!' Amanda greeted them. 'Come on in. Do you want to go into the house and get changed or are you happy hiding in the corner of the barn where the party's going to be?'

'Is it OK if we come into the house?' asked Susan, ever keen to see how other people's lives and homes were different from her own. The house had the scruffy, effortlessly flung-together look which posh people seem able to achieve without being too flashy. The combination of different styles and periods handled by a lesser mortal would have looked ridiculous, but in this house it was perfect.

'Hi, gals,' shouted Amanda's mother in a manner reminiscent of a Roedean hockey captain. 'Have an awfully good night, won't you.'

Up in a guest bedroom Susan and Rachel opened their bags and began to get ready. Rachel had a long dress from a jumble sale, which was intended for a taller, slimmer girl, and despite the fact that it looked sweet it also looked incongruous.

Susan always got it right and looked absolutely amazing in a tartan mini and black polo-neck jumper. Rachel tried very hard not to be gripped by the monster that was envy. She hoped that one day when she was older she could look in the mirror and truly feel that she was someone people wanted to look at. It was not enough having a nice personality or being brainy or good at art. Sometimes she just wanted to be gorgeous.

By the time they'd got themselves ready, it was nearly eight o'clock and the party was beginning to bubble away promisingly. The girls walked out towards the barn from which they could hear the strains of T. Rex and went in, both feeling as they entered that the occupants of the place were appraising them.

Neither of them knew anyone else there but Susan was greeted warmly again by Amanda, who introduced her to a few people and then left to circulate like a pessimistic mayfly, knowing she would never have one minute that she could say she honestly enjoyed, as is always the way at one's own party.

The abundance of alcohol was the complete antithesis to the situation described by Amanda's mother on the phone to Helen. Amanda's parents were the sort of people who start pouring decent red wine down their offspring's throats at their christening and don't see anything wrong with it, which is why many of them have big bulbous noses and gout later in life. The barn looked absolutely magical. Storm lanterns were hung all over the ceiling. 'They're just asking for the place to be burned down,' said the sensible bit of Rachel.

Bales of hay were piled up to make seats and a bar, and were covered with some expensive-looking brocade. Better than we've got in our house, thought, Susan. People were standing in groups; few of them had drunk quite enough to be dancing, but the atmosphere was friendly.

Up at one end of the room was a DJ with a record deck who kept pointing out that he took requests, particularly from pretty girls, and Rachel wanted to go up to him and say, 'Excuse me, but don't you realise what a knobhead you are, talking like that. Everyone here will think you're a tosser.' Then she realised he was being simpered over by a couple of the aforementioned pretty girls and gave up.

Susan put her arm through Rachel's and they strolled round the outside of the party assessing its potential.

'Here,' said Susan, slipping something into Rachel's hand. 'You might need this later.'

Rachel looked down. It was a condom. She laughed, but immediately felt slightly worried.

'I've got one too,' said Susan. 'You never know. Come on, let's get a drink.'

They went over to the bar and started on the cider, which was very strong, and after a couple of polystyrene cups felt quite overtaken by the night. There was someone smoking dope and eventually a joint reached Susan and Rachel, neither of whom had tried it before, Rachel because she'd never been offered it and Susan because she didn't really fancy being out of control, even though everyone who tried to pass her a joint insisted that it wasn't that sort of drug. They both declined.

After a while and a bit of a dance and a lot of giggling trying to have a pee outside behind the hedge, Susan and Rachel were both very happily having a good time and as is the way of these things, a couple of suitors wandered up and began chatting. They were two friends, Dave and Martin, and they were down for the weekend from London because they knew Amanda's older brother Stuart.

Martin was nice-looking with curly hair, a big nose and a slightly gappy smile, which Rachel thought made him look lovely, but she could immediately tell from the way that Susan had begun to talk to him that gears had been changed and Susan had moved into chat-up and be chatted-up mode. When boys meet girls like this and there is the inevitable stronger spark between two of them, the initial reaction of the second couple is resentment that there is pressure on them to fall into line and go along with the foursome for the sake of ease and convenience for the evening.

Rachel was not an easy flirter. She couldn't manage to talk the sort of bollocks you needed to signal attraction, whereas Susan could have taught it at degree level. It was subtle too. No fluttering of eyelashes or droppings of hanky but just a fixed friendly gaze, a lightness of touch in the CV department, exactly the right amount of humour. Rachel just could not manage this. She either sounded vacuous and silly or desperately stilted.

Luckily for her, Dave didn't seem to notice because he was either too drunk, too stoned, a psychopath who did not pick up social cues easily or possibly deaf.

Martin and Susan were soon in an animated discussion which isolated them from their surroundings so Rachel and Dave were forced to make the effort.

'So what do you do?' ventured Rachel, feeling she should just hit herself round the face and start again, so banal was her question.

'I'm at college,' said Dave, 'in London, doing an art degree. I'm in my first year.'

If I was doing an art degree in London, I wouldn't be at a party in Sussex with a load of schoolgirls, thought Rachel, which proved she didn't know anything about blokes.

'How about you?' said Dave. 'Still at school?'

'Oh no,' lied Rachel. 'No, I'm at college too.'

'Oh,' said Dave. 'In London?'

'No, Brighton, Sussex University,' said Rachel. 'I'm doing English.'

'How brilliant,' said Dave. 'I always wanted to do English. What books are you studying?'

Rachel panicked and then realised it wasn't a full stop, it was a comma, and Dave added, 'Chaucer?'

She nodded with relief, then re-panicked in case he asked her anything about that.

'Excuse me,' she said, 'I've just got to go for a pee.'

'OK,' said Dave good-naturedly, looking round. 'See you in a minute.'

Outside, Rachel realised that for the first time ever, and after such a short interchange, she really wanted to go back in and talk to Dave some more. This worried her as it was such an unfamiliar feeling, but as she squatted by a hedge looking up at the stars, the steam rising all around her, she had a delicious sense of future pleasures and she finally realised what all the fuss was about.

When she got back inside, Susan and Martin had disappeared and Dave was nowhere to be seen. Rachel deflated like a wrinkly party balloon, sat down and tried not to cry and wondered how easy it would be to get back home from here at ten o'clock at night.

'I thought you might like another drink.' Dave sat down beside her and Rachel began to experience emotions just like they described them in _Jackie_. Does he make your heart pound? Can you not take your eyes off him? Fucking hell, thought Rachel, they're geniuses.

She couldn't take her eyes off him and she listened with a heightened interest and attention as Dave talked about himself and about music he liked, about London, about motorbikes and about the sort of pubs he went to. He could have talked about holes in the ground and Rachel would still have been enraptured. She hardly even noticed that Susan had gone. She put her hand in her pocket and felt the condom there and mentally shrivelled a bit because its presence kind of ruined what was for her a magical evening when everything was going right for a change.

Someone clapped their hands. It was Amanda's mum. 'Attention, everyone!' she shouted. 'Please all stand to wish my daughter a happy birthday!'

Amanda's dad staggered in bearing a bloody enormous cake with seventeen candles on it and the group of party-goers broke into a necessarily tuneless rendering of that tuneless ditty Happy Birthday.

Having dispensed with that and candles et cetera, Amanda's mum announced that there were to be fireworks and hot punch outside the barn. Everyone shuffled out, some of them complaining that, 'They weren't fucking six year olds.'

The fireworks only served to create an even more surreal evening. Whilst they were watching them, Dave put his hand into Rachel's and she experienced another rush of warmth and giddiness.

Rachel just couldn't understand what was going on. It

made her smile to think of all those articles about finding true love which said there would be fireworks – and of course, there were fireworks. She felt light-headed and in control at the same time. She also feared saying anything because she was worried that any words she could possibly manage to blurt out with these momentous feelings couldn't possibly match what the situation represented to her; like a policeman saying, 'Do you want a cup of tea?' when he's just told you your whole family have been killed in a car accident.

'You OK?' said Dave.

'Yeah, fine,' said Rachel, knowing that these two words could not possibly express the elation she felt. She knew she had a huge amount of catching up and growing up to do and wished there were some guarantees that she could do it all with Dave.

'Shall we go for a walk,' said Dave, 'and have a look at the countryside?'

'OK,' said Rachel, again keeping it short.

They left the bright ring of light that surrounded the barn and headed out across the courtyard of the farm. It was cold but coats and cider warmed them both up. When they had got to a field a little way from the farm but still in sight of it, Dave suggested they sit down. He had brought something to drink with them and put it down by his side. The pair of them sat together and Dave looked hard into Rachel's eyes and she thought, Oh shit, he's going to kiss me.

In the split second before he did so, the horrible memories of Christmas 1972 came flooding back. Rachel hesitated.

She wondered if she could just keep her mouth shut and try one of those kisses they did in the old days where they didn't open up. That did look very dull and pointless though. She considered getting up and running and not risking it being appalling. Or perhaps she should come clean and say, 'Look, I think you're probably about to kiss me. Well, I just want to tell you that the one and only time it happened, two years ago, was so awful I haven't done it again since.' She thought that might be a bit too much pressure. So she closed her eyes and screwed them up tight more in apprehension than in surrender to the physicality of the moment and Dave kissed her.

What a wonderful surprise. It was soft, gentle, exciting, arousing, tender, loving, explosive, moreish, imaginative, revealing, innocent, committed and absolutely delightful in every way. Again Rachel, a fifteen-year-old, reasonably OK-looking schoolgirl, felt as if she would never have a better experience in her life than this.

The moment was broken by Dave saying, 'Shall we lie down and cuddle up or do you want to go back to the party?'

Rachel didn't want to go anywhere so they lay there with their arms round each other, drunk and happy and contented. Seemingly. After a while, Dave's hands began to move a little up and down Rachel's body under her coat. She was completely torn, because it felt lovely but she was worried about what would happen. She didn't want to stop it but she remembered all the magazines which said, Don't go all the way on the first night. She also wondered what her mum would think of her here and imagined getting pregnant, but all of these thoughts catapulted away from her like little wispy powerless burst balloons in comparison to how lovely it all felt, so she responded.

Dave took this as an acknowledgement and began to move his hands up to her chest. He delved round the back and undid her bra. Suddenly, Rachel thought of the condom in her pocket and wondered whether she had the confidence to produce it. In *Jackie* magazine, although they never explicitly recommended condoms because they never explicitly recommended sex, it was always implied that though they were necessary, actually having a condom with you made you look like a slag.

Oh, the horrible choice of wanting it to go on so badly, but knowing underneath that giving in would herald the end of it. The sensible part of Rachel's brain could not continue to operate with all these thoughts and fears so it shut down and allowed her to throw herself headlong into the experience without a second thought.

Rachel was a bit scared about the bit a teacher at school had called 'penile penetration' but she need not have worried because it felt perfectly normal and natural. The only drawback was an image of the unopened condom in her pocket failing to offer her any protection whatsoever. The noise from the barn continued all the way through Rachel losing her virginity. She thought with a wry smile afterwards that she would have liked to hear Cliff Richard's 'Congratulations' or something suitable. Rachel had to be guided by Dave who seemed to know what to do. She hoped she kissed in the right places, bit at the appropriate moment and sucked when she should, but how could she know? We don't get marks out of ten for our performance and there are so many unknowns. Did my breath smell? Did I make too much noise? Am I any good at wanking someone off? Are my tits horrible? Should I have said that in the middle of it? An endless questionnaire, which will never be filled in and leaves so many women wondering why they are never called again. And all of this is down to self-confidence. Some have it and some don't. If you don't, your list is long and if you do, your list is short.

After Dave had come in a noisy and fantastically uncontrolled way which made Rachel feel as if she had some claim over his inner self, all was quiet and self-conscious. 'Are you OK?' he said. 'I'm fine,' Rachel replied, and thought, Well, at least he didn't walk off straight away afterwards. I think I might love him for that.

Susan was having a slightly different evening from Rachel. She and Martin had decided to head for the house, given that Amanda's parents seemed to either be patrolling the barn or trying to get pissed. They took a bottle of whisky with them, which they had found under the drinks table, obviously brought by someone who had rather foolishly failed to hide it properly, and Martin had a load of dope with him. They found a quiet bedroom at the back of the house, turned the lights off and managed to wedge something against the door so at least they wouldn't be disturbed.

Susan, for all her apparent worldliness, hadn't really thought the encounter through and wanted to chat rather than do anything, but when Martin started to kiss her, in a resigned fashion she tried to join in with enthusiasm even though by this point she had decided that he wasn't her type. He was a nice bloke, probably too nice. Susan, who had always had deference on a plate from males, required a bit more of a challenge than someone who fancied the pants off her, and feared that having a penchant for bastards was not really going to get her anywhere except married to someone like her father.

In between the rather inexperienced rough and tumble they did talk to one another. Susan was not cowed in any way by older members of the opposite sex and was quite happy to relate the fact that she was a fifteen-year-old schoolgirl who lived on a council estate in Hastings with her two sisters, one of whom had an illegitimate child by a local singer.

Martin, who had led a relatively sheltered life up to this point and had a mother who held very firm feminist views and steered him in the direction of university-potential left-wingers with strong personalities, was fascinated by this lovely, rather cocky small girl with dark hair and amazingly dark eyebrows which gave her face a distinctive, almost painted quality, made up as it was of such perfect ingredients. She was perfectly formed too with a small waist, lovely bum and as gorgeous a pair of breasts as he'd ever seen in his limited experience of three pairs.

Susan liked Martin, but didn't want to have sex with

him, although to some extent she saw the losing of her virginity as something to be done, catalogued in her diary and used as a yardstick for future reference. She did not believe in romantic love because of her personal experience, although she did think that you can find a partner who is trustworthy and reliable and loving, and that is probably the best you could do.

Martin began to move towards her with a look that is very well known to all women. It says, 'I am going to penetrate you and there is nothing you can do about it.' Of course there were many things Susan could have done about it. She could have screamed. She could have humiliated him with a joke which would have been enough to ruin the moment, maybe risked his wrath but at least stopped him in his tracks, or she could have jumped out of the window. This was not necessary though. She was slightly drunk, warm and comfortable and in too cynical a way for someone her age she felt she could put up with what was about to happen because she didn't want to move and go back to the party. It occurred to her that Martin probably hadn't had sex with anyone before and she was quite right. She had absolutely no idea of the fragility of his self-confidence and her decision not to ridicule him had been a good one, as it would have shattered any sense of self-esteem he had built up over the years.

So she allowed him to have sex with her when really she didn't want to. It was pretty much what she expected, and she thought that people made too much of a fuss about it.

'Did the earth move?' is a question often asked of couples

after they have 'done it'. For Susan, it shuddered gently in a not unpleasant way and left her feeling relieved that that particular milestone was passed in as unfussed a way as possible.

Afterwards, Martin was strangely silent and contemplative but Susan didn't want to coax anything out of him; she wanted to leave and go and drink and eat something.

God, I've lost my virginity, she thought and felt strangely disconnected from the event as though it had happened weeks ago and not a few minutes ago. They lay together like two stiff little boards not really touching and waiting for the other one to make the first move.

Then there was a knocking at the door and a frenzied rattling, and Amanda's dad shouted through the keyhole, 'Who's in there and what are you doing? Come out immediately. I hope there's no monkey business going on!'

You're fifteen minutes too late, mate, thought Susan as she raised herself on one elbow, kissed Martin on the nose, got herself done up and rose to meet the wrath of Amanda's dad.

Out in the barn, Rachel had been looking round in a bereft way for Susan. Disaster. Dave had got on a motorbike and left for London, saying he had to go off on a holiday to Greece the next day with some mates and as the flight was at ten thirty in the morning, he had to go home and get his bags. Naturally he hadn't mentioned it before and so Rachel assumed he was making it up just to get away from her.

She felt a tear drip off the end of her nose. The party

had slowed right down, the mood was quiet and sombre and there were a few couples swaying together looking as though they were trying not to fall over rather than snared in an all-embracing romance.

'Rachel, where have you been?' Relief. Susan was there and to some extent the prospect of telling her what had happened brightened the evening up a bit.

'What about you? Where have *you* been?' asked Rachel.

'You first,' said Susan. 'Come on.' Rachel went through the proceedings of the last couple of hours, which could have been seven hours, or five minutes . . . she had lost all sense of time.

Susan hugged her and said, 'I'm so pleased for you. I told you it would happen sometime. Did you use the condom?' she added.

Rachel looked at the floor.

'Oh Rachel, for fuck's sake, what stage are you at in your cycle?' she said and sounded so adult and concerned that they looked at each other and burst out laughing.

Chapter 11

Rachel wasn't pregnant, nor was Susan. Dave didn't call Rachel and Martin called Susan about fifteen times and then gave up. Rachel lived in a private world of pain for some weeks after the party at Amanda's. The first few days after the party she imagined Dave in Greece even though she knew that he probably wasn't. After a fortnight, she imagined him arriving home, having thought about her a lot on holiday and trying to get her phone number. This would have taken a couple of days and once that time was up, Rachel began to get agitated because she believed that if he was going to get in touch, it would be now. She replayed what she could remember of the evening over and over again and decided that her and Dave's album was *Hunky Dory* and that the song 'Kooks' best suited them, even though they hadn't had a child yet. Rachel was desolate when a month and a half had gone by and he hadn't phoned. She talked to Susan about it but only let her have a watered-down version of how she felt as it seemed to be important even as a girl, not to show how weak you really are. Susan, however, could tell how dark things were in Rachel's corner of the world and did her utmost to try and exorcise the devil that had been Dave by any means she could come up with. This included the sort of thing her mum would say like, 'You're too good for him anyway,' or pointing out the practicalities of trying to conduct a long-distance affair with someone in London.

Rachel held it all together pretty well considering she felt there was no point in living most of the time and moved around the place like a shadow who could not muster up any positive energy to lift any muscles to make a facial expression. Helen felt very worried and said to Dick one night, 'Have you noticed how Rachel seems to have had the stuffing knocked out of her?'

Of course Dick had noticed and he knew immediately what had happened because he had suffered in a very similar way as a teenager. Before he met Helen, when he was a student in Southampton studying for his technical exams, he had met a woman who was several years older than him at a pub near the college. Her name was Diana and he didn't know much about her except that she worked as a secretary to a wealthy businessman in the town and was married with two very young children. The irresistible attraction Dick felt somehow overcame all the obstacles and the two began seeing each other and eventually sleeping together. Dick fell heavily and insensibly in love with Diana and began to pressurise her to sort something out about the situation she was in, although why he thought he, an eighteen year old with no income who was living at home with his parents in Southampton, was much of a catch for a woman of Diana's beauty and intelligence, it was difficult to imagine.

One day, Diana failed to turn up at their rendezvous and Dick assumed that her husband had prevented her. Eventually, after a couple of weeks and not being able to reach her by phone, he stormed into the office of her boss, only to be told by the receptionist that Diana had left. She and her husband and children had moved up to Manchester because her husband had got a promotion with his firm. Dick was stunned. The receptionist chatted to him, oblivious to his pain, and managed to imply by telling Dick with a raised eyebrow how much Diana was 'missed' in 'certain quarters' that she had been having an affair with her boss too. This could just have been a figment of Dick's imagination though, and he turned and dragged himself away without acknowledging the woman's cheery words of farewell.

Dick went home and spent much of the next three months lying on his bed. He ate very little, talked only in monosyllables and hoped he would die. His parents wept, cajoled, bullied and begged him to get some help but nothing made any difference. After three months, he got up one morning, cleaned his teeth, put on fresh clothes after a shower and went back to college to sort out his extended bout of absenteeism, and no one ever spoke to him about it again. But a spark of joy had been extinguished in him, leaving a man who struggled to really love anything. When he met Helen two years later, he was absolutely enchanted by her looks, intelligence, beliefs and capabilities both domestic and sexual, but a bit of him couldn't feel it. It was as though he knew he had met the perfect woman for him and he knew he was in love with her and he'd better get married to her, but he wasn't connected to any of those feelings. And so he committed himself to Helen and did his best but Diana had killed his joie de vivre and well and truly trampled on his emotional future.

Thus Dick knew exactly how Rachel felt because he truly did believe that a huge, overwhelming suffocating incomparable love like this does happen only once. One evening he came into Rachel's bedroom, turned off whatever gloomy Dylan track she was listening to and sat down.

'Look, sweetheart, I know how you feel – I really do,' he said.

Rachel raised her head in the manner of an injured lamb and tried to gather her strength to protest when Dick started to tell the story of himself and Diana, and the words and memories started to fall out of his mouth so quickly, he couldn't stop them.

Rachel listened half-amazed, half-embarrassed, to the whole thing and could not believe it when Dick, having finished the story, put his head in his hands and started to sob.

'Please don't cry, Dad,' she said. 'At least you've got me and Mum and the boys.'

Unfortunately, 'me and Mum and the boys' could not

come near the perfect love that had been waiting for Dick if only he could have got to Diana before her husband took her away, but he was more fond of his family than he ever had been of anything and that would have to do.

'Now,' he said, 'come on, tell me what happened and let's see what we can do to fix it.'

Rachel found herself unloading the lot – all the pain, longing, desperation and unhappiness whilst her dad sat and nodded as if he completely understood what she was going through.

'What am I going to do, Dad?' she said, expecting their mutual empathy to produce an answer very close to the perfect truth.

'I'd have a nice hair-do if I were you, love,' said Dick. 'Doll yourself up, get out a bit. It will help, you know.'

Rachel realised then that Heartbroken Dick who felt her pain and cried her tears with her had gone, and back had come Rachel's dad, who slapped her on the back, talked *at* her and wore the sort of underpants that act as a contraceptive.

'Gosh, you were in there a long time,' said Helen as Dick came into the sitting room and sat down.

'Mmm,' he nodded.

'Everything OK?' said Helen.

'Fine,' said Dick, and suddenly they were talking monosyllabic couples' shorthand again. This was easier for Dick who'd decided not to impart to Helen what Rachel had told him because she'd only worry about it, and what was the point of that?

Susan had decided she couldn't heal Rachel's existential problems so she would tackle things on a much more superficial level. There was an uneasy truce between her and Helen after the Fluff incident and so Helen was only too happy to have Susan's cheery presence in the flat to pull Rachel up from the depths.

Helen had rather been hoping that the flat would have been a thing of the past since they had now been in Hastings over two years, but somehow they had got stuck there and everyone seemed so busy it was too much hassle to look for a new house. They'd not got as much money as they'd hoped and Dick had decided to go self-employed as a quantity surveyor and things were a bit unpredictable so it seemed easier to stay put. Rachel thought it suited her mood and at least it was close to Susan. Alan and Clive wouldn't have noticed if they'd been resident in a public toilet. Dick was relieved because it took the pressure off him having to work his bollocks off to earn enough to pay a mortgage, although working from home as he did because he had yet to rent out a little office, was a pain for all. Helen was the only one who walked up and down the streets behind the Old Town with their high Victorian houses and almost dangerously steep gardens, which looked out over the sea, and wished they could be in one of those. She decided that if things were going to happen she would have to move now and so she thought about getting a job herself. Now the kids were older it would be easier. She decided to work in the Health Service because at least they could train her up without her having to pay for it, so she enrolled on a course to become a general nurse but thought she would get a bit of experience first by working part-time as a nursing assistant at the local General.

This spurred Susan on to do something. She and Rachel never had any money, could never afford a cab home from anywhere or only ever had enough for two drinks when they wanted four so she lined up some employment for them, as much to get them out of the house as anything. A friend of Terry's had just left a job at the local TB hospital so she sent Susan up there to see if they would have her as a replacement. There were two vacancies for a seven-hour shift on Sunday mornings as a cleaner. They were only too happy to offer the job to Susan and her friend and told her to come the following Sunday morning.

Rachel felt her mood rather suited a TB hospital and that if she caught TB, so much the better. Someone would have to contact Dave and tell him just before she died, and then he would have blood on his hands and feel the need as a matter of conscience to kill himself.

Susan also got a job at Boots on a Saturday morning working on the tills alongside Terry, but because she was so lovely-looking it wasn't long before she was on the make-up counter bullshitting to customers about what tone was right for their skin and saying things like, 'Ooh, that lipstick really suits you' – this to some poor jowly old dear to whom lipstick was about as useful as it was to a moose. Still, make-up is all about making yourself feel good, thought Susan to herself whenever she felt she was being a con merchant. And that's useful at any age.

Winter started to fade, taking the edge off Rachel's pain and self-pity, and she began to enjoy the thought of trudging to work, going out and having a laugh. Despite her fears, the TB hospital became a remarkably happy place, stuffed full as it was of octogenarians who lay in their beds as if they were already corpses and weren't much up to conversation. Between them though, Rachel and Susan developed a wartime spirit and they would clean through the wards whistling and singing as many old songs as they could remember, asking their grandmas and Rachel's great-grandma, May, who was still knocking about, what other songs they might perform.

So, on Sunday mornings the corridors and wards would echo with the strains of 'Goodbye Dolly Grey', and other old songs. They didn't know the words to most of them but would hum or fill in the gaps with nonsense. They also managed some numbers from the great musicals which they had seen as children, and which they thought the old 'uns would recognise. 'I'm Getting Married in the Morning' from *My Fair Lady* and 'I'm Gonna Wash That Man Right Out of My Hair' from *South Pacific*.

The Matron remarked to one of the Staff Nurses that there had been a noticeable change in the mood and outlook of the patients, and she was happy to have the girls there.

One of the jobs that Susan loved and Rachel couldn't abide was emptying buckets of uneaten food into the enormous pig bins outside the kitchen door. Just the smell, if the kitchen window was open, was enough to put Rachel off the Sunday dinner that was provided with the job, and she rarely ate it. Susan would tuck in with all the abandon of a porker at a trough and then go home and eat another dinner cooked by Terry. 'I mustn't have two dinners, I'll get huge,' she said to her mum, but she didn't and just seemed to get more lovely. Like bloody Snow White, thought Rachel in her grimmer moments.

When you live by the sea you can judge the seasons by the ocean's colour. In winter it is green and black with an opaque quality that makes it look solid, but as the seasons change, so does the sea and by summer, it almost looks inviting as its frothy crests sparkle, enticing the swimmer into its emerald depths. This is a con because when you get in, it's the same freezing-cold sludge that's there all year round.

In the summer, Hastings came into its own. The sun lent it an air of respectability. Rachel realised she wasn't thinking about Dave every day now, and although occasionally she would drag herself back into her bedroom to play dreary music and read some poetry by Emily Brontë and write some of her own, the pain of losing the one true love she might have had was beginning to ease.

Added to this, the town was flooded with students from most of the European countries; they studied at the language schools every summer. The local boys were slightly put out by this and in truly welcoming British fashion would fight them whenever they got the chance. They were like a bunch of extreme nationalists who believed the incomers stole their jobs and their girls. And this, to some extent, was true because the foreign boys did seem like an attractive prospect to the local teenage girl population, animated and cheerful, monied and sexually charged as they were.

Susan and Rachel often went down to the local park to saunter about, sunbathe or meet their friends. On a couple of occasions they had noticed two boys roughly their age and obviously not English, eyeing them in a friendly way. On the third occasion of their all seeing each other, Susan couldn't bear the tension any longer and approached them. 'Hello,' she said brightly. 'I'm Susan and this is Rachel. What do you want?'

'We want say hello,' said the darker, more serious one whose name was Claudio.

'We will fight them on the beaches,' said the other one, doing a fair impression of Winston Churchill and waving an imaginary cigar around. Susan and Rachel laughed and Luca, for that was his name, took this as encouragement and gave them snatches from a few more of Churchill's wartime speeches. His English wasn't quite so good as Claudio's but he made himself perfectly understood when he said, 'You girls want to fuck tonight?'

Susan and Rachel couldn't take offence at this because it was like Noddy saying it and they laughed out loud.

'Oh sorry,' he said. 'I say wrong thing?'

'Yes, you do,' said his friend, smiling. 'You like to go out tonight?'

Susan and Rachel threw a glance at each other. 'Yes, we'd love to,' said Susan. 'We see you in town by clock-tower at seven o'clock.'

The girls walked off.

'You don't have to talk in bad English as well, you know, you silly bugger,' said Rachel.

'Oh no, was I?' said Susan. 'I always do that. Do you think they minded?'

'I don't suppose they even noticed,' said Rachel.

'So, which one do you like best?' enquired Susan.

Rachel didn't want to say in case there was a clash and they both liked the same one. 'Er . . .' she hesitated.

'I liked Luca,' Susan confided. 'He really made me laugh.'

Rachel was relieved. 'I liked Claudio,' she said. 'Something about him was interesting.'

Happy with their choices, they parted at the park gates because Susan had to meet her mum in town and they agreed to see each other outside the Golden Egg just round the corner from the clock-tower at ten to seven.

Claudio and Luca walked back to their hostel laughing and joking and they agreed between them that Luca preferred Rachel and Claudio, Susan.

Chapter 12

Rachel had decided to come clean with her mother and tell her about her and Susan's date that night.

Helen, although she tried not to show it, was utterly delighted that her daughter was showing an interest in anything at all. She had almost come round to the idea of Rachel being a depressed nun holed up in a local convent; who sat listening to Neil Young all day in between telling God what a bloody awful world it was. She had been so desperate to know what was going on, but she knew Rachel wouldn't tell her, and short of pinning Dick down on the kitchen table and holding the Ronco Buttoneer dangerously close to his vulnerable bits, she did not see how she could get him to cough up any more information. All she knew was that it was about someone called Dave who had failed to phone Rachel. She had to assume that Dick could not manage to get any more information from Rachel.

So when the girl expressed an interest in going out and

seeing someone else, Helen was so encouraging it rather worried Rachel. It was like a teacher saying, 'Look, I've brought you half an ounce of dope to smoke in the break.' And when she said, 'Be home by ten,' which was an hour later than the curfew Helen normally imposed, she couldn't believe it. She could, however, believe her mother's parting words: 'Bring him round for tea next time,' and her ears reddened and the blush spread to her face as she quickened her step.

Once Rachel had left the house, Helen punched a fist in the air and shouted, 'Yes!' She couldn't wait to tell Dick when he got home.

Rachel got to the Golden Egg five minutes before Susan, who had rushed home very quickly from her cousin's to change. From the safety of the café they could look down the street – and sure enough, there were Luca and Claudio, dressed smartly and sitting patiently on a wall. Not like the scruffy buggers round here, thought Susan, whereas Rachel thought, Oh Christ, they're a bit smart. They had pullovers draped round their shoulders and this made them look ever so slightly middle-aged.

Susan and Rachel strolled casually up.

'Hello,' everyone said at once.

'Where do you want to go?' said Susan. She threw a look at Rachel.

'Well, I don't think we should go to our normal haunts in the Old Town,' said Rachel, meaning a pub she had been in three times. 'Someone might see us.' She looked embarrassed having said this as Claudio seemed to have understood. 'I'm sorry,' she said, 'I didn't mean . . . I mean, we just want you to ourselves.' But really she was thinking, We don't want our friends to take the piss or some local boys to kick the shit out of you.

This seemed to reassure him and after some discussion they decided to buy a bottle of wine and go up on the cliffs above the Old Town.

It was a warm evening in early July, and at that time of night not many people made the climb up there once the cable car had stopped working for the day. They stopped at an off-licence and Luca went in to get a bottle of wine. He bought a bottle of Lambrusco because it had a screw top. The off-licence didn't sell paper cups and everywhere else was closed so they would just have to drink from the bottle when they got up there.

As they walked along through the town, Luca tried to hold Rachel's hand and Claudio put his arm casually over Susan's shoulder.

Oh shit, thought Rachel. How do we sort this out? Both girls shook off the unwanted hand and arm in as casual a movement as possible and decided to deal with it once they got where they were going.

Occasionally Claudio and Luca would break into animated Italian, which was frustrating, and eventually Susan said, 'What are you talking about? We want to know.'

'We are saying which one likes which one,' said Claudio, 'and trying to argue for which one we get.'

'Well, we'd better say,' said Susan. 'I like you, Luca, and Rachel likes you, Claudio.'

'Oh dear,' said Claudio. 'It is opposite for us.'

This at least broke the stalemate and then some discussion ensued about how this deadlock could be broken.

'Look – I will be with you for one hour and you for one hour,' said Luca, pointing at each of the girls, 'and then for last hour we will see who like who the bestiest.'

Susan laughed. Rachel, slightly more sensitive, stifled a giggle.

'What?' said Luca.

'Your English is crap,' said Susan.

'Your Italian shitbollocks,' he said.

'At least someone's teaching him some decent words,' said Rachel, and they all laughed.

Rachel was with Luca for the first hour and as they climbed high above the town she threw the odd regretful glance back at Susan and Claudio to see how they were getting on. Meanwhile, Luca was performing his repertoire of entertaining faces and voices but it just wasn't doing it for her. She just felt irritated by him.

Susan was struggling equally with Claudio, who was running through the list of English novels he had studied at school to see whether there was anything to talk about.

'Charles Dickens,' he said. '*David Copperfield*?'

'Oh, bloody hell no,' said Susan. 'No, I prefer something more up-to-date. Have you read *Skinhead* or *Suedehead*?'

'Skinhead?' said Claudio uncomprehendingly.

'Yes. It's by Richard Allen and it's really violent,' said Susan. 'All about what skinheads get up to.' She added quickly, 'I know I dress like a skinhead, but I don't believe what they believe, I just like the clothes.'

Claudio had absolutely no idea what she was talking about.

Everyone looked at their watches at roughly the same time to see if this ordeal was over.

Thank Christ, thought Rachel. Two minutes to go.

By now they were up high above the town looking out over the fishing huts, the little miniature railway that ran round the boating lake and the narrow, higgledy-piggledy streets that meandered down towards the sea. Rachel felt some relief to be sitting next to Claudio on the grass, but this didn't last long as they spotted two boys Susan knew from the rough school down the road, coming towards them. John Mason and Stephen Moss both had a can of cider in their hands and looked slightly glassy-eyed and out of it.

'Oh, fuckin 'ell,' said John, a wiry terrier, his face a spot festival. 'Look at these two slappers, up 'ere getting some off the dagos.'

Claudio and Luca couldn't understand what he was saying but they got the sense of it and moved protectively in front of Rachel and Susan.

'Piss off, children, your mums'll be wondering where you are,' said Susan in a bored voice.

'Piss off, children,' Luca mimicked her.

'Fuck off, Eyetie,' said Stephen, the more cowardly, plump one and then exploded into a snorting giggle.

'What's the shortest book in the world?' said John triumphantly.

Claudio and Luca looked confused. Why had this boy suddenly started a quiz in the middle of this mildly threatening encounter? Susan and Rachel knew what was coming.

'The book of Italian war heroes,' said John, and Stephen let out another snort.

'And what's the longest book in the world?' said Stephen.

'Oh, go away,' said Rachel. 'We're not interested.'

'The book of plimsolls sold to the Eyeties in the war,' retorted Stephen, not really understanding the joke himself, just repeating it.

Claudio and Luca were in heated discussion as Claudio translated the sense of what the jokes were. Luca was outraged. Feeling that their national pride could not be soiled by these two pubescent louts, he prepared for action. He took a swing at Stephen, catching him in the ample stomach, not really hurting him, but winding him.

'Oi,' said Stephen, wearing the expression of a wounded seal cub. He started to snivel and retch.

John shot through the air like a missile and landed on Luca, knocking him to the ground and pummelling him as he sat on top of him. Claudio grabbed his neck and tried to pull him off. Then fourteen stone of Stephen collapsed on top of them all, causing the release of some asthmatic swearing. There then ensued a two-minute flurry of inept punching and kicking. It was impossible to tell who was getting the better of whom.

Susan and Rachel wondered if they should join in. Rachel felt slightly sick because of the Lambrusco which seemed to have the sugar content of Golden Syrup, and Susan didn't want to ruin her nails which she had just painted with black Biba nail polish, giving her hands the appearance of an Arctic explorer with severe frostbite.

Their prevaricating was cut short by a shout from twenty yards away.

'What the fuck is going on?' roared a monstrous-looking creature silhouetted against the evening sun as he crashed towards them.

'Oh shit,' said Susan. 'It's Mad Mick Mason – we'd better run.'

She kicked Stephen really hard up the arse, causing him to clutch himself in pain and roll off Claudio and Luca, and this enabled her to grab Claudio and scream, 'Run!' as Mad Mick, John's unlikely gargantuan older brother of nineteen, bore down on them. Claudio and Luca didn't need to be told twice and the four ran until they felt as if their lungs would burst, with Mad Mick in pursuit calling them a selection of names that Rachel hadn't even heard used in those combinations before.

They half-ran, half-rolled down the hill towards the Old Town in their terror until, safe in the dim narrow streets, they felt they really had shaken him off.

'Fucking hell,' gasped Rachel. 'Who is that giant?' as they all leaned against a shopfront trying to calm down and control their breathing. Luca had his head between his legs and Claudio was a khaki colour.

'That's John's brother,' panted Susan. 'He's a complete psycho, always starting fights pissed or sober. He ate a live mouse once that he found in the toilets in the Anchor, and the other week when he was off his face and really angry with no one to fight he punched himself in the face and knocked himself out.'

'Fucking hell,' repeated Rachel. 'We'd better stay out of his way for a bit. Shall we go home?'

The sun was sinking as the quartet headed warily back through the town, getting some chips as they went. Claudio and Luca got on the bus with Rachel and Susan, and Claudio alighted at Rachel's stop with her and walked her up to the door, a service not offered locally by the hippy population. Rachel turned to say goodbye and saw a mouth coming towards her. She took swift evasive action and it landed on her cheek.

'Thanks,' she said. 'I've had a really lovely time.'

'Can I see you tomorrow?' asked Claudio.

'I don't know,' said Rachel. 'Give me a call.' She got her bag out and wrote down the number on a scrap of paper with hair and the remains of a Smartie stuck to it. 'Good night,' she said, and stood at the door as the polite Italian disappeared down the street, his expensive sweater still slung over his shoulders.

The phone rang as soon as she shut the door.

'Did he kiss you?' said Susan.

'Tried,' said Rachel. 'Yours?'

'Yeah, you bet,' said Susan. 'Bloody gorgeous it was too. Like being sucked into a great big wobbly hoover and thrown round and round. I really like him, I think he's great.'

This was praise indeed from Susan and Rachel was

pleased because she liked hers too and she reckoned they could have a really good laugh this summer.

'I want to take it slowly with Claudio,' she said.

'Oh bloody hell, you're just like Amy Turtle in *Crossroads*,' said Susan.

'How am I like a tiny round old cleaning woman who belongs to the Salvation Army?' said Rachel. They both loved *Crossroads*.

'Put like that, I don't know,' said Susan.

The next couple of months were fun. Because Rachel and Susan knew that Claudio and Luca would not be around for any great length of time, they could relax and enjoy themselves with them and without them. They invented a game to play which involved charting their progress with the two boys as their relationships became more intimate. It was a competition to see who could cover the most ground before they went back to Italy. Susan and Rachel both accepted it was most likely to be Susan but it didn't ruin their enjoyment. Points were awarded for specific achievements, such as getting them to say, 'I love you,' or licking chocolate off them – a possible five- to twenty-point range depending on which part of their body the chocolate was to be found.

Susan's suggestions were much more sexual and bolder than Rachel's; Rachel tended to concentrate on the emotional progress rather than the physical. One night in Susan's bedroom they compiled a definitive list. It began with the very straightforward: Kissing.

'I've got five points there already,' said Susan.

'Yes, but I've found out all about Claudio's family and home life so I've got ten,' said Rachel smugly. 'And you know nothing about Luca.'

'Well, it's not exactly easy with his English,' said Susan. 'Still, if I toss him off in a bus shelter at the weekend I can catch up.'

Rachel shuddered.

'What?' said Susan. 'Don't go all *Sound of Music* on me.'

'Sorry,' said Rachel. 'I'm just a bit, well, you know . . .'

'A bit bloody frigid,' said Susan. 'Never mind, we'll sort you out.'

Helen and Dick found themselves surprisingly laidback about Rachel's relationship with Claudio. He came regularly to the flat and was so polite to her that Helen sometimes wondered if he could possibly be a real teenage boy. Alan and Clive, her own teenagers, were virtually impossible to contact unless there was some element of threat or force. Clive was now thirteen and spent all his spare time in his room reading science books or playing with himself. Obviously his parents thought he was doing the former all the time. Alan was now sixteen and nowhere nearer deciding what he wanted to do apart from stay in bed all day and perhaps as a sideline walk round looking like the world was about to end.

Helen was just thankful that at least Rachel was on a fairly even keel so she let Dick handle the boys. All that teenage male smell and glowering, barely controlled sexual energy left her feeling distinctly queasy.

Helen and Dick weren't really sure what they were going

to do about each other. Dick was quite happy to rub along and get on with trying to build up his business. He and Helen got on well enough, chatted every day about stuff on the news and pretty much agreed on how to manage the children, and Helen thought that was probably good enough for a couple who had been together nearly twenty years. They had sex about once every six months and the regularity of this event was affected by how much alcohol they'd both drunk. Dick could be persuaded to have a ten-minute, straightforward coupling without the trimmings if he'd had a couple of pints, but if she wanted more than that, Helen had to try and pour just enough down him to disinhibit him and allow for some foreplay, but not so much that he lay in a soggy, mangled heap that barely moved. If this happened Helen began to wish for a toasted cheese and pickle sandwich instead.

Helen felt there should be more to look forward to in her life; there must be something wrong if she would rather be at work than at home. The thought of dynamiting her marriage though, did not appeal, and as there was nothing that threatened to push things to a conclusion, for the moment she decided to potter along and see what happened with work and the kids.

The highlight of Susan and Rachel's summer was a Gary Glitter gig in the park that they went to with Claudio and Luca, who couldn't quite believe that this chubby, histrionic apparition tottering around on huge platform heels could be anything but a loser. As for the Glitter Band, they would all look quite at home detained at Her Majesty's pleasure. Just as well because Mad Mick Mason was at the gig. Looking for some action.

The fans were loyal and had dressed to look as much like Gary as they could, and so the park that day was full of people who had used up their entire supply of Bacofoil.

The stress of having to avoid Mad Mick ruined the gig somewhat, but it was worth it to see Mick disappear behind the stage accompanied by a couple of security men who had taken exception to being called 'cunting pieces of mong shit'. Huge numbers in the crowd cheered inwardly.

Although Susan had had sex with Luca on the second occasion of their meeting, their relationship managed to be low-key and still fun.

'None of this staring into each other's eyes bollocks,' said Susan cheerfully, 'especially as he's got to go back in two weeks.'

'Of course,' said Rachel. 'I'd forgotten.'

She and Claudio had done holding hands (nice and warm and friendly, 1 point); kissing (OK, 5 points); stroking each other's bodies fully clothed (fine, 0 points – 'That's just not even fucking worth writing down,' Susan said when Rachel suggested it); Claudio putting his hands on her breasts (not sure, 10 points); Claudio trying to get his hand down the front of her jeans (not pleasant at all, 5 points – and a big row had ensued ending with Rachel leaving tearfully and shouting something horrible at him over her shoulder).

A flurry of phone calls occurred after this and eventually Rachel and Claudio sorted things out in a couple of days, to the relief of Susan and Luca who enjoyed going out as a group and didn't want to function as a lone couple for the last two weeks.

Susan and Luca had found it difficult to pin down suitable venues for their efforts. Susan had allowed Luca to look at and stroke her breasts (10 points) in her bedroom, but Vince had knocked on the door and nearly caught them *in flagrante*, so that was a no no for the future,

They had been forced outside for a blow job in the bus shelter (20 points); doggy-style sex under a fishing boat (30 points); and something unsuitable with a Mars Bar at the swings (30 points, which was interrupted by two seven-year-old boys giggling).

The day before Claudio was due to return home, Rachel caved in and slept with him, not because she particularly felt she had to, but because she liked him a lot and she wanted them to do something to remember each other by that was serious. It did not occur to her to visit a museum with him. It had to be outside under the stars and took place on a slightly scrubby bit of common behind the hospital where Rachel's mum worked. They had both had a couple of glasses of wine and were slightly befuddled so it was a slow, amicable, relaxed affair with no rough corners or hysterical crying involved.

Rachel was beginning to understand all the kinds of relationships that were on offer from a series of very different men. There was nice, relaxed and friendly – a bit like swimming in warm porridge. At the other end of the spectrum was tortured and unreliable, many and varied moments of alternately crying into one's pillow, sitting forlornly by the phone and screaming abuse at each other in an unrestrained Taylor and Burton kind of way. Most relationships, however, were a combination of the two and it was a question of getting the balance right so that you did not sink into a catatonic stupor hitched to Cliff Richard or slash your wrists at every opportunity because you were married to Jim Morrison. Rachel wanted 65 per cent Jim and 35 per cent Cliff.

She and Claudio had not discussed what would happen when he returned to Italy and tonight he broached the subject.

'I would like to write to you,' he said, holding her head between his hands and looking very Cliff-like.

Rachel felt called upon to say something telling and poetic but she could only manage: 'That'd be very nice.'

'Shall we go somewhere now and drink a toast to our futures?' said Claudio. His English was definitely improving.

'Yes, let's,' said Rachel, mentally crossing her fingers behind her back. She knew a small bar that was almost a wine bar in the Old Town so they walked through the town centre. It was nine thirty and she had to be home at ten thirty.

They found a table at the back and Claudio ordered a bottle of wine that would normally have been beyond their means.

As they sat awkwardly wanting to be adults but not quite managing it and holding up their glasses to one another, a shadow fell over the table and a voice said, 'Bloody hell, I wondered when I'd bump into you again.'

She looked up.

It was Dave.

Chapter 13

Rachel didn't do the textbook move of dropping her wine or fainting off her chair; she stared in disbelief with her mouth open which, when she thought about it afterwards, was no way for a sex goddess to behave. Although, having said that, was behaving like a sex goddess the way to attract a man? Rachel, like every other woman, pretty much knew instinctively that to attract a man of Dave's psychological make-up you either had to not give a flying fuck about him or at least pretend not to. Strange that so many women know this to be the case and yet they just don't seem to be able to do it and play that poor sucker properly. There may be several reasons for this. Firstly, they may be so besotted that they simply cannot manage to pretend they are not interested. Secondly, they might find it too stressful and wearing to keep it up and thirdly, everyone is looking for someone to love and to keep pretending day in and day out that you don't care about someone when all you really want to do is envelop them with yourself is just not a viable option.

Dave spoke again. 'Bloody hell,' he said, 'I've found you.'

Rachel had no idea how to respond to this. What did he mean? How long had he been looking for her and why did he want her? She looked at Claudio and he returned a puzzled expression which said, 'Who is this arsehole interrupting our last evening together?'

Oh Jesus, thought Rachel, it's our last evening. Christ, what am I going to do?

'This is Claudio,' she said, woodenly nodding in Claudio's direction and feeling sad because she knew that she would drop Claudio like a stone and follow Dave off the end of the pier if he asked her to.

'Excuse me,' said Claudio in a dignified way, 'I must visit the . . .'

'Toilet, man – yeah, that way,' said Dave, pointing.

As soon as Claudio was out of sight Dave said to Rachel, 'Look, I'm sorry about not contacting you. I really need to talk to you tonight. Can you get rid of him?'

'OK,' said Rachel, allowing herself a fraction of a second's hesitation.

'I've just got to go and do something,' said Dave. 'Can you meet me outside the Nelson in ten minutes? No – make it twenty.'

'OK,' said Rachel again, and Dave left.

Claudio came out of the toilet and looked relieved that Dave had gone. From his point of view, a tall, older, rather scruffy wanker had barged into their blissful evening together and thank God he had gone. It took one look at Rachel, however, to tell him that there was some fairly major trauma going on.

'Look, Claudio,' she said, 'I can't explain it now but can you give me some time and I'll be back in twenty minutes or so.'

'OK,' said Claudio. 'I will wait here,' he looked at his watch, it was ten o'clock, 'until ten thirty.'

Rachel left and wondered whether to phone her mum or Susan as she had five minutes to spare before she made her way along to the pub to see Dave and find out what was going on. She went into a phone box and dialled Susan's number, not expecting to find her in because of course it was Luca's last night as well.

Surprisingly, Susan picked up the phone and Rachel pressed her money in.

'Rachel!' Susan squealed,

Obviously a bit pissed, thought Rachel.

'What are you doing?' said Susan. 'Do you want to come round? Me and Luca are having a brilliant time. Mum and Vince have gone out, Jen and Lucy are staying with friends and Kim's away. We've got the whole house to ourselves . . .'

Rachel cut across her. 'Dave's just turned up out of the blue. What shall I do?'

'Fuck's sake,' said Susan, emboldened opinion-wise by the drink. 'Don't get involved with that tossbag. He didn't even bother to phone you for months. You can't just let him walk back in and fuck everything up for you. Where are you now?'

No answer.

'Rachel?' said Susan in a warning sort of voice.

Rachel hung up, left the phone box and continued to walk towards the Nelson. She glanced at her watch. It was twenty past ten. She could see the front of the Nelson and no one was standing outside. She assumed Dave hadn't got there yet. She walked up the steps and sat outside on the stone patio wondering whether she should be nursing a drink to look more normal. After about ten seconds someone she recognised came out of the pub. It was a local hippy called Stefan who was always in the Old Town pubs. He seemed pretty harmless, although no one liked him very much. Everyone said he was a bit of an acid casualty. Anyway, he was friendly enough.

'I'm going along to the Anchor,' he said. 'Here, you need a drink, take this.' He handed her a glass. 'It's whisky,' he said.

'Cheers,' said Rachel and knocked it back in one gulp. It would only take five minutes to get back to Claudio and she was sure he would wait longer than ten thirty.

What seemed like fifteen minutes passed and she looked at her watch. Twenty-five to. Where was Dave? And was he inside the pub doing something then coming out to meet her and speak to her, somewhere else, or were they supposed to be going in when he got there?

'I'll give him another five minutes,' said Rachel to herself but she knew she'd sit there all night if she had to.

Eventually, at ten fifty-five she decided she had to do something and the sensible thing to do would be to go inside the pub. The Nelson was not a pub she particularly relished entering and there were plenty of fights happening at the weekend between the fishermen and anyone else who cared to join them.

Rachel opened the door and the dark smoky atmosphere started to escape out into the night. It took a while for her vision to become accustomed to the black lumpy figures moving about or propped animatedly at the bar, and once she had been able to recognise a few individuals, she began to scan the room to see if any of the groups contained Dave.

She couldn't see him anywhere and then her eyes rested on two people in the corner who were kissing each other. The kiss finished and the man looked round and stared directly at her. It was Dave. A big, cold fist squeezed her heart and an image appeared in her head of her shooting him.

What the fuck is going on here? thought Rachel in a semi-confused state, not even sure if she had seen what she had seen. Dave's mouth opened to speak, but she had turned and was already out through the door.

Even if Rachel had been interested in the time and getting back to Claudio, she could not have managed it because the tears had made everything very blurry and all she was able to focus on was the sight of her feet running on the pavement as she tried to get away from that scene and back home, where she could completely collapse into the cave of her room.

'You fucking cunt,' she repeated over and over to herself as she ran.

'Beg your pardon?' said a voice. She turned and there was Mad Mick Mason. Rachel didn't care whether she got killed or not.

'Yes, you, you fucking cunt,' she said, looking up at him like a child whose ball was stuck in a tree.

There were two seconds of tension.

Mad Mick burst into gales of laughter and Rachel ran on.

After a while she slowed down. She felt awful on so many counts, leaving Claudio like that, seeing Dave and then dropping everything to go and meet him, only to be presented with a scene out of a bloody soap opera. She now wished she'd screamed or said something very cutting or been violent, perhaps vomited spaghetti alla vongole onto him.

Rachel carried on along the seafront feeling a bit cold and a bit weird. She walked all the way from the Old Town past the White Rock Pavilion and the pier and then Warrior Square, and then turned up and away from the sea and started to walk up the hill.

Someone who looked extremely drunk went past her in a wheelchair, which seemed to be doing at least thirty miles an hour.

By now it was eleven thirty and the streets were quiet. Rachel had had a fair few drinks so she wasn't in that utterly paranoid state in which every small noise or footfall on the pavement made her start or turn round warily, but she realised she wasn't feeling any better having just got several hundred lungsful of sea air. She was feeling decidedly strange. Still, she was only half a mile from home so it wouldn't be long before she could try and sleep and black out the worst day of her life. So far. She was sure there were more to come.

She realised she was coming towards a familiar phone box, a landmark on her way home, and to her surprise there appeared to be someone in it. But that someone wasn't an ordinary person; that someone was a monk and not a modern monk, a monk from a Hammer horror film with a huge cowl hiding his face. The most rational explanation her brain could come up with was a fancy-dress party. Yes, that must be it. Then she realised what the monk was swinging. It was a dead cat. Her heart seemed not to beat. Now she was oscillating between being bloody terrified and telling herself not to be so stupid. She quickened her pace past the phone box just in case there was a new ecclesiastical serial killer in town and put a bit of distance between her and the phone box, then turned round. The monk had gone.

'Come on,' she said to herself, 'don't be stupid.' She started to cry. She felt lonely and scared and on top of that, of course, she'd just been seriously fucked over by the only bloke who had ever meant anything to her.

Obviously, she thought, that is probably a ridiculous thing to say to yourself when you're only fifteen.

She thought she heard a snarling noise and focused her eyes a bit harder. In a garden up ahead was a pack of wolves tied to a post and straining at their leashes with huge dripping jaws, their yellowed eyes turned hungrily on Rachel.

'Jesus Christ!' she yelled, and ran across the road. Tendrils of plants seemed to be swaying out of gardens and trying to wrap themselves ever so gently and stealthily round her. She thought to herself, I must have gone mad.

She found herself outside her front door. She lifted up her key and managed to get herself in. The shadows in the house were too much so she turned every light on downstairs. Everything was moving. The wallpaper was shrinking and expanding in a rhythmic movement. She went into the kitchen and saw that her mum (how gorgeously normal), had left some sandwiches for her. As she looked at them, they all turned into miniature Andy Williams faces and started singing, 'Can't get used to losing you.' The kitchen walls breathed in and out with her breath and she thought she should call someone.

She managed in the chaotic whirlpool that was her brain to dial Susan's number. Thank God it was Susan who answered.

Rachel described what was going on. Susan didn't say, 'Stay there, I'll call the local asylum,' she said, 'Did you see Stefan tonight?'

Rachel said, 'Yes, why?'

Susan said, 'The fucker's spiked your drink – you're tripping.'

Relief flowed down the walls of Rachel's heart. 'But why would he do that?' she asked.

'Fucked-up brain – mad twat, nasty bastard,' said Susan. 'There's three reasons. He's well known for it.'

'What shall I do?' said Rachel.

'They do say drink plenty of orange juice,' Susan advised. Then: 'Do you want me to come round? Why did you hang up before? Where's Claudio? Where's Dave? What's going on?'

Rachel hung up again, went into the kitchen, got a litre of orange juice out of the fridge and sat on her bed until a weedy sun hauled itself up over the horizon.

Chapter 14

The following day, a Sunday, not having slept all night, Rachel dragged herself into work at the hospital. She needed sanctuary and home wasn't it at the moment in case her mum and dad asked any awkward questions about why she looked as if a vampire had drained all the blood out of her face. Besides that, Susan was there to pour out the contents of her troubled heart to and try and get some sort of perspective on what was going on.

The girls filled their buckets with water and a slosh of industrial-strength disinfectant which smelled as though it could kill the hardiest cockroach with one sniff, and took their hoovers, dustpans and buckets up to the less well-supervised top floor so they could work their way down and get some privacy first to have a really good gossip.

'Right,' began Susan. 'Are you sure you're all right to work? You look like a ghost.'

'Yes, I'm fine,' said Rachel, wary that a picture on the

wall would start talking to her, or Matron would turn into a hyena. 'Just completely knackered.'

'Let's start with the acid bit then, shall we?' said Susan, who liked to put a positive spin on things. 'Was it in any way fun or enjoyable?'

Rachel shook her head. 'If I'd known what it was sooner, it might have been,' she said, 'but I was too scared and so it just terrified me all the more.'

'And has it stopped now?' Susan wanted to know. 'We must try it together sometime. I tell you, it would be really good fun.'

'Oh, give us a frigging break,' said Rachel. 'Let me recover from this and when I'm out of the straitjacket I'll think about it.'

Susan noticed with relief that there was still humour residing in the broken spirit of this careworn fifteen-year-old wraith who in the space of a few months had lived about five years of her life.

'OK,' said Susan. 'Now what about poor Claudio? He came looking for Luca round at mine in a really bad way last night. He was crying and saying you'd broken his heart.'

Rachel felt a shaft of guilt pierce through her, almost a physical sensation. 'Oh God,' she said, putting her head in her hands. 'I feel awful about that. Is he OK?'

'I think so,' said Susan. 'He's going to write to you.'

'I don't know why I did it to him,' said Rachel. 'We'd just had such a lovely time . . . you know.'

'You know . . . what?' said Susan, scrubbing vigorously at the lino with her mop.

'Doing . . .'

Rachel trailed off, never sure how to put it. 'Making love' was far too sickly, 'doing it' was so teenage, and 'fucking' was so harsh and didn't sum up what a lovely experience it had been.

'You let him nob you?' said Susan, ever the pragmatist.

'It wasn't like that,' said Rachel. 'It was lovely, really lovely. He was so kind and gentle.'

This sounded a little bit dull to Susan, who liked a good roll about and a scream.

'Bloody hell,' said Rachel. 'I've had sex with two people this year. My mum would kill me – I can't believe it.'

'I wouldn't worry too much,' Susan shrugged. 'She'll never find out and it's not that long before it'll be legal anyhow. Now, what happened with Dave?'

Rachel had had a blessed few minutes without thinking about Dave, but now in all his powerful majesty, he flooded back into her head, and as she lifted a water jug from someone's bedside table to do a bit of 'damp dusting' as Matron called it, tears began to roll down her face.

A skinny veined hand reached over and took hers. 'Don't worry, duck,' said Mrs Wilson, aged eighty-seven. 'They're all bastards, you know.'

Rachel gave her a watery smile and moved on.

'I can't believe what he did,' she said. 'What is the explanation? I mean, fair enough. If he's got someone else – fine, that's his business and I'd started to get over him a bit and not care – but then why did he ask me to meet him if he was just going to meet someone else, and who is she anyway?'

This sentence would have failed badly as an English composition test but it summed up very succinctly all the questions that were burning a hole into her brain. She had often wondered what David Bowie meant in 'Five Years' by the line, 'My brain hurt like a warehouse', and now she knew.

Susan, who was a little further down the road of not being terribly surprised by the appalling behaviour of others, tried to be philosophical.

'Perhaps it was an old girlfriend, maybe he was drunk, perhaps you didn't see it properly – there's hundreds of explanations,' she said.

'I'd better go and start downstairs or we'll never get it all done,' Rachel said shakily.

'Don't worry, it'll be all right.' Susan put her arm round Rachel and this time Rachel began to howl loudly and buried her head in her friend's shoulder.

'It's not fair! Why has this happened? Why can't I control myself? Why do I feel so much for him when I don't want to? Oh God, what am I going to do?' This set of questions, lifted from the very difficult Romance section of The Life Quiz, were impossible for Susan to answer without a considerable amount of help from the involved parties.

Susan didn't really know anything about Dave Barrett, but if he was down in Hastings fairly often there must be someone who knew him, who this girl was and what he was up to, and she would try and find out as much as she could before poor Rachel faded away and expired from grief.

The two girls worked quietly for the rest of the morning, and all the patients lying silently in their beds noticed a sadness about the young 'uns which took them back to the days before Rachel and Susan had started working there. They recalled how monochrome and depressing life was before these two breezed in once a week and the good times rolled.

At two o'clock they left work and headed home, Rachel wondering how long she could keep up the pretence to her mum that she was all right. About three seconds was the answer. As she opened the front door and stepped in, Helen spotted her from the kitchen. 'All right, love?' she enquired cheerfully, and Rachel's face crumpled like a wet flannel.

'Oh God, what is it?' said Helen, running towards her and giving her a hug. This didn't happen often and felt unnatural but Rachel was too floppy and pathetic even to pull away.

'Is it Claudio going back?' asked Helen and Rachel realised quickly that this was a convenient peg on which to hang all her madness at being humiliated by Dave.

'Yes,' she sobbed. 'I'm going to miss him so much.'

'He was here this morning with a note for you,' said Helen.

Rachel got the words out as quickly as she could. 'What did he say?' Hoping she had not been grassed up by her cuckolded Italian boyfriend.

'Oh, just that he was sad and he wanted you to read this.' She held out a letter.

'I'm going to make a coffee and go up to my room,' said

Rachel. 'I'm sorry, Mum. I just want to be on my own today,'

'All right,' said Helen kindly. 'We'll see you later.'

The note from Claudio was short and alarmingly guilt inducing.

Dear Rachel,

I am very unhappy as to your treatment of me who loves you and has just made love to you which to me means a lot. And now I must depart and cannot see you until next year. Please write and tell me what you think you are doing. Yours in sadness and love,

Claudio.

This was followed by an address in Milan, and Rachel had absolutely no idea how she was going to manage such a big lot of explaining to a basically very decent lovely bloke whom she had completely shat on.

While Rachel was sitting in her bedroom staring out of the window at a dank day, reflecting how dead she felt inside, Dave Barrett was in a pub in the Old Town wondering what he should do about Rachel.

He sat nursing a pint of light and bitter and listening to some appalling Osmonds' song on the jukebox. It was Sunday and he had to be back in London tomorrow. College started quite soon and he had not really been the best attendee the world had ever known. He had been to Greece earlier in the year with four friends from college who had just read *The Magus* and wanted some time away from London.

Dave was one of those men to whom girls are instantly attracted, but he was not particularly aware of it, although he did find himself getting into difficulties because it seemed all he had to do was be nice and chat and suddenly he was being pursued by someone who wanted to marry him. This would have given Dave the opportunity – as in the fantasy of many a socially awkward, copulation-obsessed teenage boy – to juggle enough young women on the end of his very impressive genitalia to start an elaborate fairground act. But Dave wasn't a vain person; he was a good person who came from a warm, friendly family who had been amazed that they seemed to have produced someone who was brilliant at drawing. And he was, but he had trouble not being dragged into an avant-garde group of students whose minds were turned more towards social upheaval than knuckling down and getting a good job where they could sell their paintings.

Dave knew Amanda's brother well and came down quite a bit to see him. They would meet in Hastings because they both enjoyed its narrow streets and the bohemian feel of the Old Town. Dave liked it because his favourite book, *The Ragged-Trousered Philanthropists*, was set in Hastings and he loved to soak up the atmosphere and imagine it at the turn of the twentieth century, with ordinary people doing bloody hard work and being treated like shit by complacent brutal bosses, filling the workers with left-wing zeal.

Dave thought the country was in a shit state and he couldn't work out why nobody seemed very interested in protesting about it. The son of working-class Irish parents who had settled in Swindon, he instinctively veered towards the left and even had a sneaking admiration for the IRA, although this was being severely tested by their bombing on the British mainland. He and his friends sat around and decided on one of their many drunken and stoned evenings in the pub that what was needed was some sort of new movement, one that said 'Fuck you' to all the mess that had been created up to this point. And real mess *had* been created with the three-day week, no electricity, rubbish on the streets. Old blokes said things like, 'That's what it's like living in Russia.' Dave always tried to argue, and then they'd retort: 'Why don't you fuck off there then?' Sometimes, he wished he could. He thought Mother Russia would be great, given the amazing literature her writers had produced.

Dave had recently been toying with modern art, which was frowned on by the grown-up art world. He believed that, because it could be dreamed up and sometimes executed relatively quickly, in the eyes of the art conservatives, this demonstrated a woeful lack of talent. If an artist hadn't suffered like Michelangelo in the Sistine Chapel, they might as well call it a day.

Rothko, an artist Dave loved, apparently just painted big splodges of colour onto canvas, something anyone could do, and it was taking a section of the establishment a very long time to acknowledge the emotional power contained on these huge canvases. Dave got really angry when he heard reactionary views expressed and wanted to take people by the hand and drag them round a Picasso exhibition to show them how absolutely brilliant Picasso's early representational art was, and that it was his choice to paint abstract pictures. He despaired of people's cultural taste. The number of student walls he had seen adorned with the execrable piece-of-shit poster of a woman in a tennis dress scratching her arse made him want to weep. And women his age made him want to weep too, with their minds full of superficial rubbish. It was only recently that some of their number had made the first steps on the road to liberating themselves and gaining some real power – a move Dave admired and thought was long overdue. However, many girls he knew seemed to be unaffected by this. The ones he mixed with on the whole continued to absorb all things facile and silly. He would chat to what he supposed were relatively intelligent women, and find their knowledge of politics and world affairs on a par with a child of five. He felt like giving them a quiz when he met them and then not bothering if they scored under 50 per cent.

He remembered saying to a girl at a party once, 'What do you think of the three-day week?' and she'd said, 'I didn't know that was happening. What days are they getting rid of then?'

And that was why Rachel had been such a breath of fresh air. She didn't simper or talk bollocks. She didn't constantly ask him if she looked OK, and she'd never wanted to know what star sign he was. She didn't drone on endlessly about things she didn't know much about and she had read the odd book. Added to that, though, she wasn't just his mate, she had something about her which interested him and made him want to discover more and more of her; like exploring a continent. She seemed to be interested in something a bit more substantial. She knew about the Dylan concert at the Free Trade Hall in Manchester, for instance, when he was heckled with 'Judas'. Most women only knew 'Blowin' in the Wind' and the lyrics of 'Just Like A Woman' and couldn't even see the political flaws in it. They could only trace him through his singles and his 'cuteness', as one woman had once described him. He'd nearly thrown up and hadn't gone back there again.

But Dave was a man after all and so found it difficult to align his intellectual needs with his sexual ones. Dave's ideal partner was a left-wing sex kitten who just happened to have a first-class honours degree from Oxford. In the way that gay men all want a straight man who wants to have sex with them, and lots of women want a bastard who treats them well. And so since he had first had sex at the age of fourteen with a friend of his mother's, Dave had been on a fruitless but enjoyable mission to find a woman who fitted the bill. This was made easier by Dave's unconscious magnetism and he was never lost for bedmates, However, the vast majority of them were sloughed off after the first encounter, which he did feel bad about but not bad enough to keep seeing a woman who drove him insane with her lack of interest in anything.

Rachel had lingered in Dave's affections for a long time

after their encounter outside the barn. There was something about her manner, her shyness and her ironic perspective on the times in which they lived which he had not come across before. He thought about her a lot while he was away and wondered if he should phone her. But of course there is no point in calling anyone when you are not going to arrange anything, and he thought he would do that when he got back. Several women drifted through his bed in Greece, a couple in Athens and two more out in the islands, but it was always Rachel who plopped into his mind at the most unlikely times and niggled him.

And so Dave had decided when he returned from Greece that he would go to Hastings and try to find her. He wanted to see her face and he wanted to see how she would look when he appeared. On a couple of occasions he had tramped round a few Old Town pubs and wine bars. He was sure she'd mentioned that's where she went . . . and so he kept a lookout for her. And that was where he'd met Sally.

Sally came at him one night in a little pub up towards the higher reaches of the town with her eyes slightly mad, some alcohol on her breath and a huge appetite for stirring up trouble. She was muscular and athletic and had cropped, very black hair; in a way, she looked like a doll you might buy to replace Barbie because Ken had got bored with her anodyne good looks, her stereotypical blondness and her saccharine manner. Sally, whose boyfriend Timbo had just left to join his ship at Southampton, was at a loose end and needed something to happen in her life. Dave couldn't help being transfixed by her expressive hands and her incredibly long and lithe body. He sensed that she was dangerous as she made her way imperiously through the pub like a warrior queen, shoving someone here, telling someone to go fuck themselves there and exuding an attitude of tigerish aggression coupled with drunken good humour. To some extent her Nutty-Woman-Out-Of-Control-And-Liable-To-Damage-You-Physically-If-Angered demeanour put him off as he'd had his fill of semi-suicidal drunken women either calling him at 3 a.m. or telling his parents how he'd destroyed them, or even arriving mid-embrace with another woman and launching into a melodrama that both terrified and embarrassed him.

However, although Dave knew what he wanted and what he liked, he was hugely flattered by the attention of most women and enormously attracted to Sally, and those were two major reasons to spend the night with her. Within half an hour they were at her flat and naked on her bed in a flurry of limbs that made Dave feel there were several extra people there. It was wild sex and he was absolutely amazed by the things Sally did to him and how little she expected in return. He felt like an emperor being serviced by one amphetamine-fuelled courtesan after another. But a few seconds after he had come he felt a slight shiver of unease about what she might expect from him now and what she would do to him if she didn't get it.

The next morning the wild sex happened again, and a phone call from Timbo was taken while it was going on as well. Dave couldn't help but be fascinated by this madwoman, but he was relieved she had a permanent partner and when he left her flat, he planned to stay away unless by some chance he bumped into her and she beat him into submission.

And he did meet her, the night he found Rachel. Again, he was patrolling Hastings in a slightly nervous way in case Sally cropped up when he saw Rachel going into a bar with a young guy. A surprising stab of jealousy poked at him. Who was this? Brother? Tutor? Student friend? He couldn't tell. He went in and asked her to meet him, realising he had encroached upon some romance but still chancing his arm because he had thought about her so much. He had then gone along to the Nelson, got there early at the bar and Sally, who was quite pissed and not to be argued with, had appeared.

And sometimes it's easier to kiss someone than to give them a fifteen-minute explanation of why you don't want to.

Chapter 15

Rachel desperately wanted to believe what Dave said about the girl she had found him with in the pub, and when you want to ignore the most glaring shortcomings in someone's character because you are so mad for them, it's very easy to do.

Dave finally did something that could be classified under the heading *Making An Effort*: he called a few people and got Rachel's phone number.

The transformation in Rachel that morning after she got the phone call was miraculous and Helen somehow doubted, despite her tears of the other day, that it was anything to do with that polite Italian boy who was so sorely missed – but only by her and Dick as a longed-for clean and predictable escort for their daughter.

Dave and Rachel had sat down on the beach, finally, one afternoon in early September. It had taken that long for Dave to come up with Rachel's number and for Rachel to do the requisite amount of hesitating as advised by Susan. Had she been taking her own advice, she would have gone down to meet Dave one second after the call, with her nightie on.

They sat staring out to sea with the pier to their left looking rather sorry for itself in the unforgiving September light. Now they were together and Dave had, to some extent, formalised their relationship he wasn't quite sure how to proceed. Rachel, although she was tense, was speaking in a confident and easy manner and he didn't know which set of signs to believe. Had he known the strength of her feelings he would have run for his life, but Rachel, as well as not wanting to fuck things up, had been tutored very thoroughly by The Queen of Ice, Susan, and was somehow managing to do tortured casual as she chatted away to Dave as if they were friends, not lovers whose aspirations about one another were several miles apart.

Dave's natural inclination was to underplay his part in bringing them together, to the point that Rachel almost began to believe that she had organised the meeting. She pounced on any nuance in his language that might demonstrate some commitment and was hugely wary of seeming too keen about anything. And even though it was artificially created, Dave was surprised by the fact that she didn't immediately try and manoeuvre herself into a series of meetings with him.

He had come down for the day and had to get back to college, but he wanted Rachel to stay with him in London for the weekend. Rachel wanted to do this more than anything else she had ever wanted, including meeting Marc Bolan or Bob Dylan, but she stayed monotone.

'Not sure,' she said. 'Yeah, possibly. When were you thinking?'

'How about next weekend?' said Dave. 'One of my friends is having a party at his squat. It'll be a laugh.' He didn't enquire whether Rachel's parents let her run riot or if they were Victorian in their guardianship of her, because he didn't feel like getting involved and assumed she would work out some way of getting up there if she wanted to do it. At least he now knew her true age.

They covered such diverse topics as politics and whether Neil Young would make a good werewolf, and the big hand on the clock whizzed round to cram three hours into what seemed like twenty minutes. During this time they sat side by side and Dave had his arm round Rachel who was so happy to be back and soaking up the Dave smell again. Now and then they would kiss and it was just as overwhelming as she remembered and made poor Claudio's efforts evaporate in her memory without even taking a detour through regret first.

'Whatever you do, make sure you leave first,' Susan had said. 'Don't let him leave you sitting there watching his back disappear into the distance like some poor cow waving her husband off to the war.'

Rachel thought this was slightly melodramatic but made a supreme effort to heed her words and said to Dave, 'I'm really sorry, I've got to go now.'

Dave looked pissed off. 'Can't you even walk me to the station?' he said.

Rachel immediately caved in and ended up on a bench

at the station sobbing uncontrollably like someone who *had* just seen their husband off to the war. She had tried to get herself into the mindset, because their relationship had not been a particularly committed one to date, of believing that every time he went away, she might not see him again – but that inevitably meant it was always going to be as traumatic as *Brief Encounter* every time.

Susan was suffering a bit from the departure of Luca although she never let things get to her or buried them so deep that they didn't surface. She called Rachel immediately.

'How did it go?'

'Oh Christ, it was fantastic,' said Rachel. 'He's brilliant and I just . . .' Rachel often trailed off for fear of being too enthusiastic.

'I'm so pleased,' said Susan, 'but you will be careful, won't you?'

'I don't know if I want to,' said Rachel. 'Part of me wants to dive headlong into it and bugger the consequences.'

'Rachel, please watch it,' said Susan.

'All right, Mum,' said Rachel. 'He wants me to go up next weekend. How am I going to swing that one?'

'When?' asked Susan.

'Friday night till Sunday,' said Rachel.

'What about just going Saturday? It'd be easier to get away with.'

'No, I can't.'

Susan could hear how utterly Dave had clamped himself round Rachel. 'All right, I'll ask my mum if she'll help,' she offered. 'We could say we're going to stay with my auntie or something.'

'Would you?' Rachel felt relief flooding over her.

'I'll do my best,' said Susan.

Terry, surprisingly, wasn't keen.

'What if anything should happen to her?' she said. 'I don't mind covering for the odd party down here, but two nights in London, it's too much.'

'Oh please, Mum,' said Susan. 'Dave's a really nice bloke – she'll be fine.'

'No, she'll have to find some other way.'

'What about if I go too and we stick together?' said Susan.

Terry wavered. 'Maybe, let me think about it.' Two seconds later, she relented and agreed.

Rachel was ambivalent about the news. On the one hand she was pleased she would be able to go, and on the other she wasn't sure how easy it was going to be having Susan around. I mean, where would her friend go when she and Dave were together? In the wardrobe?

I can't be ungrateful though, thought Rachel. 'Oh, that's fantastic! Are you sure?' she said.

'Yes. My mum will talk to yours and say we're both going to stay with a relative of mine called Auntie Lil,' said Susan. 'And I have got an Auntie Lil and we *will* go and see her so your mum can have a number to ring.'

Then there was a silence.

'What's the matter?' asked Rachel.

'Oh shit, Martin,' said Susan. 'I'm bound to bump into him. Isn't he Dave's best friend?'

'We'll think of something,' said Rachel, 'and if the worst comes to the worst, you'll just have to give him a blow job or something.'

Some seconds elapsed before Rachel started to laugh and Susan realised she was joking.

Rachel sat just inside her bedroom door in the dark while Helen spoke to Terry on the phone.

'So, Lil will keep an eye on them and make sure that they behave themselves and don't stay out all night, will she?' Helen was saying.

After a few tense minutes in which Rachel was convinced Helen would blow the whole plan wide open, her mother eventually said, 'OK. Thanks, Terry. Yes, I'm sure that'll be great. Let me have Lil's number, would you?'

Rachel appeared out of her bedroom. 'Is it OK then, Mum? Can I go?'

'All right then,' said Helen, 'but you're to phone me when you get there and call me on Saturday.'

'OK, Mum. Thanks.' Rachel hugged her.

The two girls took the train together on Friday night. Dave was waiting for them at Charing Cross and so was Martin, much to Susan's disdain, both with suppressed grins on their faces in an effort to look cool. The boys were at St Martin's School of Art in Central London, but like most students who study in the bit of London that tourists tend to concentrate on, could not afford to live near there, so had a very cheap rented flat in Stockwell which they shared with two other blokes, Bill and Wes. After a slightly terrifying Tube journey in which Rachel witnessed a couple of fights, sat next to some poor bloke who was mentally ill and talking to himself, and saw more black people than she had ever seen in her life, they arrived at the flat. The smell of joss sticks was heavy in the air, overlaid with patchouli – an attempt, Rachel felt, to disguise the lack of commitment to domestic chores rather than any aesthetic nasal choice.

Dave had been a little surprised when told that Susan was coming too, but Martin was overjoyed. After a snatched meal notable for value for money rather than nutrition, they headed off across London to the party, which was in Hackney. They started off at a pub with a band playing in the background. Hardly background, thought Rachel, as the noise was so loud that it felt like a psychological experiment on tolerance rather than a sound to relax with and have a laugh. Dave sat next to Rachel and they held hands under the table. Rachel was ecstatic. Susan sat next to Martin who looked at her intently, and had she not poured quite so much vodka down her throat, she would have felt extremely uncomfortable.

Then to the party and after getting a bus on which everyone seemed exotic in some way, either because of their skin colour, bad language or unwashed urban aroma, they all arrived in Hackney. Rachel noticed that as they entered the house where the party was, a big Georgian affair that looked like it belonged to someone's parents, Dave let go of her hand. She began to panic because she wondered what this meant. She turned to Susan for some support and noticed that she and Martin were holding hands, mainly to keep Susan upright and stop her going face first onto the pavement.

The next few hours were a jumble of new experiences. Rachel had never been to a party with a load of art students before and everybody exuded a studied scruffiness (men) and a charity-shop chic (women). Rachel, still clothed in a long skirt, baggy T-shirt and clogs, felt like a poor relation but not quite as weird as Susan felt; she, for all her elfin loveliness, stuck out like a sore thumb in her new tonic suit and wedge lace-up shoes. A very tall girl dressed entirely in black said to her, 'Wow, lady, look at you. Is that fascist garb or what?'

'I don't know what the fuck you're talking about,' said Susan and the girl laughed and walked off, saying to anyone who would listen, 'And she's got an accent and personality to match.'

Rachel felt protective towards Susan, caught in the middle of this pantomime like Little Red Riding Hood with the wolf's clothes on. It had dawned on her that Dave was not the sort of person who was going to take her round the party and say to everyone, 'I'd like you to meet my new fiancée, Rachel,' and that she pretty much would have to fend for herself.

She looked at her watch and something about that action jogged her memory. Shit, she'd forgotten to phone her mum. It was eleven thirty. She'd have to do it or Helen would be on her way up to London riding shotgun on a police motorbike. When she asked where the nearest phone box was, everyone looked at her as though she had asked the location of the nearest sewage works, so being unable to find Dave – something else that worried her – she took off with the bravado that seeps into you courtesy of alcohol to find a phone box. She had told Susan where she was going in case a search-party had to be sent out. She found a phone box and tried to get herself together so she wouldn't be too drunk to talk to her mum.

The phone was answered on the first ring, a very bad sign that meant Helen had been sitting next to it and waiting for it to ring, and even in her cloudy-headed state Susan could detect a note of hysteria.

'Thank God,' said Helen. 'I was thinking of calling the police.'

Rachel tried to inject as much light-heartedness and sobriety into her voice as she could manage. 'I'm really sorry, Mum,' she said. 'We're just having such a lovely time it went right out of my head.'

Helen was so relieved that Rachel was spared a full-scale interrogation. Helen had had questions lined up too, because she was slightly suspicious about what was going on in London. However, she did accept that Susan was a good companion because sometimes the head on her shoulders was positively middle-aged. Little did she know that at this precise moment, having ingested some speed, Susan was lying in the garden of a very upmarket house in Islington being rhythmically penetrated by a delighted Martin.

Despite thinking it was unlikely she would get murdered

on the way back from the phone box (another anomaly her mum hadn't commented on), Rachel got back to the party safely. She was in the kitchen getting a drink when she heard someone say, 'Martin's fucking that skinhead tart out in the garden,' and a combination of alcohol and indignation caused her to position herself right in front of the woman

'Excuse me,' she said quietly, and everyone turned round. 'I would just like to point out to you toffee-nosed arseholes that my friend is not a tart or a skinhead and you can all fuck off.' She turned to get out of the room and realised Dave was standing in the doorway.

Oh piss, she thought. I've really done it now and Dave's going to be angry with me for slagging off his friends, realise I'm not quite the person he thought I was and give me the boot. She began to prepare for tragedy.

But Dave started to laugh. 'Well done,' he said. 'That silly twat deserves to be told. Come on, let's go. I'm bored. Where's Martin?'

'Last spotted fucking the skinhead tart in the garden,' said Rachel and they laughed and walked out to get them and take the night bus home.

When they got back to the flat, Dave took Rachel up to his bedroom, leaving a semi-conscious Susan and Martin to sort themselves out. He rolled a huge joint and took off his boots. They had an exhausting and unrepeatable night together and didn't get to sleep until five. As Big Ben struck one on Saturday afternoon they roused themselves, happy and sticky.

'Let's go walking round London and see some things,' said Dave.

Rachel had been on a couple of school trips to London and done the Tower and the Houses of Parliament. But she had not been whisked along the King's Road and through Kensington Market, or round the Tate in the way Dave introduced these places to her, and of course on all those other visits she had not had Dave's sperm inside her. If things had been different she'd have wanted to phone her mum and tell her all about it.

They spent the whole afternoon out, holding hands, laughing, talking and kissing, and Lou Reed's heroin anthem 'Perfect Day' echoed in her head. When they got back to the flat Susan had her 'It's all gone wrong' face on.

'It's all gone wrong,' she said.

'What do you mean?' said Rachel.

'Well, I just phoned Mum to say hello and that I was OK, and she says she's had your mum on the phone saying she's phoned Lil and Lil doesn't know anything about it.'

'Fucking hell,' said Rachel.

'Mum only bloody forgot to let Lil know.'

'Oh Christ,' said Rachel, hating Terry with all her heart and soul.

Susan continued, 'Apparently your mother wants to know where you are and what you are doing, and she wants you to phone her and come home now.'

'Shit, shit, shit,' said Rachel, twisting the black plastic bangle she'd just bought from Biba.

'What are you going to do?' said Dave. 'Do you think you should go back?'

'She's going to fucking kill me,' said Rachel, forgetting temporarily to look calm and in control in front of Dave. 'Look I'll go and phone her,' she decided. 'I'll be back in a minute.'

'Cheer up, love,' said a bloke, as she headed towards the phone box

If only you knew, thought Rachel.

She dialled her home number. Again, Helen picked up on the first ring.

'Rachel, I am extremely angry and disappointed in you,' said Helen. 'I want you to get on the first train and come home right now and Dad will pick you up at the station.'

Rachel couldn't believe that all the gloriousness of this sex-and-alcohol-and-love-filled weekend was slipping away and it was all bloody Terry's fault. She took a calculated risk.

'I'm not coming home today, I'll come home tomorrow evening,' she said. 'And if you do anything like call the police to come and get me, I'll never ever speak to you again and as soon as it's legal I'll leave home. You can do whatever you want to me tomorrow but I'm not coming home till then.' And she put the phone down. Afterwards, she couldn't believe what she had said.

Back at the flat, Susan and Dave were waiting for news.

'I told her I'd go home tomorrow,' she said.

'Your dad is going to kill you,' Susan warned her.

'I don't care,' said Rachel. 'Let's have a bloody good time.'

And that is exactly what they did.

Rachel often discussed with Susan how she would behave if she thought she didn't have long to live, or if a news flash informed her, along with the rest of the world, that there were three minutes before the world exploded. Everyone reckons they would have sex but realistically, not much could actually be achieved in three minutes. For a start you've got to find someone suitable, get them to have an erection and by that point you're probably up to about two and a half minutes, so unless premature ejaculators are your thing you'd be better off with a shedload of chocolate and fags.

But Rachel didn't have three minutes, she had one evening and one whole day, and in the first couple of minutes she came clean with Dave. How she had lied to her parents and the gaff had been blown and how it was very likely that she would be kept in until she was at least thirty so they probably wouldn't be seeing each other for a while. Normally Dave would have been relieved by this and seen it as a highly convenient full stop to the relationship which was starting to get slightly tedious. He'd often wished this option were available generally for those slightly mad drunk women who are very hard to get rid of.

In this case, I don't want to tick the Unavoidably Prevented From Continuing The Relationship box, he thought grimly. He knew he was becoming more and more interested by Rachel and seeing in her something that was difficult to find in the girls he mixed with: a complete lack of pretension.

'Look,' Rachel said, 'I'm convinced my mum won't send the Old Bill up here to get me and will await my return tomorrow with a good deal of sadistic pleasure, so I may as well make my last hours of freedom ones to remember.'

'It's totally up to you,' said Dave. 'You have carte blanche to say what you want to do. Go on.'

'Right, first of all,' said Rachel, blushing very slightly, 'loads of kissing and sex.'

'Taken as read,' said Dave. 'Next?'

'Well,' said Rachel, 'some food, some drink, some drugs, and tomorrow some art, some sex, some strolling around and then a great movie to finish it off.'

Susan seemed to be handling Martin by being so pissed that she could be spending the weekend with a real boyfriend. They were happy to continue.

And so the rest of the evening, the night and the following day were a never-to-be-forgotten cornucopia of great experiences for Rachel, starting with some mindblowing sex, which made her want to forget all the other things they had planned.

On Sunday morning they all went to a greasy spoon café down the road and Dave ordered everything on the breakfast menu on one plate for Rachel, who manfully tackled a fair bit of it before they ran for a bus to take them up to the National Gallery in Trafalgar Square. While Martin and Susan went off to have a look around, Dave showed Rachel his favourite paintings and explained why he loved the artists in here and why it was OK for a scruffbag art student like him to look at traditional art without being censured for being a right-wing tosser.

At this point, Susan and Martin peeled off for a while.

'Are you sure?' said Rachel, looking into Susan's eyes and trying to spot some tiny clue as to her irritation with the situation or her exasperation with them doing love all over London. But there was nothing there and she happily winked at Rachel and said, 'See you under Nelson's Column at five?'

Dave and Rachel went to St James's Park and managed to achieve intercourse in a reasonably subtle manner under his big coat, a ridiculous but essential accessory for every self-respecting art student in the summer.

They saw a film in the afternoon, *Last Tango In Paris* (Very appropriate, thought Rachel. Marlon Brando is very good at doing realistic stranger-fucking, thought Dave.) Rachel sat with her mouth open through most of it.

Then they met Susan and Martin at Nelson's Column. And it was time to go. Everyone suddenly felt hungover and had gone a weird grey colour. Martin looked miserable; Susan looked slightly relieved. Dave was more fed up than he had predicted.

They walked across the Strand to Charing Cross and at the platform, Susan turned to Martin. 'It's been really nice,' she said. He didn't notice she said 'nice' as though she was saying 'shit'. Regret was souring her memories of a very good time with him.

'Can I phone you?' he said.

'Maybe.' Susan turned and started to walk towards the train.

God, how does she do that? thought Rachel. I could never

be that casual. She didn't realise she was being like that too.

Martin grinned. 'Maybe' was a result in his book.

Rachel turned to Dave. 'See you then,' she said, trying to be as nonchalant as possible.

'Yep, right,' said Dave. 'I hope they're not too hard on you. Shall I call?'

'I don't think so, that would just wind them up,' said Rachel. 'I'll write or something.'

That was as much as she could manage without dissolving so she turned and started to walk down the platform. She tried to do the Liza Minnelli wave from *Cabaret*, a cheeky flourish of the fingers without looking back, but she had neither the nails nor the glamour for it so she just hoped Dave hadn't even noticed and turned round to wave.

He'd already gone.

Chapter 16

Dick was waiting at the station for Rachel, and Susan decided it was probably best that he and she didn't exchange pleasantries so she waited in the café until she saw them disappear then began to walk home.

Dick was more reasonable than Rachel had imagined he would be. She had had visions of some sort of terrible scene played out between them on the station platform and so felt slightly more optimistic than she had on the train. Big mistake.

Even though it was the Sunday service, the train journey from Charing Cross to Hastings had been far too short for the time the two girls needed to analyse the weekend's proceedings, to laugh about some things and cry about others.

'What do you think your mum and dad will do?' Susan had asked.

'I don't know,' said Rachel, adding hopefully, 'There's only so much they *can* do.'

'If you're not allowed to see me, we can develop a code by which to communicate.'

'I'm sure they won't stop me from going to school,' Rachel sighed, 'so they'll have to let me see you.' She started to panic at the real possibility that her parents would move just to spite her, and prayed this would not be the case.

'What are you going to do about Dave?' said Susan.

'What can I do? I'll have to see what happens and take it from there.'

'I can also pass you messages from him if you want,' said Susan.

'No, it's all right.' Rachel couldn't bear the idea of Susan seeing or communicating with Dave, but she didn't tell her that because it was too hurtful.

In the car, Dick said, 'Your mum is absolutely incandescent.'

Rachel wondered where he'd got that from because he wouldn't normally say things like that, but she kept quiet. So far, her dad seemed to be playing the good policeman because he had not made any threats or warned of any punishment. That was, no doubt, all to come when they got home.

Rachel went into the flat and was vaguely aware of the admiring faces of Alan and Clive at their bedroom doors; her brothers gave her a supportive sibling wave before she was whisked into the front room, the door was shut and the session began. And when it did begin it was a bit like being in a pantomime.

'First of all,' Helen said, 'I want to say how utterly

shocked I am at the degree of duplicity you have displayed. I have almost accepted the fact that you are going to try and get away with as much as you can, but for me to discover you have gone up to London completely unchaperoned' (Fuck, she's doing big words as well, thought Rachel), 'and then when I tell you to come home, you refuse – well, that really is the limit as far as I'm concerned.' Rachel felt like saying, 'Can you just tell me the punishment and I'll be off then?' but she knew she had to give her mum the opportunity to sound off. She did not deny that what she had done was appalling.

'. . . And us sitting here . . .' (Rachel realised her thoughts had blocked out quite a big chunk of the speech) '. . . having absolutely no idea who you were with and where you were. Your father nearly phoned Uncle Phil' – Helen's brother whom Dick loathed – 'when Terry told us where you were because he lives in that area, to go and look in the pubs for you. And you know how humiliating that would have been for him.'

'I was with Susan,' pointed out Rachel.

This caused her mother to go nuclear. 'What!' she said. 'You're trying to say to me that just because you were with another child, because that's what you both are, and a child from a family of liars like Terry, *that that makes everything OK*?'

'Well,' began Rachel.

'Just keep your mouth shut,' Helen said viciously. 'It's my turn to talk now and you bloody listen. Added to that,

I have managed to get Terry to admit to the fact that you were both seeing two older boys.'

They're nearly nineteen, Mum, said Rachel in her head. They're not boys.

Her mum continued, 'And two older boys at art college who are involved in God knows what on the drugs front – they could be heroin addicts for all I know.'

Rachel had to let this happen. The most important thing about the parental rant is that it just has to be endured.

'So what is this young man called?' said Dick.

'Dave,' said Rachel.

'Ah,' said Dick, 'the one who . . .' He trailed off, unable to remember how much he had told Helen at the time of the barn-party incident.

'The one who what, Dick?' his wife asked harshly.

'The one who was at that party,' said Dick.

'What, Amanda's party?' demanded Helen. 'So it's been going on all this time, when I thought you were with that nice Claudio.' If Helen was truly honest with herself, she had thought Claudio a bit too nice, but this was not to be revealed. Did Rachel want to explain the complexities of her relationship with Dave? Helen asked. No, she didn't.

'Right,' her mother said. 'I suppose you want to know what we are going to do about all this.'

'Yes, please,' said Rachel, which seemed rather inappropriate.

'Very well,' announced Helen. 'You're not to go out at night on your own without one of us for six months.'

Rachel started to say, 'Fucking hell,' and managed to

turn it into, 'Fine,' but inwardly, her blood pressure was plummeting and she thought she was going to faint.

'Also, I am going to ask your Headmistress to move you to a different class away from that Pigg girl, and if this cannot be done we will arrange a private tutor for you at home. Dad will meet you from school, every day.' (Room starting to spin.) 'Also, I am going to contact this Dave's parents and tell them what has been going on and you will not be seeing him again under any circumstances once we have finished with them.' (Falling into a big black pit.) 'And I want you to dress properly and to have nice clean hair and stop wearing that dreadful perfume. You are to throw away all your records and just have books in your room, and if you do badly at school in the coming months we will extend the curfew.' (Rachel landed at the bottom of the cavernous abyss which was her future.) 'Right,' said Helen. 'Now go up to your room and start packing up your records. And no using the phone,' she shouted after her, as Rachel left the room.

Rachel dragged herself to her room, but couldn't muster up enough energy to respond to the urgently whispered questions from Clive and Alan about what had happened. She sat on the bed, stunned. She wouldn't be able to tell Dave any of this unless she wrote to him; she couldn't phone Susan for some solace, and everyone at school would know that something had gone on.

I should kill myself, she thought, and that would teach them all a lesson.

Helen and Dick were rather stunned by what they'd

done too. Helen was shocked by the tone and content of the sort of things she'd said to Rachel. She had intended to be a laidback liberal mother who accepted the fact that her daughter was growing up and kept quiet about her worries, but she found herself to be an anxious and rather reactionary person she didn't recognise or particularly like. She had ascribed the latter characteristics to Dick, who seemed remarkably sanguine about the whole thing.

Helen started to cry as soon as Rachel got out of the room.

'Oh Christ, love,' she wept. 'Have I been too harsh with her? Is this only going to make things worse? Will she only rebel more?'

'I don't know,' said Dick, putting his arm round her. 'Don't worry – I'm sure it'll work out OK.'

Even such a banal platitude as this and the action of putting his arm round her made Helen feel as if there was still a connection between them and she felt slightly comforted by that.

She wanted to go into Rachel's bedroom and say, 'Look, I hope you realise how hard this is going to be for us, policing your life and Dick having to take you to school and pick you up every day. I hope you appreciate we're only doing this for you.' But she didn't think appreciation would be top of Rachel's list of reactions to her punishment.

She was wrong to a certain extent because Rachel could understand how worried they must have been to overreact like this. But there is no way of reassuring your parents when you are fifteen that the life you are leading is in any way acceptable and the man you are sleeping with is all right.

Rachel got into bed and pulled the covers over her head. She couldn't believe it was only a few hours since they'd all been in London, and she wondered whether she should try to run away. But what if she got to London and Dave was with someone else – or, even worse, what if he was not with someone else, but he didn't want her? The police would find her easily. It wasn't worth it. No, she somehow had to get through the next few months and hope that Dave would hang about, that Susan wouldn't make new friends and that this wasn't the end of the enormous, brilliant, exhausting, unpredictable and at times frightening ride she'd been on.

That night, Susan sat at home telling Terry, Kim and Jennifer all about the goings-on in London. Terry felt like a naughty schoolgirl who had been caught out, and although her untidy beehive had nearly blown off when Helen had called her immature and irresponsible, she couldn't help but agree. When she thought about the fact that she had let her teenage daughter and friend go to London for the weekend, and lied to the other child's mother, she felt ashamed and thought if she had read a letter in the *Woman's Own* problem page about what she had done, she would have tutted along with the rest of the readers.

She had said to Vince, 'Let's try and rein things in a bit with the girls, shall we?'

Vince was shocked but gave thanks as he lay in bed, for

the turn of events and the fact that the adults in the house might exert a bit more control.

In Stockwell, South London, Dave lay on his bed feeling morose and bereft. Then Martin put his head round the door and said, 'Coming for a pint?'

They went down the pub and smiled at two girls who were sitting at the bar and trying to catch their eye.

Chapter 17

Rachel endured the curfew with extremely bad grace and made her parents feel like prison guards doing work experience at Butlin's. They had confined their daughter to barracks but were nevertheless expected to be maniacally cheerful about it as if life was progressing normally. Rachel was monosyllabic and surly most of the time, causing Dick to remark to Helen one day that she had turned into Alan.

Helen had smiled weakly at this but inside felt like she was floating unanchored in the huge sea of parental responsibility, not really having a clue about what she was doing. Rachel could hear her sitting at the kitchen table crying occasionally but she just hardened her heart and wished she had the wherewithal to run away from home.

Running away was a possible in her list of *Where now for the heartbroken teenager?* but where to, and who with? She'd hinted at it to Susan on the train journey back from London but Susan wasn't stupid enough to substitute a bedsit and a job in a shop for the home life she had with Terry and Vince. Besides, Rachel felt too tragic to do anything constructive and spent her time staring at the wall, listening to Leonard Cohen and Dylan over and over again and wishing she could waste away, if only she didn't feel so hungry all the time.

She was now in a different class at school. Initially this had raised a few overplucked eyebrows until more interesting pubescent concerns flew in to settle them down again. She and Susan initially accepted the lack of contact at school, occasionally passing in the corridor and managing the odd, 'All right?' but Rachel felt her life was so dull there was nothing to talk about anyway, and Susan missed Rachel and the chance of joint adventures which were so much better than single ones.

Rachel often wondered why Helen and Dick had been so hard on her. What did they fear? And if Clive or Alan had bunked off to London for the weekend, would they have been given the same treatment? But Alan and Clive wouldn't have bunked off to London. Alan was seventeen now but could still barely match a pair of socks; he had had a couple of girlfriends who hadn't lasted long because he didn't realise it was rather inappropriate to ask them to clean his room while he watched the football.

Clive at fifteen was painfully shy of girls. He still spent a long time in his bedroom and no one in the family liked to dwell on what he might be up to.

Dave had managed a few secret communications via a series of cryptic postcards. Dick never even noticed their arrival but Helen was fully aware who they were from and didn't have the heart to withhold them. Rachel had desperately wanted to call Dave, but felt if she got through she might explode in a tirade of emotion so powerful it would frighten him off for ever. So instead she cast herself in the role of tragic heroine and revisited some books which seemed apposite like *Anna Karenina* and *Jane Eyre*. She hoped Dave and she would eventually get together and this kept her going.

Helen did attempt to change Rachel's appearance to that of a secretary at a small building firm. This meant colourful yet somehow dull blouses with Crimpleney skirts, flat shoes and those tights that make your legs look as if you have died from the waist down. Rachel felt like a freak in them, and wearing a bra again gave her some idea of what it was like to be in a straitjacket. She had been only too happy not to wear bras. They created such an obvious line under a T-shirt and felt all pointy and unnatural. Susan, who had always worn slightly twee Berlei bras with little rosebuds or bows at the front, had constantly teased Rachel about letting everything wobble.

'They don't fucking wobble, they are perfectly firm,' Rachel had said crossly. 'Give it a couple of years,' said Susan.

Rachel had forgotten the torture that was tights. She had been so used to long skirts with no knickers, no socks and often no shoes, that wearing tights made her legs feel as if they were wrapped in elastic. She could almost feel the thrush starting to crank up as soon as she put them on. And it was round the crotch area where tights never quite managed to stay up that they caused the most grief, because that void between crotch and tights as they started to sag was impossible to ignore. Rachel always ended up wearing two pairs of pants, one under and one over just to stop this yawn away from the line of her body. This made her feel as attractive as an elderly nun.

At the end of six months Rachel had metamorphosed into a young lady who was conservatively dressed and morose but with a tiny little glimmer of hope about the future spluttering like a wet firework in the far reaches of her mind.

Dave didn't try to see Rachel as soon as she was allowed out. She was desperate to see him, but she knew six months at their age was a long time in a romance and she tried to suppress her feelings and wait for what she hoped would be a momentous meeting.

Time slid on and Susan, to whom she now had the opportunity to be much closer but of whom she felt inexplicably wary, seemed unable to bring news of him.

'Where is he?' asked Rachel.

'I don't know,' said Susan. 'He must be away at the moment.'

It was July and Rachel had hoped that she could get him to come and see T. Rex with her. They were playing on the pier on the twenty-fifth, and time to organise it was running short. She had avoided discussing it with Susan because she didn't want to arrange to go with her and then have to cancel it. Susan had not discussed it with Rachel since she had assumed that Rachel wouldn't be allowed to go.

Rachel decided she might as well ask Helen if she could go. It was a very special night, after all. Helen, who'd been out all day shopping and seemed more content, hesitated. Rachel held her breath.

'No, I don't think so,' she said, and however much Rachel pleaded she seemed unmoved.

'You don't understand,' said Rachel. 'It's really important for me to see them. Please, Mum.'

Some hours later Helen had come up with a solution.

'All right,' she said. 'You can go to the pier to see T. Rex, but I'll have to come with you.'

This was the ultimate in double-edged swords and conjured up many images in her head of humiliation, ranging from gangs of her peers from school pointing and laughing to perhaps the most unimaginable – Marc, singling her mum out of the heaving crowd and having her taken to his dressing-room for drug-fuelled sex.

Where the fuck did that image come from? thought Rachel.

'Are you going?' she asked Susan. They were chatting at the bus stop, because Dick had finally eased up on collecting Rachel from school.

'No,' said Susan.

'Me neither,' said Rachel. She found herself not wanting to explain even to Susan that she was going with her mum. Six months ago they would have had a good laugh about it, but things were still awkward and Rachel couldn't fathom why this was. It seemed that the regime imposed by her parents had achieved one of its aims and caused a fracture in their relationship.

On the night, Rachel didn't know if she could go through with it. She wondered how much her mother could and would humiliate her. She was worried because Helen hadn't laughed when a woman in the queue in Sainsbury's said, 'Oh, I see they've got that Trex on the pier tonight.' She seemed distant and preoccupied.

Rachel decided if they went in after the support act had started, steered clear of the bar and stood at the back in the dark, it would be bearable as long as she didn't bump into anyone from school.

It was a warm night and despite looking like a youthful primary schoolteacher with a knee-length flowery skirt and a pink blouse, Rachel felt the old excitement start to creep over her as soon as her foot landed on the first plank of the pier. Helen had had the good grace to dress down and not come in a mum-type outfit and also not to say mum things like, 'All these young people, they're not very sensibly dressed, are they?'

They got along the pier without being recognised, although at one point Rachel saw someone in her class and ducked behind a wall pretending to do up a shoe lace on her platform sole which didn't have shoe laces.

'Would you like a drink?' offered Helen as they approached the bar. 'It's all right, you can have a proper one.'

'No thanks,' said Rachel, who'd decided sullen was appropriate for the early evening.

'Well, I'm having one,' said Helen.

'All right,' said Rachel. 'I'll have a vodka.'

'I meant half a lager or half a cider,' said Helen.

'Half a cider then,' said Rachel. 'I'll be at the back of the hall.'

Rachel stepped in just as the lights came up and Marc Bolan appeared and it took her breath away. She could not believe that he and she were in the same room, this pixie man whose delicate features and haughty manner put him in a parallel universe populated by those with cheekbones and ethereal beauty. The girls at the front went mental. Rachel wanted to be up there with them but she held back, and when Helen came in with the drinks she was the picture of subdued sophistication.

'So this is what all the fuss is about,' yelled Helen in Rachel's ear and instantly regretted it because the look she received back withered her. It was so easy in such a short time to become a grown-up, Helen thought, and hated herself for a while because she had intended to be the mother whose children did things because they respected her rather than because they were terrified she might keep them in at night.

Rachel turned and concentrated on the man onstage as he launched into 'Jeepster' and a thousand sighs combined to send one great big longing groan up towards the stage. Suddenly it seemed as if everyone in the front row was fainting and being dragged up onto the stage because of the crush. A few hadn't really fainted and as soon as they were laid on the stage, they instantly came to life and tried to rush their hero, without much success. Security were obviously familiar with the fake fainting routine and men with hands the size of frozen chickens lifted these fifteen-year-old sirens up and away from the adored one with the greatest of ease.

There were a few casualties who were taken back and laid behind the stage. Rachel started to look around, and as the band launched into 'Raw Ramp' she noticed the back of a head that looked very like Susan's. So she did come, after all, thought Rachel. Great. She turned to her mother.

'Mum, I've just seen someone from school. I won't be long,' she said and before Helen could protest, she was gone.

The crowd around Susan came into focus as she moved towards them and as Marc Bolan screamed out, 'Girl, you ain't nothing but a raw ramp!' a phrase Rachel felt lacked sensitivity, she realised that someone familiar was standing next to Susan. Dave.

The punch hit the back of Susan's head so hard that it threw her forward and into a couple in front who turned uncomprehendingly to see a girl of about sixteen snarling and foaming at the mouth. She was now attempting to hit a tall man next to her with all the force she could muster, and he stood there with a look of helplessness and defeat as though the whole world had caved in on him.

Rachel had allowed hysteria to get the better of her, and when security realised there was some sort of scuffle they moved in quickly and carried her towards the backstage area where there was some space. Rachel was aware of several girls lying semi-conscious on the floor, and stupefied, she sat against a wall while a security man went off to find some help. A policeman who had been attending the faintees looked round and then knelt down almost on top of a girl of about fifteen and pulled her T-shirt up, exposing her breasts.

Rachel wondered if her drink had been spiked again and for the second time that night, hit the back of someone's head. She didn't take into account that it wasn't the greatest idea to hit a copper. Still, she was beyond worrying about that sort of trivia and when Helen, who had come looking for her, having seen a fight and wondered if her daughter could possibly be involved, saw Rachel hitting the policeman with all the force she could manage, she wondered how her sixteen-year-old daughter who played the piano and spoke French had reached this point. Several explanations ran through her head.

That Rachel was on drugs.

That she and the policeman were having some sort of relationship.

That Rachel had espoused left-wing politics a little too enthusiastically and was doing her duty and hitting 'a pig'.

The one thing that never occurred to her, an intelligent middle-class woman, was that the policeman could have been doing anything wrong.

The copper by this point had swung round and caught Rachel by the wrist and wrenched it away, hurting her.

Helen intervened. 'I'm terribly sorry, Officer,' she said.

'This is my daughter. I have no idea what came over her and I apologise. I'll take her home and punish her accordingly.'

The policeman stuck his face right into hers. 'What do you think this is?' he screeched at her. 'Fucking Toytown? Who are you, Margot Fucking Leadbetter? This girl has just assaulted me, an officer of the law, and that's a very serious offence. I will be taking her down the station and she'll spend the night in a cell. Now piss off home, you stupid bloody tart, and leave me to do my job.'

He grabbed Rachel by the hand and led her through the crowd and to the end of the pier where a wagon was waiting to receive the hordes of people who'd been unable to contain themselves during the T. Rex gig. Rachel was unceremoniously thrown into the back of the van.

Thank Christ he didn't come in with me, she thought as she realised she was sitting next to a small, rather inoffensive-looking policewoman who gave her a wan smile, and then looked at the floor.

As the adrenalin drained out of Rachel's nervous system, it struck her what she had seen tonight and she began to sob – huge, heartrending sobs that shook her whole body.

'Don't worry, love,' said the WPC. 'It'll be OK.' And that was the extent of the counselling skills of Sussex Police.

At the police station Rachel was charged with assault and put into a cell while Helen was contacted to come and get her.

Rachel sat there and mulled over the evening's events. She wanted to know what was going on, what had gone on and what would be going on, but unfortunately the only people who could tell her were Dave and Susan themselves, unless Susan had confided in one of her sisters or her mum. It was odds on that Susan's family had no idea whatsoever what was going on. In theory, Susan should be ashamed about this dirty little betrayal. Rachel was filled with hate and despair, and what hurt the most was that Susan, knowing how she felt about Dave, had still gone ahead and done what she had done. Of course she had explored the option that it was all totally innocent but her instincts told her that she was being over-optimistic because:

They would have told her about it.

Dave would not have had his arm round Susan.

If it was innocent, knowing that Rachel loved Marc Bolan so much, they would not have done it on this particular night, but maybe when Showaddywaddy was on.

What she didn't know was that, ironically, Dave had only contacted Susan because he was desperate for news of Rachel and what was happening to her. He had sent a couple of cards and had no reply, and although he continued to flourish at college and girls continued to throw themselves at him at parties, he felt a bit empty and he thought that was down to the lack of Rachel.

He got hold of Susan's number and called her and they arranged to meet. Susan filled him in on the curfew and punishments and it was while she was talking to him about it that some jealous feelings rose up in her throat when it occurred to her that this man did really seem to care for Rachel. He didn't want to just keep her in his bedroom all day or show her off to his friends, there was a genuine concern which, looking back at all the men who had drooled over her throughout her short life, was something Susan had never experienced. A little bit of her wanted Dave to direct that at her. She promised him she would try and get a message to Rachel, although she had no intention of doing so, and arranged to meet him several weeks later to report back. When she did, she made up a whole load of things which amounted to the fact that Rachel couldn't see him or didn't really even want to at the moment, and as Dave was teetering on the brink of trying to wait outside school for Rachel, this stopped him in his tracks.

They met again a few weeks later and this time he looked again hard at Susan and thought how pretty and sparky she was. Susan flirted a bit with him and then disappeared, leaving him wanting to see her again.

The next time they met was the night of the Marc Bolan gig, in a café near the pier. She persuaded him to take her, saying she had no one else to go with and reassuring him that Rachel wouldn't be there. He had had a few drinks and started to feel warm towards her, the irony being that he was putting his arm round her to kiss her during the gig and hadn't at that point done anything untoward, when Rachel made her presence felt.

After the event, Dave felt more guilty than he had ever done before, as if he had had sex with a bridesmaid at his wedding. Over the months he had come to realise that he had very strong feelings for Rachel, but hadn't considered how easy it was for him to jeopardise his relationship with her for the sake of a smile that hinted at some crazy sex. He had always ignored the less attractive aspects of his personality in the vain hope they would go away, but lately because of Rachel this had started to change. Even though he could hardly bear to admit it to himself, the idea of marriage had occurred to him. He wondered whether just the thought of a giant commitment at his age had been enough to tip him into immediately being unfaithful. End result, he hated himself, and hated Susan for making herself available, and was miserable and depressed.

Susan was angry with herself for letting what she called 'petty jealousies' wash over her and control her. She cringed when she recalled how she had been with Dave, teasing him and jokily challenging him about some of the things he said to snare him with deliberately inconsistent banter and the occasional brush of her hand across his. She feared she had become one of those women who can't bear anyone else to be happy or has to have what other people have. All this knowledge was bubbling just under the surface and she didn't want to drag it up any further for fear of looking in the mirror and seeing someone she should punch, or at least send for counselling.

But Rachel didn't know any of this and sat in her little cell listening to the shouts and protests of the night's crop of lawbreakers. After what seemed like the whole night, the door swung open and Rachel was ushered out.

'Your mum's here,' said a young PC gruffly, 'and until further notice you are free to go.'

Helen and Rachel walked silently out to the car. Rachel

didn't want to tell Helen what was going on and Helen didn't want to tell Rachel what she had agreed at the police station. The charges had been dropped and Rachel would go before the Chief Constable at the station for a formal warning. Helen wanted Rachel to think something worse than this might happen, in order to shock her into not starting fights with policemen. But something much worse *was* happening to Rachel and she was barely aware of the assault incident. Her best friend had betrayed her with the love of her life. Somehow that doesn't sound corny when you are devastated. She began to cry. Great gulping sobs that threatened to stop her breath.

Helen softened. 'All right love,' she said. 'Don't worry, everything will be OK.'

Rachel buried her head in her hands and howled – not really the effect Helen had hoped for with her reassuring platitude.

Chapter 18

Rachel's battered heart began to turn her into a person who was nihilistic in outlook, unconcerned about what others thought of her and searching for a way to express herself outside the small town of Hastings which seemed to be getting even smaller. She loved her parents and wanted to get on with them but could not forgive them for not putting right what was wrong. She felt as though she needed to get away from everyone and everything: her mum and dad's stale marriage, her brothers' low aspirations, and the constant reminder that the place that she loved had not turned out to be the fantasy town she'd had in her head in which she would find what the teenage magazines called 'luv'.

Since T. Rex, she had lived a frozen sort of existence for six months or so, because she didn't want to see anyone or talk to anyone, and so she went about her life in a robotic way with the minimum amount of human contact. She didn't know what to do. Either she could hang on and make an effort in her exams, or she could leave home and travel, or she could do what so many had done before her – Dick Whittington, David Bowie and her next-door neighbour Mrs Winch's niece included – she could go to London. She decided that was what she would do and that she wouldn't come back until her head was on the right way and her shatteredness was mended.

Over the next few months, Rachel hatched a plan. Money was the main problem. She had some savings in a post office book which amounted to a hundred and eighty quid, which she had put in there from her TB hospital job. She nicked a bit here and there, and found it surprisingly easy, dipping her hand in her mum's handbag or taking the odd pound note from her dad's wallet. She had decided to go up to London on her own which, although it scared the shit out of her, hugely excited her too, and being in that no-man's land of blunted emotion, she didn't really give a toss whether she was attacked or killed, although had she thought about the dangers, she would have crapped herself. She needed a head start before her mum and dad realised she was gone, and she definitely wasn't going to do that runaway living on the streets and then having to become a prostitute stuff; she was going to get a job as soon as she got there.

She owned an old *A-Z*, which she pored over every night, looking at street names and imagining what it was like in that area. She didn't want to be anywhere near Dave or bump into him because she had managed somehow to persuade herself that any connection with Dave must be severed. On the other hand, his bit of South London was the only bit she knew so she would hover near there and keep her distance from his flat and locals.

To save money, she decided to travel out a bit on the bus, then hitchhike. This was risky because it meant if her mum and dad had realised she'd gone then the police would pick her up at the side of the road waving her thumbs, but if she set off on a seemingly innocent day out, she would have a start of several hours. She had been cultivating the appearance of a stable persona so that since the policeman-whacking incident her mother would assume she was dull and settled rather than at risk, and because that was what poor old emotionally battered Helen wanted to see, that was what she saw and over a couple of months Helen believed that Rachel was at last getting over whatever it was that was going on. She had begged her to confide in her, but given all the bad blood between them, Rachel could not bring herself to do so.

And so it happened on a cloudy June day with everyone going about their business that Rachel, got a bus out to Sedlescombe and sat at the edge of the A21 with her thumb out waiting to be taken to a life that was better than the shitty one she lived at the moment.

As it was the weekend, she'd told Helen she fancied going on a long walk and together they'd looked at the map and planned a route. Helen had even made sandwiches and said to Dick, for the seventh or eighth time in Rachel's teenage years. 'I really think we are turning the corner now.'

Rachel's thumb was stuck out for the first time at ten thirty in the morning and it was not until five past eleven when she had virtually given up and decided to walk to the station that a blue estate stopped with a woman in it and two Labradors in the back.

'You shouldn't be hitching on your own,' she said. 'I have two daughters and I hate to think of them doing anything like this.'

'Are you going to tell me off all the way?' said Rachel, half-morosely and half-teasingly.

'Cheeky bugger,' said the woman, laughing. 'I'm going as far as Tunbridge Wells, take it or leave it.'

'Take it, please,' said Rachel, thinking, If I get murdered and robbed by this woman it will at the very least be the most interesting murder and robbery story for a long time.

They chatted together fairly happily, Rachel telling more lies than she had in her whole life in that thirty-five-minute drive. Mrs Posh knew she was lying, but rather admired her nerve and so didn't challenge her.

After she had been dropped off in Tunbridge Wells and the posh woman had gone off to some terrible gentlemen's outfitters to buy something that would identify her husband as a member of the aspiring aristocracy, Rachel got a bus out towards the A21 on the other side of Southborough and stood in a lay-by waiting for a lift.

Her next travelling companion was a bloke in a van and Rachel hesitated about getting in with him because he looked rather dodgy. A lot of men suffer the lifetime burden of looking as if they might have just nicked the battery out of your car or driven their mate away from a bank job. However, nine times out of ten, they are perfectly well-adjusted, law-abiding citizens as was her van driver, and he rather helpfully was going as far as Bromley to drop off a load of bathroom appliances. His van looked official, with some writing on the side of it, so Rachel settled down and enjoyed the forty-minute ride.

At Bromley she was able to get a train into London and was standing in Trafalgar Square at about four o'clock and thought she had better look for somewhere to stay for the night. Two hours later, she felt extremely depressed, having tried a few grim-looking hotels and a couple of letting agencies only to find they were too expensive.

Suddenly, in the middle of that big anonymous city she felt very lonely, very frightened and very fed up.

I'm not sure I can do this, she thought to herself. I don't want to sleep on the street or go on the game or end up in a hostel with a load of girls my age who are running from something much more serious than I am. I want to do something and get paid for it.

She went back to the station and decided to blow her money on a train ticket home and take it from there. She looked up at the big board in the station to find out the time of the train, and the word 'Bromley' caught her eye again. She was probably the first person to be able to relate this later that week without the slightest hint of irony. On a whim she got on the train back to Bromley, desperately wanting to say to the assorted group of shoppers and their offspring. 'I'm a runaway. What do you think of *that*?'

Within a very short time she found herself standing outside Bromley station. In the newsagent's window near by was a postcard advertising a bedsit, and Rachel realised she could afford a month's rent in advance and still have a fair bit left over for food and some essentials, although she hadn't thought what an essential for her might be yet.

She phoned the number on the postcard and asked if she could come and look at the room straight away. A slightly crabby old bloke at the end of the line said it was a bit late, but relented because she sounded desperate.

The bedsit was above a shop on the High Street, reached by a dingy set of stairs which also led to a couple of other flats and bedsits. There was a shared bathroom and four other rented rooms. The place had that smell which is a combination of unwashedness and damp flannels, and the room had not been lovingly restored by a craftsman. There was a very basic bed, a nasty wardrobe, a table and chair, and the walls were peppered with tiny bits of Blu-Tack.

'I'll take it. Can I move in tonight?' asked Rachel.

'If you give me some cash,' said the man, who turned out to be called Mr Flint.

Rachel was glad Mr Flint was the kind of man who asked no questions, and once they had agreed a price, he grunted. She got rid of him as soon as she could and sat down on the bed in the small rancid room, wondering whether to cry or bounce up and down on it in celebration.

Then, at nine o'clock that night, she thought about calling her parents. It was the first time Rachel had considered the sort of fracas that might be going on, down in Hastings.

She felt compelled to go and find a phone box and ring. It might keep the police off her trail whilst she established herself and got a job. She was seventeen now and it wouldn't be long before she could do what she liked, without her parents' permission.

Just down the road was a urine-perfumed phone box. She expected Helen to pick up the phone on the first ring and was disappointed when it took three. However, her mother did sound suitably distraught.

'Oh God, Rachel,' she said, biting back the tears and the frustrated rage of a parent who would just like a couple of years of quiet in her life.

'I've left home, Mum,' said Rachel. 'I'm sorry to put you through this and I know how pissed off you'll be with me, but I can't live in Hastings any more. There are too many things that have happened to me there to make me low and I want to get away and sort myself out.'

'Come on, love,' said Helen pleadingly. 'I'm sure we can iron it all out and talk about it. Can't you come home and we'll start again?'

'No, I'm sorry I can't,' said Rachel, the soft bit of her brain that was still left, tempted by her mum's concern. 'I'll keep in touch but you mustn't try and find me.' She put the phone down, leaned against the door and cried.

'Oi, Lady Macbeth,' shouted someone outside. 'Hurry up, I'm dying of a heart attack! Let me in, I need to phone an ambulance!'

Rachel turned and pushed the door open to be faced with a round red moon grinning at her.

'Only kidding, darling,' said the man. 'Got you out though, didn't it?'

Rachel smiled and walked on. She got some chips at a chip shop several yards from her front door and a can of Coke and sat upstairs on her bed, eating and thinking about Susan.

She and Susan hadn't seen each other to talk to since the night of the T. Rex show, and the times when Rachel managed to separate Susan from the Dave incident, she missed her badly. She thought back over some of their nights out and their hilarious times together. It was really hard to survive without a best friend.

Rachel assumed that Dave and Susan must have been having an affair with each other and that was why neither of them had got in touch. It did not occur to her that maybe they had gone their separate ways and were missing *her*.

And that is what had happened. Susan felt so badly that she had coveted what her best friend had that she could not bear to talk to Rachel or Dave for fear they would hate her for it. The fact that Rachel absolutely loathed her already and had pretty much promised herself she would do so for eternity didn't really seem possible. Dave felt soiled by the whole affair because he'd got carried away with how lovely Susan looked, and he promised himself that if Rachel would let him back into her affections, he would never do that sort of thing again. Their separation increased his sense of how desperately he needed Rachel, and every day he wondered if he should go round to her house, talk to her and her parents and try to repair the damage. Dave's problem though, for all his easy manner and intelligence, was that he was terrified of rejection,

Rachel had no inkling of this, sitting in her grubby little room in Bromley. She made a list of things she would need to make her life bearable and first on that list was something to play music on. She decided to go out on Monday and look for a job so she could at least buy the basics. Wrapping her coat around her, she tried to sleep, and just before she dropped off felt a small surge of satisfaction that she had done something on her own without anyone either sanctioning it or forbidding it, and that lit a tiny little light in the darkness of her future.

In Hastings, for the first time in ages, Helen and Dick, Alan and Clive were sitting round talking. Somehow Rachel's flight had changed the household and they were able to chat fairly amicably. Alan and Clive hadn't had much parental attention over the last couple of years because it was all taken up with worry about Rachel, and if your presence as a teenage boy tends to consist of coming to meals, making a mumbling noise, looking bored and staying in bed a lot, you don't exactly encourage your parents to come running headlong at you for a bit of top-drawer dinner-party conversation.

Clive and Alan, through custom, communicated that evening in monosyllables with their parents, but were planning great things in the conversation department for the future. Eventually they sloped off to their room where their hitherto pent-up eloquence was given free rein.

'Silly cow,' said Alan.

'Yeh, silly fat cow,' said Clive.

Alan laughed. 'Silly, fat, dozy cow,' he said.

Clive laughed. 'Yeh, silly, fat, dozy, daft cow,' he said.

Alan laughed. 'Hope she's all right though,' he said.

'Yeh,' said Clive.

'Night,' said Alan.

'Night,' said Clive.

Chapter 19

Susan, doing her toenails with a dark crimson polish that looked slightly obscene, with a facepack on and her hair in a towel, heard the phone ring from her bedroom. There was no one else in and being unable to leave a ringing phone alone, she almost somersaulted down the stairs to get it. She always presumed it was going to be a really important call which would change everyone's lives for ever.

It was Helen.

'Rachel's gone and I don't know what to do,' she said. Then she started to cry.

Susan knew that from the first minute Helen had set eyes on her, she'd felt that she wasn't good enough to be her daughter's friend, and now she was in this terrible mess – mostly, Susan thought, of her own making. The girl was tempted to say, 'I'm sorry, I can't help,' and put the phone down, leaving Helen to bake gently in her own guilt and sorrow, but Susan had a warm heart hidden away from the male species and was a sucker for a female trauma, so she arranged to meet Helen in town to talk about it.

Terry had developed a near-psychotic hatred of Helen over the years because of the fondue incident, and because Helen reminded her of a teacher she had loathed. Also, Vince seemed to admire Helen and that made Terry seethe, because she saw herself as the one Vince adored and couldn't live without, and he as the weak dependent one. For this reason Susan made up a story about meeting a friend in town to Terry and sat on the bus looking out at the sea and wondering why she and Rachel had wasted the last two years falling out and pursuing the same man, even though in Susan's case it was mostly in her head.

In Demarco's café, scene of so much skiving from school, the two sat staring at each other with a cappuccino each as Helen, who looked like she had suffered last night, laid out the reason for the meeting.

'I've got to find her,' she said. 'She has phoned me and even though she sounds happy and things are easier at home because she has gone, I can't let her live wherever she is without knowing what she's doing and how she is. Can you help me to find her?'

Susan wondered at this point whether it was a good idea to come clean about the Dave business and paint herself an even worse shade of black than the one she was already. She decided yes, and told Helen what had been going on between her and Rachel for the last few years.

Helen was astounded. She had had no idea her daughter

was having such a difficult and sad time. When Susan had finished speaking, she looked up nervously, expecting Helen to give it to her with both barrels.

There was silence and then Helen started to laugh, the laugh building until the tears were running down her cheeks.

'Are you OK?' asked Susan, worried that her revelations had triggered an acute mental illness in Helen.

Helen was doubled-up. 'I'm fine,' she gasped. 'It's just that I've spent the past few years worrying about Rachel and how unhappy she was, and I thought it was down to me and that I was doing something wrong.'

Susan was shocked at her naïveté. 'Surely you must have realised something was happening with her and blokes,' she said.

'I suppose I tried not to think about it,' Helen said. 'Rachel always seemed so young and not interested in that sort of thing.'

Susan made a snorty noise to signify her disdain.

'Do you think we can find her?' said Helen.

'I don't know. Any idea at all where she's gone?'

'Well, I'm sure it's London,' said Helen. 'I thought maybe she'd gone back to the area where you went for the weekend. She could even be with Dave.' She pondered for a moment. 'Still, I suppose after what's happened it's unlikely.'

'Sorry,' Susan said humbly. 'I don't know why I did it, I really don't.'

'Water under the bridge,' shrugged Helen. 'Now will you help me have a look or at least ask some questions for me?'

'OK,' said Susan hesitantly. 'Maybe we could get the Salvation Army involved.'

'Pardon?' Helen looked puzzled.

'Well, they helped to look for Amy Turtle in *Crossroads*,' said Susan.

Helen nearly said, 'I don't watch that rubbish,' but stopped herself.

'Look,' said Susan, 'I'll make a few calls and see if anyone knows anything, and we'll take it from there, OK?'

'Thanks,' said Helen. 'I'd really appreciate it.'

'But if no one knows anything, we'll have to wait until we have more clues, or until she calls me,' said Susan.

'OK,' said Helen.

Susan quite looked forward to having to go to London to find Rachel. She wanted to go down the King's Road and have a look at the punks who hung around looking like dirty black parrots with their Mohican haircuts, leather gear, chains and safety pins. There were only three in Hastings at the moment and their embarrassed cringing when stared at meant they weren't taken very seriously.

Susan had gone to see the Sex Pistols perform on Hastings pier, supporting Budgie, a band who were very close to the heart of her latest suitor John, a fisherman from the Old Town. Their earsplitting rock had been bearable, but the Sex Pistols had really unsettled her. There was bad language and a bit of stuff she didn't understand about politics and royalty, and for some reason loads of the audience had started spitting. She'd kept well back. She'd wished Rachel was there (she suspected Rachel would love the Sex Pistols), so that at least they could have had a laugh and not taken it quite so seriously as the headbangers seemed to be doing.

Rachel was too busy sorting her life out in Bromley to go to any gigs, but she did love the punk movement and in fact had seen some punks around locally whom she vaguely recognised, but she couldn't remember where they were from. She had been to the Dole Office and found that Woolworths were after staff, so immediately put her name down for an interview. She loved the familiarity of Woolies in Hastings, the smell of the place, the enormous variety, as if a factory making inexpensive and gaudy products had blown up and as the contents came down to earth they landed in a higgledy-piggledy state on the shelves. Rachel particularly liked the Pick 'n' Mix counter and always got some flying saucers, shrimps and bananas, which she could feel actively decaying her teeth as she ate them. So off she went along to Bromley Woolworths, and after what seemed like an extremely cursory interview with a man with moist hands and a greasy moustache that appeared to be acting as a soup-catcher, she got the job and was told to report there the following morning.

She felt lonely in her bedsit, which by now she had scrubbed and polished until its shabbiness was at least presentable, like a tired old tramp who's been given a secondhand set of clothes at Christmas.

Moonface, whom she had met outside the phone box, came in on her second day at work.

'Oh, hello you,' he said in exaggerated camp.

'Hi,' said Rachel, who was working on the record counter.

'I'm after Bette Midler,' said the man, who was probably about twenty but could have passed for thirty-five. 'Well,' he added, 'not *after* in that sense – not my cup of tea, know what I mean?'

Rachel did. She had never met a very camp gay man. They tended to keep their heads down in Hastings as homosexuality wasn't encouraged, especially amongst the fishermen whose sexual politics were lifted from *The Canterbury Tales*.

Rachel had made her first Bromley friend.

His name was Paul ('but you can call me Pauline if you like') and he lived in a bedsit not far from hers, having moved out of home because his mum's new boyfriend 'didn't like fucking poofs'. He worked at a clothes shop up the road where the boss was cruel to him and instructed him to stay out the back in case he frightened the customers.

Rachel felt sorry for Pauline. She suggested he leave that job and come and work at Woolies. It was a casual suggestion but within a week he was there.

Musically and culturally, Rachel and Pauline were at complete odds with each other. Rachel was interested in punk, which seemed to have sprouted up from the ashes of glam rock, producing children who looked like the bastard sons and daughters of David Bowie, bringing with them a new disrespect for adults, and putting two fingers up to any kind of conformity.

Pauline was scared of punks but he was scared pretty

much of anyone who was drunk or stoned and wanted someone to pick on. He and Rachel developed an unspoken agreement that they would look after each other at gigs. Rachel, it has to be said, did not really need much looking after at the sort of gigs Pauline began taking her to – drag queens at the Vauxhall Tavern or personal appearances by Lorna Luft, the less well-known Judy Garland offspring – but Pauline always needed huge protection at punk gigs which inevitably seemed to get out of hand.

Rachel thought his life up until now sounded terrible. Paul came from a big estate in Bromley, one of a family of eight children, and his father, on realising his son was not going to be quite the Charles Atlas he had hoped for, set about undermining him in any way he could until, as a teenager, his confidence was so shattered, he withdrew from relationships and his family, eventually leaving home at the age of eighteen. So many people were so horrible to him and yet he seemed to have retained this chirpy cheerfulness that made Rachel sad when she realised how much shit he'd waded through. Pauline had never had a boyfriend or a best friend and he'd never gone out until he met Rachel. Occasionally he made cheeky comments to strangers, as he had to Rachel outside the phone box, but he was usually told to 'Fuck off, you freak,' or something similarly well-constructed and imaginative.

Rachel was in need of a friend who didn't threaten her, someone whose good looks didn't force all eyes towards her, or whose flirting drew men from miles around. Whatever it was, the two became close friends very quickly and after a couple of months Rachel would quite happily have stabbed anyone who abused him.

The transformation in Pauline was lovely to see. He was more talkative, funnier, full of ideas and such good fun to be with that Rachel couldn't imagine him not ever having been around.

The wages at Woolies did not provide much of a luxury lifestyle for Rachel and Pauline so they had to put up with going to the pub a couple of nights a week and the odd gig when they could afford it.

Rachel, who hitherto had been somewhat ethereal in her dress (before that awful building-society period imposed on her by her mum), started to get interested in the hard look that was punk. It seemed to her she had spent her formative years running around in a flowery skirt and T-shirt, and it had got her nowhere.

'That's 'cause you look like some old hippy with saggy tits,' said Pauline, not meaning to be unkind, just telling it like it was, when she asked for his opinion on her style.

Although Rachel felt her emotional hardness was softening a bit – she missed her mum and would have liked to know what Dave was doing – she still wanted to look hard on the outside. She spent the last of her saved money on a pair of tartan trousers, a ripped shirt, some massive scruffy boots, and had her hair cut so she could spike it up with sugar water. It was three months since she had arrived in Bromley and she had a job, a friend and some kind of real happiness in her life. A couple of times she had phoned her mum to say that she was all right, and Helen had begged her to say where she was, or at least come home and visit. Rachel wanted to, but she still felt there were some things to be done on her own first.

'At least phone Susan now and again and tell her how you are,' said Helen.

Bells rang in Rachel's head. 'How come you've been talking to Susan?' she said.

'Well, we both want to see you and we both worry about you.' A short pause. 'Look,' said Helen, 'I know what she did – she told me.'

This was too much for Rachel. It meant her mum knew what was happening with Dave and she wasn't sure if she wanted her to know. She wondered if Dave was a punk. Whether he had seen the Sex Pistols at college. Whether he still wanted to see her.

Pauline's advice was very straightforward. 'Fuck 'em all,' he said.

'And is that considered answer based on any scientific evidence?' enquired Rachel.

'Just the evidence that they're all cunts,' said Pauline, and Rachel had to admit that somewhere inside that boy there was a psychologist trying to get out.

One day, she bit the bullet and phoned Susan out of the blue.

'Hello,' she said. 'It's Rachel.'

'Rachel! Oh my God, how brilliant to hear from you!' Susan really wanted to say, 'Do you forgive me, can we be friends again, I never did anything with Dave, I'm sorry about my bad intentions, I really miss you,' all in one breath, but she was aware of a certain coldness in Rachel's voice. I suppose I don't blame her, she thought.

'Why don't you come up to London?' Rachel went on. 'It'd be good to see you and we could try to thrash things out.'

Pauline felt threatened by this, because as soon as Rachel told him he began to come up with increasingly weak reasons why Susan shouldn't visit.

'She's crapped on you from a great height,' he said. 'Let her stew for a bit longer.' Then: 'I won't be able to stop myself slapping her.' Finally: 'She might get lost.'

Rachel sensed his fear. 'It's all right, you silly sod,' she told him. 'It's not going to make any difference to us.'

'Just say the word and I'll punch her out for you,' said Pauline, who couldn't have punched out a six-year-old girl.

Rachel didn't want Susan to know where she was living in case she told Helen, and it just wasn't time yet for Helen and Dick to come up in the car and leave it parked outside the grotty row of shops whilst they climbed the grimy stairs and tried to persuade her to come back home. So the girls agreed to meet up in town outside Vivienne Westwood's shop Sex in the King's Road.

Pauline refused to come in the end. 'I'll just spoil things,' he said. 'I always do. Especially when people have to fucking look at me.'

'Stop it,' said Rachel, laughing. 'For Christ's sake you're bloody gorgeous.' But she and Pauline both knew this wasn't true.

Susan got to the shop first and spent some time looking

open-mouthed in the window at the selection of bizarre clothes. She hadn't really changed her look in all the years that she and Rachel had known each other, and it was odd but because of her perky little face, much of the time no one seemed to notice what she was wearing, particularly blokes who fancied her.

'Hello.' A punk was standing next to her at the window and seemed friendly. She vaguely recognised her and then she knew it was Rachel. Gone was the long hair parted in the middle and tied back with a bit of coloured string. Gone were the baggy earth-coloured clothes and clogs. In front of her stood someone in tattered combats, DMs and a torn T-shirt. No safety pin though.

'Fuck,' was all Susan could manage. Then she said, 'Look at you, you silly bugger.'

A big grin spread over Rachel's face and she held her arms open. The two of them hugged for ages, almost like reunited lovers and said things like, 'I missed you.' It was as if they had never been apart.

'I'm so sorry,' was all Susan kept saying and wondered how, in the weirdness of it all, she could have resented this lovely person and considered hurting her. But how lovely a person is has nothing to do with envy. In fact, if they're lovely it makes it worse.

'Oh well,' said Rachel with a trace of regret but a harder face on it all than Susan remembered, 'It's all in the past now. Come on.' She pulled her into the shop. 'Let's buy something to celebrate our reunion.'

Of course the price of artful scruffiness was too high for

a couple of Hastings girls and they came out empty-handed. Susan was aware of some male eyes on them – a common occurrence but nonetheless one she always picked up. She didn't mention it to Rachel because she thought it might worry her – then Susan realised that the new Rachel was more likely to take the piss.

'Let's go and get a coffee, shall we?' Rachel suggested and they stopped off in a café grubby enough to admit Rachel but smart enough for Susan not to be tarred and feathered.

'So,' said Susan. 'Tell me where you've been and what you've been doing.'

Rachel deliberately left out where she was living and was surprised at how strict she was with herself. Several times during their meeting she wanted to throw away her caution and reveal everything about her strange life, living on the edge of London and dabbling in a scene which made her increasingly uneasy.

Eventually they got round to the prickly area of Dave and Rachel had had enough time to prepare for this so that she was able to control her heart-rate and her breathing and didn't worry about fainting when the truth was revealed.

'Look,' said Susan, 'there was never anything going on between us. It was all down to me being envious of what you two had with each other and trying to get some of that. I didn't really mean to hurt you. You weren't around and it just seemed so strange I got carried along with it all.'

'So you didn't sleep with him?' said Rachel.

'No.'

'Did you kiss him?'

'No.'

'Touch his penis?' said Rachel with a perfectly straight face.

'No!' Susan was shocked.

Rachel's face crinkled into a smile and then a laugh came out. Susan was forgiven.

'I'm sorry I hit you round the head,' she said. 'I just couldn't fucking believe it when I saw you next to him, I jumped to all sorts of conclusions, I suppose. I expected to be shat on. It's because you're so pretty and so confident, you've always made me feel like your best friend the baby elephant who always has to make do with the weird mate, and when I met Dave I couldn't believe that he was interested in *me*.'

'Oh Rachel,' said Susan. 'I never knew you felt like that.'

'Well, it's not exactly the sort of thing you go round telling everyone, is it?' said Rachel. 'Not even your best friend. I always put on a front and pretend that I'm not affected by things that threaten to overwhelm me, and when I think back I can't honestly remember how *I* felt about Dave. I was just so carried away with the fact that a grown-up like him wanted to be with me.'

'I'm sure he still wants to get back together,' said Susan.

'Oh, don't say that,' said Rachel. 'I've only just got him out of my system and it's taken years. Look at me – I don't even know what I'm doing. I made a lot of bad decisions because of how shit I felt. I should have hung on in there, gone back to school, got some decent results and gone to university. That's what my mum and dad wanted me to do. But instead I'm in a bedsit and working in Woolies. Not exactly the future my parents dreamed of for me.'

'Why don't you come back home,' said Susan quietly. 'We all miss the old you.'

'I don't even know if there is an old me any more,' Rachel told her. 'I know I'm only seventeen, but the last few years have hardened me up and I'm not as porous as I used to be.'

'Eh?' said Susan.

'Well, I don't soak up all the old crap like I used to,' said Rachel. 'It washes off a lot more. Is that a good way for a girl to be? I don't know.' She started to cry.

'Oh, this is all down to me,' said Susan. 'I hate that I did this to you.'

'No, it isn't,' said Rachel. 'I made bad choices, got carried along by all the high emotion like I was in some film. Maybe you did me a favour and Dave would only have crapped on me with someone else later.'

'Why don't you write to him?' said Susan. 'Maybe he still wants to be with you.'

'Oh, I don't know,' said Rachel tiredly. 'Maybe he'll just fuck me up again.'

'Anyway,' said Susan, changing the subject, 'shall we go out somewhere tonight? I can get the milk train home, or whatever. Why don't we have a bloody good night out and go mental and try and forget what's messed us up in the last few years.'

Rachel hesitated. 'I don't know.'

'Come on,' said Susan. 'Let's buy an *NME* and see if there's something we can go to.'

'It's not going to be some old shit like Budgie,' said Rachel. 'We'll go and see a really scary gig, shall we?'

They decided to go to the Screen on the Green in Islington and try to get in to see the Clash, the Buzzcocks and the Sex Pistols.

Chapter 20

Outside the Screen on the Green, Rachel felt like she was on a different planet. She was excited and ready for anything. Susan felt like a stranger in a strange land and was frightened. She had seen the Sex Pistols in Hastings, but the audience there had been the familiar bunch of half-drunken old herberts she'd known for years. Up in London they seemed more scary. This was to some extent because of the clothes that she was wearing, and here more than ever, she realised she was identified as a skinhead and that the attitude towards her was aggressive.

'I feel like everybody wants to give me a kicking,' she said. 'You go on and I'll just get the train home.'

'No way,' said Rachel. 'Come on – they'll see you're with me, it'll be perfectly all right.'

Skinheads had colonised a section of punk and were turning the anarchic messiness and good-naturedness into one of alienation and violence. Sometimes it seemed to

Rachel that what had started as a fairly relaxed and even comical move against the older generation who were concreted into their beliefs and alliances, was turning sour and there wasn't much of a welcome in punk, particularly for girls, any more. She had always shied away from the excesses of the punk ethos because they seemed so blokey. Many women agreed with her and were happy to accept a watered-down, more female-style punk. And now the shops were getting in on the act and even places like Dorothy Perkins were nodding towards it and stocked clothes that although vaguely punk in character, could still be worn to your grandma's funeral.

None of this had occurred to Susan. She just didn't like the fighting, spitting, abuse and the feeling that things might quickly get out of control, even though she'd always seen herself as a wild girl who'd take on anyone. She hoped for a more well-behaved youth, so young people could be different from adults but still smart, and for girls to be allowed to look pretty. Susan was appalled by the look of Poly Styrene from X-Ray Spex. She deliberately made herself look ugly when underneath it all she was quite attractive. Where would that get her?

She said this to Rachel, who commented, 'You sound like someone's mum,' but understood what Susan was getting at.

'Slag.' She was brought back to the present day by a chunky, spotty punk with his face maybe an inch away from hers. 'Piss off, you're not welcome here,' he said. 'You and your trouble-making friends.'

'Fuck off yourself,' replied Susan feistily. Not being a natural Christian, she could not step back from an insult. The punk threw a punch at her which she managed to duck, and then she and Rachel ran as fast as they could inside, as if indoors would be any safer.

Inside, Susan felt even more intimidated, and suggested to Rachel that they hide in a dark corner. Rachel, who'd had a few barley wines in the pub beforehand, wanted to go up the front and get stuck in but Susan was wary, again finding herself in the maiden-aunt role. As they stood with their plastic pint glasses of cheap cider, Rachel shouted above the din, 'Look, we'll find somewhere safe for you to be and then I'll go and have a dance for ten minutes and come back and get you.'

This new Rachel was a shock to Susan who had always been the leader, but was now a pale shadow, reduced from Peter Pan to Wendy in a few short months. She wanted to cry and grab Rachel's hand and ask her not to go. A weird thing had happened – the clothes she was wearing had totally cancelled out her good looks, and no one seemed to care any more that she was sweet and fanciable. It was as if she was wearing the combats of a foreign army. People snarled past her and one or two punk girls looked like they wanted to scrape their nails down her face.

Rachel pushed her into a corner and said, 'I'll be back in ten minutes, OK?' Susan nodded numbly. She wanted to go back to Hastings and order a snowball in the Crypt. She wanted to go out with someone called Brian who worked on a building site and she wanted to have two children called Oliver and Emma and go round for dinner with her mum and Vince on Sundays. She did not want to be at the forefront of a youth movement in London full of alienated acne on legs and borderline personality disorders.

The atmosphere up at the front of the stage was something Rachel had never really experienced and she was exhilarated by it. The sweaty, loud, uncontrollable, surging, spitting, pissed, vacuous, ebbing and flowing mass of humanity heaved her backwards and forwards as the deafening noise of 'Pretty Vacant' seemed to physically hit them. After a couple of minutes though, Rachel had had enough and wanted to get out, but couldn't. It was like struggling in a very rough sea and being flung onto the beach only to be dragged back in again by the tide. She started to panic and push against the crowd of youth that seemed to have no aim in life apart from going more mental than they had ever gone in their lives. Rachel shoved against the wall of leather, keeping her head down after a huge gobbet of phlegm had landed on her eyelid and she'd been so tightly held on either side she hadn't been able to wipe it out of the way. She elbowed, kicked, pushed and punched, but the same was done to her with more force. In the end she was exhausted and began to think she wouldn't be able to get out alive.

'Help me, for Christ's sake!' she started screaming. 'I can't breathe, I'm going to die.'

She realised this was a little melodramatic, but no one could hear anyway as everything was drowned out in the deafening roar of human voices, feedback and a noise that seemed certain to explode heads.

Rachel started to faint, but just before she went down on the floor, a big male hand grabbed the back of her shirt and somehow hauled her through the testosterone spasm and sat her down at the side. She looked up and saw a slightly familiar face.

'Hello,' said the face. 'I'm Barry Nesbitt.'

Fucking hell, thought Rachel. What is this weirdo from my dad's old workplace doing here? He was the bloke she'd heard her parents rowing about, when they'd just moved to Hastings – the bloke Dick went on about having burnt down their house.

She remembered Susan. 'Quick,' she said. 'My friend – I left her over there. I hope she's OK.'

They spotted Susan, who seemed to be under threat from two big punk girls who had backed her into a corner. One had already thrown a punch and the other had produced a knife from somewhere. Susan had a vision of herself twenty years down the line, scarred and unmarried.

Barry Nesbitt steamed into the fray with all the enthusiasm of a TA reservist, which he actually was. He didn't hit the girls, just manoeuvred them out of the way very forcefully, and with a Hastings girl on each arm he fled outside, hailed a cab, and they got inside before Rachel managed to say, 'What the hell is going on?'

'Your mum called me,' he said to Rachel, 'and told me that she thought Susan was coming up to London to meet you. I'm afraid I spotted her at Charing Cross and I've been following the pair of you since the King's Road.'

Barry Nesbitt seemed surprisingly nice, contrary to what

her dad had said. She'd only caught sight of him once, walking along a street in town, and when her dad spotted him, he started swearing and looking thunderous while her mum said, 'Calm down, Dick, for Christ's sake.'

'So my dad didn't phone you then?' said Rachel.

'No,' said Barry, and Rachel could see he was uncomfortable. She made a mental note of this and thought she would explore it further later.

'Right,' said Barry. 'I'd better get you two young ladies home.'

'I'm not going back to Hastings,' said Rachel.

'I am,' said Susan.

It was only ten o'clock.

'I'm all right from here,' said Rachel, realising they were heading past King's Cross. 'What about you, Susan?'

Susan was crying, her immaculate make-up smeared across her face and her clothes torn. Like a real punk, thought Rachel.

'What is it, love?' said Barry.

'Oh, it was so fucking awful in there and I was so scared,' said Susan. 'I'm never coming to London again.'

Barry laughed a kind laugh. 'It's not all like that in London, you know,' he said. 'There's a few of us don't piss everywhere and bite people.'

Susan smiled.

'That's better,' said Barry. 'We'll drop you off at the station first, Susan. Will you be OK?'

'Oh Christ, yes,' said Susan. 'Once I'm pointing towards Hastings, I'll be fine.'

'Are you sure you don't want to stay at mine?' Rachel asked. Having been reluctant to tell Susan where she lived, she now had a much more relaxed attitude to revealing her secret hideout.

'No way,' said Susan, and without even realising what she was saying, went on, 'I want my mum.'

Rachel tried to explain that she and Pauline had been to loads of gigs with no trouble.

'Who's Pauline?' asked Susan, wondering if Rachel had a new best friend.

'Tell you another time,' said Rachel.

They dropped Susan at Charing Cross just in time for the ten-thirty train. She looked traumatised but said she was happy.

'Where to now?' Barry turned to Rachel.

'Just drop me down here,' said Rachel. 'I'm fine from here.'

'Certainly not,' said Barry, sounding like a provincial headmaster. 'I'm making sure you get home safely.'

Rachel wondered if she still had to fight against this. Would Barry tell her mum where she was living and even if he did, would that be such a problem?

'I live in the high street in Bromley,' she said.

'Yum,' said Barry. 'That is real urban sophistication, young lady.'

'Are you taking the piss?' said Rachel.

'Just a bit,' he said, grinning.

When they pulled up outside Rachel's flat she opened the cab door. 'Thanks,' she said, and went to get out.

'Not so fast,' said Barry. 'Aren't you going to ask me up for a coffee?'

'No,' said Rachel. 'It's too late.'

The cab driver raised an eyebrow. He had no idea what was going on. The girl looked like a teenage prostitute to him and the man looked like your average punter, but what did he know. He was always getting it wrong.

'I'm coming up,' said Barry, 'whether you like it or not.'

The cabbie heard this. 'You all right love?' he said to Rachel.

'Yep,' said Rachel in a resigned way. 'He's a friend of my parents.'

Barry's first sight of the bedsit, about which, if he managed to get in, he had promised to tell Helen, made him feel very protective towards Rachel. The girl had made as much as she possibly could of the dingy little room. It was clean and the walls had been covered with cheap Indian bedspreads to disguise their muckiness. There was an Elton John poster with the words *Fat Jess* scrawled across it and another of a wild sea. There had been plenty of joss sticks burned to disguise the smell, and Rachel had cleaned the carpet to the point where it was becoming threadbare.

Rachel put the little kettle on in the corner and gestured to Barry to have the only chair. He seemed a friendly, helpful guy and the combination of alcohol and her own trusting nature made the fact that her dad reckoned Barry had burned their house down seem hazy and outlandish.

'I'm only worried about you on behalf of your mum who misses you and wants to know what you're up to,' he said.

'Can't you just tell her I'm OK?' Rachel asked. 'This is hardly in the gutter with a syringe hanging out of my arm, is it?'

'I don't know,' said Barry. 'She's very persuasive, your mum.'

Once Barry had finished his cup of tea and they had chatted in a friendly way about his family and home in Putney, he got up to leave.

'Thanks for rescuing us tonight,' said Rachel. 'That was beyond the call of duty, an old git like you having to go into the Screen on the Green, wasn't it?'

'Cheeky bugger,' said Barry and laughed.

'How did you get in, anyway?' Rachel asked. 'Surely you didn't pay?'

'I pretended I was CID, flashed my library card – you can get away with anything if you look the part,' he said.

'You can get me into a few gigs if you like,' said Rachel. 'Have you seen the Damned?'

'No, but I can well imagine,' said Barry. 'Not my cup of tea. Give me a bit of James Taylor any day,' and he went out humming 'You've Got A Friend'. He had given Rachel his number. 'Call me if you're ever in trouble, won't you,' he said.

'Don't tell my mum where I am,' Rachel warned him.

Barry didn't answer, but just smiled.

Rachel lay awake in bed for a long time, going over the events of a day which had seemed two weeks long. She felt a surge of real fondness for Susan, someone she had hated so much at certain times in the past few months. But now this bad feeling seemed so silly, and she could understand her better, having heard the real story of what had happened with Dave. She realised she hadn't thought about him since they had dispensed with him in their conversation earlier, and that was a huge improvement as her ruminations on Dave often stretched over hours. It is true, even though it is a cliché, that time is a great healer, and time spent dwelling on someone you love unrequitedly gradually shrinks down to nothing if you give it long enough.

However, Rachel still felt that things weren't finished yet with Dave.

Her mind then turned to Barry Nesbitt, whom she had always viewed throughout most of her life as a villain of massive proportions. But it seemed he had some sort of fond relationship with her mum.

All at once it struck her like an electric shock. Maybe he was having an affair with Helen! That would explain all the bad vibes about him at home, the reason they had moved away from London and her mother's stonewalling about it all. How long had the affair been going on? Maybe for years and maybe her dad had only found out just before they moved. Maybe before. Residual alcohol fuelled the quantum leap Rachel then took. Fuck, say Barry Nesbitt was her dad! Jesus, could that be the case? She couldn't bear to think of it. She wanted to know and she wanted to know now. Throwing on some clothes, she rushed down the road to the phone box. It was two thirty. She dialled her home number and a sleepy Dick answered, 'Hello, who is it?'

Rachel dropped the phone back in the cradle as if it was red hot and sobered up. What the hell am I doing? she thought. I must go to bed then in the morning perhaps I won't be living in a bad soap opera any more.

Chapter 21

The next morning, Barry phoned Helen. Same old routine. If Dick answered he would put on a different voice each time and say, 'Wrong number,' rather than hanging up, as he thought that was less suspicious. However, this time Helen answered.

'It's Barry,' he said. 'I found her.'

'Oh thank God,' said Helen. 'Is she OK?'

'Of course she is,' said Barry. 'She's a sensible girl, why wouldn't she be?'

'Where is she?' said Helen. 'Soho? Islington? Brixton?'

'Bromley,' said Barry, and she could hear him laughing at the end of the line.

She laughed too. 'And what is she doing in Bromley?' she asked.

'She's got a job in Woolies,' said Barry. 'Seems remarkably happy and she's got into that punk thing a bit – cut her hair, got different clothes.'

'Oh God,' said Helen.

'I wouldn't worry,' said Barry. 'She's not on drugs or anything, drinking a bit like any teenager, but very normal – very together, actually.'

'Barry, I don't know how to thank you,' said Helen. 'I couldn't be sure Susan would spill the beans about where she was. I'm going to go and see her.'

'OK,' said Barry. 'I'm glad I could help. Any chance of a drink soon?'

'I don't know,' said Helen. 'I'll call you – and thanks.'

Not surprisingly, Helen decided not to tell Dick about the Barry Nesbitt connection. She phoned Susan to tell her she knew where Rachel was and that she was going up to see her.

'How was Rachel?' she asked Susan.

'Oh, she's great,' said Susan. 'Looks really well, seems to love it up there. Yeah, good.'

'And how about you?' Helen asked politely. 'Did you enjoy yourself in London?'

There was a silence.

'I don't really want to talk about it,' said Susan. 'See you.'

The following weekend, Helen got the train up to see Rachel. She arrived outside her address at about two in the afternoon, her plan being if Rachel wasn't in, just to sit around and wait for her. She stood outside the dingy row of shops feeling a bit depressed, thinking, I feel a bit depressed.

She rang the only doorbell that didn't have someone

else's name on it and there was no answer. She wondered whether to go along to Woolworths and see if Rachel was working, but thought it might give her too much of a shock if she just turned up, so she found a bench over the road, got a too-hot coffee in a polystyrene cup and a newspaper and sat down to wait for her.

She ploughed her way through the *Guardian* which she hadn't read for ages and it was hard work, as over the last few years the inside of her head seemed to have been replaced with some gauze dipped in jam which wasn't conducting electrical impulses very efficiently across her nerve-endings. This, she thought, is the result of reading the tabloids and watching soaps. Looking up for a moment, she saw a small but chunky punk walking down the road accompanied by the roundest, campest young man she'd ever seen. She squinted and realised it was Rachel looking masculine, her lovely hair dyed black and spiked up, and her eye make-up too heavy. She and the boy were laughing and looked happy.

Helen crossed the road towards them.

Rachel spotted her. 'Mum, what the hell are you doing here?' she said. 'Oh bollocks, Barry bloody told you, didn't he?'

'Don't use that language,' Helen said to Rachel. 'Please.'

'Never mind the bollocks,' said Rachel, and she and her friend started to laugh uproariously.

'Sorry,' said Rachel. 'What do you want?' The tone wasn't aggressive at all, just interested. It felt awkward between them.

'Oh come on, give me a hug,' said Helen.

Rachel hesitated and looked at her friend

'Go on then,' he said, as if he was presenting a game show. 'Give her a hug.'

Rachel's face broke into a smile and she hugged her mum.

'Can we talk?' Helen said.

'I'll go,' said the boy.

'Sorry,' said Rachel. 'Mum, this is Paul.'

'Hiya,' he said, proffering a hand like a pasty.

Helen took it. It was warm and strong.

'See you later?' he said to Rachel.

She nodded and they headed towards the bedsit.

When Helen saw it she said, 'Oh Rachel,' and her eyes filled with tears. She couldn't bear the thought of her lovely daughter existing in this swamp of a room – damp, dark and depressing – even though she could see the efforts she'd made to disguise it.

'Oh, come on, Mum,' said Rachel. 'Just 'cause I'm not living in a bloody Georgian terrace studying to be a doctor . . . I'm having a cracking time, you know.'

'We want you to come back,' said Helen. 'Alan and Clive really miss you.'

'Bollocks.'

That word again, but Helen had to admit she was right – it *was* bollocks.

'I bet the house is much more cheerful now I'm not there,' said Rachel. 'It is, isn't it? I can see it on your face.'

Helen said, 'I've lost track of what this is all about. Is it me and your dad? Susan? Or this Dave character?'

'He's not "this Dave character", he's a real person,' said Rachel. 'And it's a bit of everything.'

'Well, why didn't you tell me at the time,' said Helen, 'talk to me about it? We could have sorted it together.'

'Come on, Mum, can your mother really discuss with you the fact that you are mad about someone because you've had the most brilliant sex with them and you can't get them to commit themselves in any way to you?' she said.

'I see what you mean,' said Helen, having been told too much just in that one sentence.

'And you never told *me* about your affair with Barry Nesbitt,' Rachel went on.

Shit, how does she know? thought Helen, and said, 'What do you mean?'

'Look, Mum, I'm not twelve any more. I know something went on but I don't want to know the details, I just want to know if he's my dad.'

'Jesus Christ,' said Helen. 'Wherever did you get *that* idea?'

Rachel laughed. 'Don't know really. Well, I didn't know how long it had been going on for, did I? Was it the reason why we left London?'

'Yes,' Helen whispered.

'Do you still like him?' said Rachel.

'Pass.' But Helen might just as well have said yes. 'Think about coming home, will you?' she went on. 'We do miss you, we do really.'

'How are you and Dad getting on?' said Rachel.

'We'll survive,' said Helen grimly. 'And what about Dave?'

'I haven't seen him for ages.'

'Do you want to?'

'I don't know any more,' said Rachel. 'I was on the brink of calling him several times, but that's worn off a bit now. I think he wants to see me.'

Then Helen said something which surprised her daughter.

'Go and see him,' she said, 'and sort it out, or else you'll never know and you'll never completely move on.'

'OK, I will,' Rachel decided, the fact that it had been sanctioned by her mum somehow giving her the impetus to do it.

Helen said, 'I'd better go. Look – keep in touch, come back soon.'

'I will come back soon, but maybe not to live,' said Rachel. 'I feel as if I've only just got away.'

'What about school and what about college?' Helen asked cautiously.

'I can finish my A-levels anywhere,' said Rachel, and Helen realised she'd thought about it more than she expected.

On the train back to London, Helen sat looking out of the window, and for once didn't feel stressed or anxious. All through the Rachel Trouble as it came to be called, she hadn't trusted her daughter to be sensible, and now she realised that in fact Rachel would never take the sort of drug-fuelled alcohol-sodden risks that ended up with your death being reported on the front of the local paper if you were pretty and round about page four if you weren't. She wondered how Rachel and Susan had got on and hoped they had sorted out their differences, although it seemed possible that the two friends had grown apart. Helen had heard that when Susan came back to Hastings after that weekend she'd started looking for work and had got a job in the big civil service building at the back of the town and was going out with someone from the office called Mark.

Susan felt her visit to London had been like a brush with death and she had narrowly escaped being maimed for life. She didn't like London people; she didn't like punks or skinheads. Even the hippies in London seemed like vicious, uncaring versions of the ones everywhere else.

Vince and Terry, who had both only been to London twice in their lives, had listened open-mouthed to Susan's description of the night in Islington. Terry thought it sounded like hell on earth and could just imagine all the smelly punks with halitosis and gum disease all spitting on each other while they went gradually deaf.

Concepts like the freedom of self-expression or the rejection of the stagnant status quo didn't really feature in her imagination and for the sake of their parents she hoped it was just a phase these poor kids were going through. She and Vince had looked round at their family, Jennifer doing well at the hairdresser's part-time while young Lucy was at school, Kim a supervisor in Marks, and Susan having started at the Department of the Environment, and Terry felt happy that she'd kept them all close. Not one of them had ever even considered putting a safety pin in their ear. She breathed the relieved sigh of the housebound housewife and mother.

Chapter 22

Rachel had explained to Pauline about Dave and they had spent many evenings in her bedsit when they couldn't afford to go out chatting about Dave and the days when Rachel was running around in Hastings with him and Claudio.

'I don't know, that Claudio sounds much nicer to me,' said Pauline.

'Why?' said Rachel. 'You never even met him.'

'Well, you said he dressed nice and smelled nice,' said Pauline. 'That's the sort of fella I like.'

'Oh, you're so predictable,' grinned Rachel. 'You only go for the well-heeled, you do.'

This was all a fantasy anyway, as Pauline and Rachel both knew it was highly unlikely that Pauline would ever have sex with anyone, let alone have a boyfriend.

'So what's it like?' said Pauline.

'What's what like?' said Rachel.

'Having sex,' said Pauline.

'Well, it depends who it is really,' said Rachel. 'It can be the most gorgeous fantastic thing or it can be like being crawled over by a huge slug, depending on whether you actually like them or not, and if you love them they can be the crappest at sex in the whole country and you'll love it.'

'I like the sound of the huge slug,' said Pauline. 'I'll have to try that.'

'In that case you've got to break the cycle of misery/eat/misery/eat,' said Rachel.

'That's not quite right,' Pauline corrected her. 'It's misery/eat/happiness/misery/eat/happiness. Shall we get some chips?'

On the way back from the chippie, Rachel told Pauline that she was going to go and find Dave and that she would not really be able to relax and move on as her mum had said until she did. Pauline felt uneasy about this because anything could happen if Dave came back on the scene including, horror of horrors, marriage, or at the very least, moving away. He lay in bed at night and entertained fantasies of killing Dave but unfortunately, always at the end of them, there was poor Rachel crying her eyes out and saying something like, 'I loved him.'

Pauline eventually offered to go and find Dave with Rachel, because he realised the Dave situation wouldn't go away so he might as well put up with it, and so they set aside a weekend to do it in. Rachel phoned Susan and asked her if she could get in touch with Amanda to see if her brother knew anything, and the answer came back that nobody had seen or heard anything of Dave for a couple of years.

Rachel decided she would have to start at the flat in Stockwell where she had stayed that weekend and take it from there. She imagined he must have left college by now and so was either working or had gone away travelling.

She met Pauline in the pub to plan their itinerary. He seemed a bit upset.

'What's the matter?' asked Rachel.

'Someone called me names,' he said.

'Who?' said Rachel.

'One of the hangers-on with Siouxsie Sioux.' He wiped away a tear because although he had been called 'fat' five thousand six hundred and seventy-two times in his life, it still hurt. Siouxsie was a local girl who had her own band and looked like a glorious black-fringed cockatoo as she strode round town with her entourage positively glowing with otherness.

Rachel was ambivalent about Siouxsie and the Bromley contingent of punks who occasionally strolled past them into the pub or in the town. She didn't like the fact that Siouxsie used swastikas to decorate herself with, and even though she said she wasn't making a political statement Rachel thought the symbol of the swastika was too evil to use in a throwaway shock-your-parents decorative fashion.

Pauline and Rachel decided to go into London the following day, a Saturday, and if they didn't have any joy there then they'd maybe hitch out to Swindon in Wiltshire, which was where Dave came from, Rachel remembered.

At the flat in Stockwell the following morning a rather stoned girl answered the door. She was beautiful and Rachel had a fear that she might be Dave's new girlfriend. She crossed her fingers behind her back.

The girl had an American accent. 'Dave,' she drawled. 'Yes, I think he was here last year. Nice dude – art student at St Martin's?'

Rachel looked hopeful.

'No idea where he is now,' the American girl said. 'Sorry. Perhaps you could try the college?'

'She was pretty,' said Pauline, who even after all the shit he'd been given about his looks still found it in himself to be positive about attractive people.

'Yeah, pretty fucking vacant,' sniggered Rachel, and they carried on down the road singing, 'You're so pretty, I'm so pretty. We're vacant,' at the tops of their voices.

'What are we going to do now?' Pauline wanted to know.

'Let's go to the college and see what we can find out.'

They ended up in the Admissions office with a rather stern-looking man who said, 'Yes, David Barrett was a student here but I cannot divulge any information on his whereabouts at all, I'm so sorry.'

Rachel, without any advance warning to Pauline, said to the man, 'I respect absolutely what you are saying, and if I wasn't carrying his child I would completely agree with you and abide by your rules, but I'm afraid time is of the essence' (What the fuck does that mean? thought Pauline) 'and I *must* track him down within the next two weeks.'

The man wanted to say, 'Well, you should have thought

about that before you had sex with him,' whilst simultaneously eyeing up Pauline and thinking, Wouldn't touch *that* with a fucking bargepole, dear.

'Wait outside,' he said. 'I'll see what I can do.'

He came out of the office with an address in Swindon, not the birthplace of many artists it has to be said, but it was good enough for the jubilant Pauline and Rachel. They decided to get a bus or a tube to Hammersmith and try hitching from there.

They arrived at Hammersmith Broadway in thirty-five minutes and started to walk round to go up the slip road and onto the road out of town. A group of punks eating ice creams were strolling towards them, no doubt coming from the Clarendon in the middle of the roundabout, thought Rachel, who had been there a couple of times and on one occasion had seen the Damned, whose soundcheck she'd managed to gatecrash. They'd invited her into the gig – oh, the envious eyes of the crowd who came in after! The other time she'd been to the Clarendon she was so pissed she couldn't remember who she'd seen. Was it the Slits or X-Ray Spex? Who knows?

She expected the punks to acknowledge her likeness to them and just pass by, but they were looking for trouble, having consumed (she hazarded a guess) some drugs and alcohol.

'And what the fuck have we here?' said one of them, who'd managed perfectly to mimic the nasal twang of Johnny Rotten. 'A little punk girl out with a fucking balloon.'

Pauline started to shrink against the wall.

'Come on, leave it out,' said Rachel, who'd been expecting some faint expression of camaraderie.

'Don't know what you're expecting from your boyfriend,' said one of the others. 'Not a fuck, surely?' The whole group laughed at his comic genius.

'Oh, fuck off the lot of you, you big girls' blouses,' said Pauline, irrationally combative for the first time in his life.

There was the inevitable scuffle then, with seven of them on top of Pauline giving him a bit of a pasting, but that wasn't enough, they hadn't humiliated him quite enough. He was left, trousers down round his ankles, arse in the air with an ice-cream cone sticking out of it as they walked away.

Pauline grinned at Rachel. 'Not as bad as I expected,' he said.

Rachel's love for the anarchic ethos of punk started to slip away at that point. Why did it always have to be so fucking full on? Couldn't they water punk down a bit? Did they have to gob? Could they not just swill it round a bit and swallow? Why safety pins in their various bits? Why not clothes pegs that didn't hurt so much? No chains. No militaria – something a bit more stylish and historical was called for. Rachel wasn't sure how much she wanted to identify with the gang that had just done what they'd done to Pauline. Take Sid Vicious and Nancy Spungen. She was a groupie. He was off his face most of the time and treated her like shit. Were they such great heroes? Was she turning into her mum?

Pauline was getting himself together and being very matter-of-fact about it.

Probably, thought Rachel, because it's happened to the poor old bastard more than a couple of times. In fact, from what Pauline had told her, he had been beaten up by strangers on more than ten occasions, by his family members about fifty times. Oh, the comfort of one's nearest and dearest.

'Do you want to go home?' said Rachel. 'I wouldn't blame you. I can always take you back and hitch on my own.'

'No fucking way,' said Pauline. 'A delicate little flower like you? I wouldn't dream of it. Come on, let's go.'

They walked up to the slip road and along the A4 and eventually found a garage they could wait outside where people could pull in and pick them up.

Is anyone ever going to pick us up? thought Rachel to herself. Look at the state of us. Still, she continued to herself, if we looked smartly dressed like Sunday school teachers, then we wouldn't be hitchhiking.

They waited a surprisingly short time before a rickety old van stopped with a really whiskery old hippy in it on his way down to the West Country.

'Hey man. Look at you. Too far out,' he said as they climbed in.

It was obvious he spent a lot of time on his own, thought Pauline, judging from the rather strange aroma of over-cooked vegetables emanating from the floor area. He looked down to see a pair of very old plimsolls that were barely managing to contain the driver's ripe feet.

Still, once they had got accustomed to the stench, it wasn't too bad and they chugged down the M4 at about fifty-five, in the fast lane, trying to ignore the furious beeping of horns from Capris coming up behind them and the angry faces of boy racers as they flew past gesticulating wildly.

The hippy's name was Cat and he came from Devon. He'd been up to London to see his mum who was in hospital with liver disease.

'Poor old mare,' he kept saying to himself and shaking his head. Rachel and Pauline tried to engage him in conversation but he was difficult to understand, possibly because of the combination of his accent, his stonedness and use of words like 'fantabulousaroonie'. Rachel thought he would have got on well with Susan's nanna.

By the time they got to Junction 15 just outside Swindon they were both really fond of Cat and promised if they were ever down near the tented community in which he lived, they would drop in. He left in a cloud of exhaust, beeping loudly and shouting, 'See you, cats!'

Two hours later they were at the top of Dave's road and Rachel's heart was beating faster to the accompaniment of Pauline's stomach rumbling. She said nervously, 'Oh God, was this such a good idea? Oh, I don't know now,' and wished she was wearing slightly more neutral clothes.

'Let's go and eat first then, shall we?' said Pauline. 'And then we can do it.'

'Oh God, I couldn't eat a thing,' said Rachel, not noticing his face drop.

'Come on then,' he sighed. 'Let's get on with it.'

Dave's home address was number fourteen in a very ordinary-looking road of council houses.

Rachel took a deep breath and knocked on the door. Nothing happened for ages and then a tall thin bloke, who Rachel convinced herself immediately looked very like Dave, roughly fifty in age but somewhat haggard and neglected, answered the door. He didn't seem in the least phased to see a punk and a big fat camp bloke standing at his door.

'Hello, love,' he said to Rachel. 'Can I help you?'

'Is this where Dave lives?' said Rachel, feeling as if she might faint.

The man looked confused. 'Dave?' he said. 'I don't know anyone called Dave, love.'

Rachel felt as if she had been stabbed, even though she didn't know what that felt like.

'Oh,' she gasped. 'Sorry to bother you,' and she turned and headed up the concrete path with pebbles in it, hardly noticing the scrubby garden.

'Here, love!' shouted the man. 'I'm only kidding. Course he lives here, and you must be Rachel. I know all about you.'

Pauline's face became a big smile. Despite his shitty life, he just wasn't able to resent people's happiness or, as many have a tendency to do, start to try and assess how much damage his best mate's romance might do to their friendship. This wasn't bad, considering Rachel was his only friend.

'Come in,' said Dave's dad. 'He's not here at the moment, he's at the shops and he'll be back in about half an hour.'

Dave's dad, Pat, made them a cup of tea and heard the story of their journey from London with little comment. He explained to Rachel that his wife had died a year ago and he had asked Dave, who had finished his course, to come back home and help out because Dave's sister, Marion, lived in Canada with two young children so couldn't really travel.

He said Dave hadn't been too happy about it, but being a good lad had come home then never went back to London. He had a part-time job in a bookshop in town and was in a local band.

He sounded a bit settled. Rachel wanted to ask Pat if Dave had a girlfriend but she couldn't bear to find out yet. She also wanted to ask, 'Does he miss me? Does he still want to see me? Does he love me? Do you want to live in Hastings with us?' And a host of other questions which had entered her overactive mind, which was now convinced that she and Dave were intended for one another.

Pauline could contain himself no longer and said to Pat, 'Could I have a piece of toast, please?'

'Go on, lad, help yourself. It's all in the kitchen,' said Pat.

Pat put the racing back on the telly and he, Rachel and Pauline sat and watched some races from Sandown Park and awaited Dave's return.

About three-quarters of an hour later, Rachel heard the front door open and her heart lurched so much she thought it had swapped over to the other side.

'Hello, you old bastard,' shouted Dave. 'I've got your fags.'

Rachel stood up, wobbly, and ridiculously thought, Does my hair look all right?

The door of the little front room opened and Dave walked in. He saw Pauline first and wondered in that split second whether his father had been keeping a huge secret from him and had a boyfriend. And then he turned and saw Rachel, who had not the slightest idea what effect her arrival would have on him. It could be anything from casual indifference to a catastrophic rebuttal of her feelings.

Dave's mouth started to open to say her name and then he sank to his knees with his face in his hands and began to cry. Rachel, oblivious to the rather embarrassed looks of Pat, who mumbled something about the kettle and Pauline, whose eyes were also starting to fill with tears, crawled across to Dave, hugging him.

'Thank Christ,' he said. 'I can't find anyone else like you anywhere.'

The two of them sat in a heap together and soaked up the fact that after so much time and ridiculous separation they were together, while Pauline and Pat rather pointedly discussed racing, with the tacit acknowledgement that Pauline knew as much about racing as he did about hod-carrying.

'I'm sorry about your mum,' said Rachel.

'Thanks,' said Dave. 'It's been really hard for my dad . . . and me,' he added.

There was silence.

'So what have you been doing?' he asked.

Rachel said, 'I'll tell you all of it eventually, but for now let's just . . .'

'All right,' said Dave. 'Anyway,' he added, 'I'm doing a gig tonight. Are you going to come?'

Rachel looked at Pauline questioningly.

'Great idea,' said Pauline. 'We haven't got to go back to work till Monday.'

'Work?' said Dave. 'You've got a job? You left school?'

'Woolies in Bromley,' said Rachel. 'Don't ask any more. What's your band called? Your dad couldn't remember.'

'Dogmeat,' said Dave.

'And what stuff do you do?' asked Rachel.

'Oh, you know, anything that comes into our heads,' said Dave. 'We're a cross between the Pistols and Floyd.'

'Bloody hell,' said Pauline. 'That's quite an achievement.'

'Where shall we stay then?' said Rachel, looking at Pauline.

'Oh, you must stay here,' said Pat. 'We've plenty of room and David'll knock you up some tea before you go out.'

'Do you mind if I don't go out?' said Pauline. 'I've had about as much ice cream up my arse as I can stand for one day.'

'Pardon?' said Pat.

'Just a local Bromley expression,' said Pauline.

'You stay in with me,' said Pat, 'and we'll watch a film or something, OK?'

'Brilliant,' said Pauline, who'd just made his second friend.

Dave and Rachel were desperate to kiss and tear at each other's clothes, but in this cosy family environment it just didn't seem appropriate, so Dave sent Pauline to the offie to get some beer and crisps for him and Pat for the night, while he cooked egg and chips and they all watched telly.

Dave's appearance had changed little and he still seemed able to fit into any style he chose. He wore a slightly scruffy T-shirt and had ripped jeans, and his hair looked a bit like Johnny Rotten's. For the gig, however, he changed into a pair of tartan trousers and a T-shirt that said *Dogmeat* on the front. Rachel thought he looked fantastic but she was so captivated by him she was unable to see him through ordinary eyes. He would have looked fantastic lying in a bath of offal.

That night they walked hand-in-hand down to the bus stop and Swindon glowed with their love; everyone seemed to be smiling or at the very least contented. Teenage boys on the streets didn't shout abuse, men in pubs didn't feel the need to fight and at Dogmeat's gig a hippy layer of love and peace spread over the proceedings. Well, at least that's how it felt to Rachel. She and Dave got to the grimy pub where Dogmeat were playing, and to Rachel it looked like a small, golden palace. She met the rest of the band who seemed like nice guys but paled into insignificance next to Dave, and she stood at the side of the stage as they thrashed their way very averagely through some Sex Pistols and some Ramones to the delight of the semi-drunken audience, half of whom had bought some duff drugs off the same dealer two streets away.

Rachel, tinged with love, truly believed Dogmeat had a future and sounded better than a lot of punk bands she'd heard before, forgetting to remember that most punk bands sounded like they couldn't play and that was their attraction.

Somehow the Swindon punks seemed a bit more naïve and rustic than their London brothers and the evening passed off without any nasty incidents. Most people at the gig had adapted punk to suit their own style. A lot of girls just had a hint of it but had retained their feminine appearance. They were wearing perhaps a safety pin brooch or were dressed in a smart biker's jacket and had backcombed their hair a bit. They reminded her of Susan, and Rachel thought for the first time that day of her friend and how she must phone her and tell her what was going on. She also wanted to stop herself being constantly threatened by Susan's good looks, and short of a facelift wondered how this could happen. She and Dave had not discussed Susan at all yet. Maybe there wasn't anything to say.

On the way home under the Swindon stars, Dave and Rachel were on an equal plane of happiness. They were both quite drunk and Dave was sweaty and happy after the gig . . . perhaps his perfect night.

Swindon, unfortunately, wasn't blessed with sylvan acreage for young lovers to trip into and make love in as the moon lit their smiling faces, but Rachel and Dave didn't want to indulge in a noisy tryst back at his place, with Pat and Pauline either snoring or trying not to listen, so they resolved to find somewhere on their way home. It was a warmish night and Dave led the way into a small industrial estate where they found some packing material and piled it up against a wall and there poured out all the longing they had suppressed for the last two years.

The alcohol had made them bold and eventually, after

kissing and touching and licking and sucking they managed to get each other's clothes off and despite the chill that ran along the surface of their skin had the most ferocious, brilliant and unforgettable fuck. Sometimes they were standing, sometimes lying down, Dave was on Rachel's back, Rachel was underneath and as they stood together after each had come in an explosion of hitherto unexperienced feeling, a voice said, 'I'm sure you're having a lovely time but if you don't get your clothes on and fuck off, my dog will bite your bollocks off, sir.'

It was Ted, Swindon's only humane security guard, with Lady, an Alsatian that showed no mercy at all and was straining at the leash to get a mouthful of Dave's genitals.

The alcohol insulated them from embarrassment and Dave and Rachel put their clothes on very quickly considering how pissed they were, thanked Ted for not giving them too hard a time and walked, giggling, with their arms round each other, back to Pat's.

When they arrived home at about three thirty they found a scrawled note from Pat which said, *Paul in Marion's old room, me on settee. Your welcome to mine and Mum's bed.*

'Bloody hell,' said Dave.

Of course, once they were in bed they couldn't resist carrying on where they had left off and at about seven thirty in the morning they drifted into a happy sleep.

The next morning, Pauline got up and made a huge fry-up for everyone, and was pleased to see that these two men living together had filled the fridge with exactly the sort of food he loved and very few vegetables.

Rachel and Dave hadn't had a chance to talk about what they were going to do so they sat outside in the tiny back garden, both drinking a cup of tea, and chatted.

'Well, I suppose I've got to get back to Bromley and go to work,' said Rachel, still slightly wary of jumping the gun and expecting too much.

Dave said, 'Look, Rachel, I think we should be together and by that I mean live together. What do you think?'

'I want to do that as well,' said Rachel, 'but where will we do it? London, Swindon or Hastings?'

'I don't know,' said Dave. 'There's Pat to think about, and what about your mum and dad?'

'It doesn't matter right now,' said Rachel, 'but I wouldn't want to be too far away. What about our jobs?'

'What about college? You gave up school,' said Dave. 'Shouldn't you finish your A-levels?'

'I really want to be by the sea,' said Rachel.

'I'd like that,' said Dave. 'I didn't like London. I preferred the countryside at that party. Do you remember?'

'I don't want to tie you down,' said Rachel.

'What about Pauline?' Dave wanted to know. 'He seems so besotted with you.'

'I don't know,' she said. 'I suppose I feel a bit of a responsibility for him.'

'We'll see how it pans out,' said Dave.

'But I have to go back to work tomorrow and whatever we're going to do, I must work out my notice,' said Rachel.

Rachel wasn't a very good punk in many ways. She was shot through with the work ethic. She felt she could not let people down, even though many would have said, 'Oh fuck it, it's only Woolies.' Nor could she quite get the clothes right. People like Johnny Rotten, Siouxsie Sioux, Jimmy Pursey, Captain Sensible and their satellites looked as if they had spent the whole day achieving that look, and either they didn't have jobs or they worked in places that positively encouraged you to put in all that effort. She just wasn't much good at it. Dave wasn't very good at being an art student either. Great artists aren't meant to go home to look after their dads and work part-time, they are meant to go to an island in the Mediterranean and forget about everyone except their muse. Dave had finished his degree but he didn't know what he was going to do with it, as no one seemed to have noticed what a genius he was yet.

Rachel and Pauline had planned to hitch home, but now Dave and Rachel had been Blu-Tacked together by love, Dave could not bear the thought of Rachel risking her life so he asked Pat for a loan and got them some coach tickets. Just before they were due to set off for the coach station they talked again about where to live.

'What about Swindon?' said Dave.

'Wherever you are, I'll be there too,' said Rachel, using words that you can get away with when you are in love because the person who loves you doesn't notice that they sound like the corniest line from a cheap romantic novel.

'It's just that I'm worried about Dad,' said Dave.

'Can't he come too?' said Rachel. 'Wherever we go, I'd be very happy with him living with us.'

Dave kissed her. 'But you've only just met him. You don't know what it's like when—'

Rachel stopped him on the grounds that any talk of Pat's shortcomings would ruin their last few minutes together.

'I'll talk to him,' said Dave. 'You talk to your mum and dad, and Pauline of course, and we'll meet next week. I'll come up to London for a couple of days and we'll make a decision.'

On the coach Rachel spent a lot of time doing that staring thing that people in love do and smiling to herself. Pauline thought it was very sweet. They got back to Bromley at about nine thirty.

'Shall we have a drink on the way home?' Pauline suggested.

'Yeah, come on then,' said Rachel. 'Work in the morning.'

In the pub they talked about the future and what they wanted to do. Rachel was loath to broach the subject of moving away because she thought Pauline was so fragile that he would dissolve, get angry or walk out.

They wandered home together at about ten thirty. Pauline gave Rachel a peck on the cheek and said, 'I'm really happy for you, truly. See you at work in the morning.'

When Rachel got home there was a note pinned to her door from her next-door neighbour, whose phone number she used in emergencies.

It said: *Please phone home immediately. There is a problem. Dad.*

Chapter 23

Rachel was absolutely shattered, having had no sleep the night before, and all she wanted to do was drag her tired body into bed. However, the adrenalin surge from the note turned her round and sent her sprinting to the nearest phone box. What on earth could it be? Why hadn't her mum phoned? There must have been an accident or something. She dialled the number and a man who sounded like her dad, his voice thickened by some emotional battering, answered the phone.

'What is it, Dad?' she said, thinking, It sounds like he's been crying. Most people never hear or see their dad cry. It's happened to me twice in the space of a few years and I don't like it.

'What is it, Dad?' she said again.

'Mum's gone,' he said.

'What do you mean, Mum's gone? Gone where? What – died? Do you mean died? For Christ's sake, Dad, *what's going on?*' And Rachel started to cry. This stopped some of the cracking in her dad's voice.

'No, she hasn't died, sweetheart,' he said. (She hated him calling her this.) 'She's left home.'

'Well, where's she gone?' Rachel asked. Reasonable question.

'She's gone off with that fucking Barry Nesbitt,' Dick said.

'How . . . when . . . what . . .' Rachel delivered a quick-fire round of interrogatives that her father couldn't possibly take in or answer and so he stopped her and said, 'Look, just come home, will you? I need you. Clive and Alan are fucking useless. The house looks like a bomb's hit it and I can't cope.' He began to cry again.

Rachel thought, I wish Pat was my dad. 'All right, Dad,' she said 'I'll come home.'

'Oh, thanks,' said her father, so grateful it made Rachel feel bad that she'd been so irritable with him.

'I'll jump in the car and come and get you now,' he went on.

'No,' said Rachel. 'I'll come tomorrow. I'll have to explain to work and everything. I'll see you about lunchtime. Can I talk to Clive or Alan?'

'No, they're not here,' said Dick. 'They're both at the pub.'

Exactly where I'd be if my mother had pissed off and my dad was falling to pieces, thought Rachel. 'Look,' she said, 'just go to bed, all right, and I'll see you tomorrow.'

In the morning Rachel went into work as usual and having

told Pauline about the trouble going on at home, she had a word with her supervisor, who was sympathetic but obviously pissed off that they seemed to be leaking staff so copiously. She was allowed one day of compassionate leave – unpaid – but after that they would have to see it as her voluntarily having left the job, so she couldn't claim the dole. At the moment, this was the least of her worries.

Pauline told Rachel to keep in touch and pointed out that her erstwhile spiky hair had almost flattened out. Rachel wondered if this meant her punk days were over, but she couldn't be bothered to do her hair. She wanted to be in a movement that didn't give a toss what your hair was like or what you were wearing, but she didn't think that would ever exist.

She decided to hitch home from Bromley to Hastings to save money and was picked up by a man who had gone out for a paper but didn't like his wife very much so decided to drive Rachel all the way there. Rachel kept saying, 'Are you sure?' to which the man kept cheerily replying, 'Oh, absolutely, dear. Absolutely.'

One of the joys of being able to afford public transport and not hitch is that you don't have to talk to anyone if you don't want to, thought Rachel. The peril of hitchhiking wasn't being attacked by the occupant of the car but being bored to death by them as they droned on. In fact, she suspected the picker-uppers were people who couldn't find anyone to talk to or whose partners had ossified over the years.

This bloke, Gordon was his name, rambled on and was

happy as long as Rachel said, 'Mmm,' every five minutes or so. Eventually, he dropped her right outside her door. Rachel got out of the car and thanked Gordon who was bereft that she was leaving him and drove off in a bit of a huff. Rachel felt like Julie Andrews in *The Sound of Music* going back to the convent. She took a deep breath and opened the door with the key she still had.

Shock ran over her as soon as she stepped inside the door. She didn't know how long her mum had been gone, but she had assumed it was only a couple of days. Her dad wouldn't have left it any longer than that before he tried to get in touch with her.

The house smelled of a combination of feet, unflushed toilets – and cabbage. Strange as this was something their family never ate. The carpet had that bedsit look about it and was covered with crumbs; some clothes were strewn on the chairs in the hall and it looked as though Dick, Clive and Alan had dropped stuff where it lay and hoped at some point that someone would come along and sort it all out. On the hall table where the phone was, were a couple of cups and a tin of baked beans with a fork stuck in.

Rachel went into the front room. Dick looked like a tableau from a work called *Deserted Husband*. He was slumped in front of the telly staring at a programme about tulip growing in Holland. He was unshaven and had a dirty shirt on, with a flattened baked bean perkily placed just below the collar. He was also smoking a cigarette – something Rachel had never seen him do and sipping from a can of Special Brew. Rachel wondered if Pat had done this for the first few days when his wife died and thought she must remember to ask Dave. Dick didn't even notice Rachel standing by the door and so she went to explore the rest of the house.

The kitchen had turned into the set for a sitcom called *Dirty Old Buggers* and Rachel thought if her mother came home now she would go right back out of the door again never to return.

In the marital bedroom, grimy coffee cups were lined up on her dad's side of the bed and there were pants strewn around, those horrible dad pants that you have to wear when you get over the age of thirty, not to mention slightly yellowed vests and a couple of cans of lager. The bathroom was grim too; toothpaste was smeared round the sink and the aroma of a men's public toilet had overtaken the place.

Rachel went down to her dad and sat next to him feeling ambivalent about his misery when she was so happy, but he was her dad and somewhere inside she loved him and worried about him even though she had thought over the years that he didn't really deserve her mum.

'Tell me what happened, Dad,' she said.

Dick stared at his feet. 'I don't really know,' he muttered. 'Your mum started to seem a bit anxious and laden down with worry for a couple of days and I wondered whether I should say anything.'

The longer the relationship, the longer the timescale before anything is sorted out, thought Rachel, who decided she'd get stuck in with Dave right away if there was even the slightest hint that something might be going wrong. Longer-term married couples have a habit of leaving things to fester until they are on the point of divorce. Dick and Helen's marriage had been this way for years and they had always found something to distract them from what was important about their relationship.

'So you wondered if you should say anything . . .' prompted Rachel.

'Yes,' said her dad, 'and I decided against it.'

'And?' said Rachel.

'And I came down on Wednesday morning to find a note saying she had gone and she wasn't coming back,' said Dick.

'How do you know it's Barry Nesbitt?' asked Rachel.

'Oh, I've spoken to your mum and she's told me it is,' Dick said dully. 'I can't believe he's done this to me.'

'But Dad,' said Rachel, 'you and Mum haven't been getting on with each other for ages.'

'That's not the point,' he said. 'I love her and it will kill me if she chooses that fucking wanker Nesbitt over me.'

Rachel felt she must have crossed over the adult threshold as her dad had never spoken to her like this before.

'Dad, don't,' she said. 'Come on, let's look on the positive side of things and try to work something out. Let me clean up the flat and get you something to eat. When are Alan and Clive coming home?'

'I don't know,' said Dick in a sad way. 'Who knows anything?'

Rachel had the flat cleaned up in about two hours. She then peeled some potatoes and put a frozen pie in the oven and opened a tin of beans. Her dad looked like he hadn't eaten for two days. She was just about to turn the radio on when she heard Dick crying out in the hall.

'Please come back,' he was saying. 'I am begging you, Helen, begging you.' He cried again and Rachel took the phone.

'Mum, is that you?' she said.

'Rachel!' Helen was surprised. 'What the hell are *you* doing there?'

'Dad called me and asked me to come home,' she said. 'He's in a terrible state. What are you doing, Mum?'

'I'm not really sure I want to talk to you about that sort of stuff,' said Helen.

'Oh, for Christ's sake, let's cut the bullshit,' Rachel said. 'This is serious. Dad's falling apart, Alan and Clive are out God knows where, and you don't want to talk about it. What's going on? Are you with Barry Nesbitt and what are you going to do?'

'I'm living in the Old Town,' said Helen, 'but don't tell your dad or he'll come down and cause no end of trouble. Alan and Clive have been here – they can tell you where I am.'

Rachel felt pulled two ways. Pathetic and wan as her father was, she had some loyalty to him.

'You've got to tell him all this,' she said.

'Tell me what?' said Dick.

'When I'm ready,' said Helen.

'Oh Mum, you can't do this. Come home and talk about it properly, please.' The phone went down and the dialling tone buzzed in her ear.

'What did she say?' asked Dick, a spark of hope in his bloodshot eyes.

'Oh nothing,' said Rachel. 'Nothing. Let's get things together, Dad, then we'll do some talking.'

The door opened and in rolled Alan and Clive, 'roll' being the most appropriate word to describe the sort of swaying plus a forward motion which characterised their progress towards the kitchen.

'Hi, sis,' said Clive, not yet sixteen and off his face.

'Hi, sis,' said Alan, also off his face but at least legally allowed to be.

'For Christ's sake, you two,' said Rachel. 'What are you playing at? Everything is falling apart and you're just pouring stuff down your throats.'

'Well, drunk and vile as we are,' said Alan, 'at least we have been here watching the decline and fall of pater.'

'Oh fuck off,' said Rachel. 'This isn't *Upstairs Downstairs*.'

'It's *No Stairs*,' said Clive, laughing uncontrollably at his bad joke.

'Anyway, I'm back now and we should do something,' said Rachel.

'I think you should go and see Mum,' said Alan. 'Let her tell you what's been going on and then perhaps we can do something.'

'Can't you just tell me?' said Rachel.

'No, she needs to tell you,' said Clive. He put his arm

round her. 'I know we're a hideous pair of boozers,' he said, 'but we do care and we will get ourselves together.'

Rachel felt ill when his sickly, whisky breath swooshed up her nostrils but kept a fixed grin on her face. Clive gave Rachel the address where Helen was staying and Rachel told her dad she was going to the shops. Instead she went to see her mum.

As she walked along the seafront she realised how glad she was to be back in Hastings. For all its suburban character and unfashionableness it did have the appeal of the familiar and made the outside world seem uninviting and alien.

When Helen answered the door, she was secretly pleased to see that the harsher edges of her daughter's hair and clothes had been replaced by a more casual appearance that signified her weary progress back into the fold marked 'conventional'.

'Come in,' she said. 'Barry's out, he'll be back in half an hour or so.'

The little flat was dingy and slightly squalid. Helen Weston had done her best to make it homely, but the unpleasant Formica surfaces in the little kitchenette, the damp smell emanating from the bathroom and the crusty orange shagpile had defeated her.

The two women were both acutely aware that the last time they had met, it was Helen who had been assessing Rachel's rather shabby living quarters and turning her nose up at them. But seeing her mother in these circumstances, it was not in Rachel's nature to enjoy the Schadenfreude that would wash deliciously through some other personalities. She just felt sorry for her. Her mum made some tea.

'Look,' said Helen. 'I'm sorry about on the phone and treating you like a child. You deserve to know what's been going on. I've told the boys and you should know too.' She sat down and motioned to Rachel to sit on the cheap beige-coloured settee that must have been difficult to live with.

Rachel sat down, feeling strangely tense and embarrassed about what she was going to hear. Part of her wished she could spirit her mother back to their home without any fuss and just get on with her own life.

There was a pretty long silence that no one attempted to fill. Then Helen said, 'I don't know where to begin.'

'Perhaps just tell me some facts then,' said Rachel, wanting to keep it businesslike.

'All right. Well, I met Barry through Dad's work,' said Helen, 'and over the years, at various work "dos", we got to know each other a bit better.'

Rachel knew she was being shallow but felt some admiration for her mum being able to have a relationship with someone called Barry. Had Dave been called Barry she was sure things would have been very different.

'Then,' said Helen, 'I suppose your dad and I were going through a bad patch and I bumped into Barry up in Oxford Street when I was doing some Christmas shopping. We went for a coffee and had such a nice chat and a laugh, it just sort of went on from there.'

Rachel, briefly a Puritan, heard herself say, 'But what about your marriage vows? What about us kids? What about

Dad? And isn't Barry himself married with a couple of kids?'

'Was married,' said Helen. 'It's never been right between him and his wife.'

And you really gave them a chance to sort it out, thought Rachel.

Rachel, now a divorce lawyer: 'So how long did it go on before Dad found out?'

'A couple of years maybe,' said Helen. 'I thought it could just stay like that and I could keep the family together.'

'So what did you do?' said Rachel. 'Where did you go to . . . you know?' She didn't want to say anything about her mother having sex or even acknowledge that was the case.

'I don't think I need to go into those sort of details,' said Helen primly.

Rachel felt like saying, 'Well, *I* think you do.' She wanted something to tell Susan about.

'How did Dad find out?' she asked instead.

'He was supposed to be at a business meeting in Kent one day,' Helen said, looking embarrassed, 'and Barry came round to the house.'

Rachel felt rather alarmed at the thought of her mum and Barry Nesbitt going up and down coitally under the newly acquired duvet with its understain-concealing, flowery pattern.

'Anyway, Dad forgot his sandwiches and as he was virtually going past the house on his way to this job, he stopped in to pick them up.'

Rachel found herself wanting to know what was in the sandwiches. She put her hands over her face as if this would somehow shut out the image of the tragic-farce that had been the beginning of her parents' marriage break-up.

'So what happened?' she managed.

'Turned out Dad had seen Barry's car outside and assumed he'd dropped in for a cup of tea or something. We didn't hear the car, Dad came in and found us, you know . . . and was quite upset.'

'Quite upset' was hardly accurate. In fact, Dick had been a homicidal, Barry-seeking missile when he realised that there was no polite tea-drinking going on downstairs.

'And then?' Rachel prompted.

'Dad saw Barry off the premises,' said Helen, failing to mention that it involved Barry in his pants, clutching the rest of his clothes, being hit and punched and kicked by Dick in a rhythmic pattern reminiscent of a Status Quo single, all the way down the stairs and through the front garden to his car.

'Fuck! Poor Barry,' said Rachel.

Helen gave her a stern look because of her language. This seemed totally inappropriate to Rachel, considering what they were discussing.

'So why did you and Dad decide to stay together then?' Rachel asked.

Helen looked as if she had no idea, but said, 'For you and Clive and Alan. We thought it might be worth one more try. I agreed not to see Barry, Dad said he'd leave the firm and that we'd move away and make a fresh start.'

'So how did Barry get hold of you then?' Rachel wanted to know.

'Well, I phoned *him* actually,' said Helen.

'Oh, for Christ's sake, Mum.' Rachel was slightly depressed that maturity didn't seem to have contributed to the stock of commonsense Helen had been allotted.

'I know,' said Helen. 'When I came down to the new house the day before we moved he met me there and . . . well, you can guess.'

'You had sex?' said Rachel, horrified.

Helen looked at the floor.

Out of the blue, the answer to a mystery shot through Rachel's mind. 'Did he have a fag afterwards?' she said.

'He left a cigarette burning in the ashtray and it must have fallen onto the carpet. The whole house went up in flames,' said Helen. 'Your dad hasn't got a clue, and neither have the boys so don't you go telling them.'

'And then Barry moved down here,' said Rachel.

'Yes. He got this bedsit in the Old Town to be near me. We'd been meeting a bit. Your dad found out.'

'How?'

'He followed me last week because he wanted to know where I was going when I went out. Thought I was doing an evening class or something on the side.'

Every woman's perfect evening class, thought Rachel. Barry Banging.

'Dad saw me going into this place, rang the doorbell and Barry answered. Dad punched him, Barry shut the door, Dad shouted some threats through the letterbox and then he left. I haven't been home since, except to get a few bits and pieces.'

'So what are you going to do?' asked Rachel.

'Well,' said her mother, 'I've got another bit of news.'

'What, as well as leaving Dad and moving in with your lover, there's more?' said Rachel.

'I'm pregnant,' Helen told her.

Rachel's face flared bright red. 'Oh God, you're not going to keep it, are you?' she croaked.

'Of course I am,' said Helen.

'Christ, Mum, how will that all work out?' said Rachel, thinking, I'm the one that's supposed to get irresponsibly pregnant, not you. 'Does Dad know yet?'

'No,' said Helen. 'I've told Clive and Alan but I can't bring myself to tell him.'

'Mum, you'll have to,' said Rachel.

'I know.'

'Come on, Mum, phone him up now and tell him. Go on you'll feel better.'

Helen shivered. 'I can't, it'll destroy him.'

Thinking of the state of Dick, Rachel was forced to consider that she might have a point, but he had to know sometime. Rachel took the phone and held it out to her mum, who looked at it as though it was a big scary vibrator.

'No,' she said. 'I'll do it in my own time.'

It occurred to Rachel that so far, their entire conversation had been about her mum's life, her mum's boyfriend and her mum's unplanned pregnancy, and Rachel started to resent Barry Nesbitt for pushing himself into their family even though he had seemed like such a lovely bloke when she met him. Her mother's worries about Rachel had been completely replaced by Rachel's worries about her mother, and Rachel had a cursory ten minutes devoted to Dave before the front door opened and in came Barry.

'I'd better be going,' said Rachel, and got up.

'Oh don't go,' said Barry. 'It's lovely to see you.'

Rachel didn't know if it was lovely to see Barry or not. Up in London with the benefit of ignorance she'd felt very warm towards him. Now, sitting next to her mother on the beige sofa and holding her hand like a twelve year old, he looked like a tosser. Occasionally he said things to Rachel about Helen like, 'I adore this gorgeous woman,' and Rachel feared her half-digested biscuit might be thrown up.

The force of their middle-aged passion made Rachel frantic to get away but she could see how that would look, so she forced herself to stay in the chair while her mum made some more tea and Barry mused in a daft way about their future with lovey-dovey asides to Helen in the kitchenette about three feet away.

Eventually Rachel felt as though she might either laugh hysterically or start to scream at them to grow up, and this spurred her to act.

'I've got to go,' she said. 'Let me know what's happening, Mum, won't you?'

Walking down the street, she had a really strong urge to phone Susan. It was a while since she had spoken to Susan and Rachel missed her. She went into a call box, and looked for some change.

Chapter 24

Terry answered the phone. 'She's at work,' she said, 'up the DOE.'

'Has she got a number there?' said Rachel. 'I'd love to meet her for a coffee.'

Terry gave her a number and Rachel was eventually put through to Susan's little section.

'Brilliant,' Susan said, when she heard Rachel's voice. 'Do you want to come up here and meet me during my lunchbreak tomorrow?'

'You're on,' said Rachel.

The staff on the door at the DOE looked a bit suspicious of Rachel as they did of everyone who didn't have a suit or a beige jumper and skirt on. But they let her through.

Susan and Rachel hugged and both realised they were really pleased to see each other.

'Let's go to the bar and have a drink to celebrate,' said Susan. There was a subsidised bar on the premises and it also did food which doubled as an emetic. Susan ordered them both a vodka and lime and this was knocked back in seconds after they had raised their glasses. 'To us!' they said simultaneously, and laughed.

There was a great deal to catch up on.

Terry and Vince were fine, although Vince had had some treatment for the lump in his testicles and was absolutely mortified when it was Helen, working part-time as a nursing assistant at the local General, who had turned up with a gown for him to put on.

'I'm not showing my bollocks to that woman,' emanated very loudly from behind the curtain.

Helen hadn't actually told Rachel about this and she thought how much of this sort of gossip she must have missed, being away from home. Jennifer was still working at the hairdresser's, doing very well and almost earning enough to buy a small bar of chocolate, said Susan. The money was appalling. Lee Greenwood had returned after being treated in a drug clinic and was doing his best to be a bit of a father to his daughter, Lucy. Jen was still besotted with him because they'd never spent enough time together to get bored with each other sexually.

'How's Kim doing?' asked Rachel. 'Still at M and S?'

'Bored shitless,' said Susan. 'I think she'll end up going to college in the end. She's got a nice new bloke who wants to get married to her so maybe she won't. And what about your lot?' Susan asked for politeness' sake, assuming there would be nothing to report and wondering why Rachel had come visiting.

When Rachel told her about Helen and Barry, Susan was open-mouthed with shock. Helen was the last person she would have expected to be leaving her husband and getting pregnant.

'What's going to happen?' she asked.

'I don't know,' said Rachel. 'She hasn't told my dad yet.'

'He's going to go fucking mental, isn't he?' said Susan.

'Yep, but hey – listen to this,' and she told Susan all about Dick's love affair and how he had cried in front of her.

'Blimey, your parents have been right up to their necks in rampant sex,' said Susan. 'Lucky bastards.'

They both laughed. Then Rachel filled Susan in about Dave. Not so long ago she had wanted to strangle Susan with her bare hands when it looked like she might be responsible for stealing her only chance of a decent relationship. But now she was convinced it had been a fleeting fancy between Dave and Susan.

'What about you?' said Rachel.

'I'll just get us another drink,' said Susan. 'Vodka and lime again?'

'OK,' said Rachel, 'but haven't you got to go back to work?'

'Oh, it's all right,' said Susan. 'I could do the job blindfolded.' She didn't seem unhappy about this. 'I've met this really nice bloke called Mark,' she went on. 'He works in my office.'

'Isn't that a bit weird?' said Rachel.

'What?' said Susan.

'Being with him at work all day long . . . in fact, all the time.'

'Well, we don't go out Thursdays or Tuesdays 'cause he plays footer on a Thursday and I do my washing on a Tuesday,' said Susan.

Rachel balked at the shocking suburban content of Susan's routine. 'But don't you ever feel like getting out and going mad?' she said.

'No, I don't really,' said Susan. 'We did going mad in London, didn't we, and it scared the shit out of me.'

'It was exciting though, wasn't it?' said Rachel.

'The bingo's exciting enough for me,' Susan told her.

'You don't,' said Rachel.

'I bloody do, with Mum and Jen,' said Susan, 'and it's a bloody good laugh.'

'What about Kim?' said Rachel.

'Oh, too embarrassed to be seen there,' said Susan. 'Right snobby, she is.'

Rachel started to laugh even though this wasn't funny. So did Susan and it then occurred to them that they were pissed. It was five past two as well and Susan should have been back at her desk at two.

'Oh fuck it, let's just go down town and have a laugh, shall we?' said Susan.

'No way. I'm not being responsible for you getting the sack.'

'But I want to get the sack,' said Susan.

'No, you don't,' said Rachel. 'What would Mark say?'

'Oh fuck Mark,' said Susan. 'He's just like bloody Vince.'

'You don't mean that,' said Rachel. 'That's just the drink talking.'

'No, it isn't,' said Susan, and fell off her chair giggling.

'Come on,' said Rachel. 'Try and sober up.'

They got up and headed out of the bar and to the main entrance that led to Susan's office.

'Are you sure you're OK?'

Susan snorted to signify that she was, and some snot flew out of her nose, which started another crescendo of giggles.

'I'll see you later,' said Susan, and Rachel watched her staggering towards the lift trying to look as if she was in control of her limbs.

On the phone to Dave that night, Rachel surprised herself by saying that she'd like to stay in Hastings to be with her parents until they had sorted themselves out. Dave agreed that this would be a good idea. He then said that he would come down and wondered, if he brought Pat with him, whether Rachel could find them anywhere to live. What with her mum gone and her dad currently barely noticing that life was happening through his bifocals of beer, Rachel thought it might be a possibility that she could squeeze them into the flat although how this would work out she really wasn't sure. Still, she could only ask.

'Dad,' she said to Dick the following night as he sat slumped in front of the telly.

'Can my boyfriend Dave come and stay?'

'Sure,' he said without thinking and carried on watching telly.

'And can his dad come too?' said Rachel as fast as she could, knowing that the quicker she said it, the easier it would be for him to agree to.

'Whatever,' he said, which Rachel took as a yes.

Back at Susan's house, all was not well. Susan had been asked to leave work early because she was so pissed, and Mark her boyfriend, who had worked through his lunch-break, wasn't too happy to see her virtually on her hands and knees giggling, then proceed to fall asleep and dribble all over her desk.

'God, Suze,' he said. He was twenty-three and very responsible – 'responsible for fucking pissing me off,' Susan used to say jokingly to members of her family when Mark got obsessed about some small thing or other and went on and on about it for days, weeks sometimes. 'God, you could get the sack.'

Something about that statement cheered Susan up but she pushed it aside and apologised for the eleventh time in the last five minutes.

'Mark's right,' said Vince, ecstatic at having another grown-up in the house. For too long he had felt that he was the only one who noticed the behaviour of these adolescent women and tried to improve their standards. Terry raised her eyebrows at Susan across the room and made a wanker sign behind Vince's back. Mark spotted it and winked at Susan.

Thank Christ, she thought. At least he hasn't turned into Vince just yet.

'Don't worry, love,' she said. 'I won't get the sack. I'll

sort it out and apologise and all that bollocks. It'll be fine.'

Mark thought she was probably right. He knew she only had to point her little angel face at someone and smile and they would do anything for her. He still couldn't believe that out of all the potential suitors in the world, she had chosen him. But that was the precise reason she had chosen him – because despite being a really good-looking bloke, he didn't spend most of the day either looking in the mirror or counting the minutes until he got to one. Mark wasn't ambitious or cut-throat and he wouldn't end up with his own business or running an empire, but he was bright and good fun and he was relentless in the bedroom, which Susan could not resist. Very occasionally though, she had small moments of terror when she imagined the future with Mark and herself – a tableau of bored, frustrated unhappiness. She tried not to think about it.

Terry understood this; after all, she had been living it for the last twenty years. Every week she scanned the *Woman's Own* problem page, looking for an answer to her sense of hopelessness about her future with Vince. It didn't occur to her to actually write a letter herself. She envied Helen and hated herself for feeling that way, but the effort you'd have to go to for a new man put her off. She was comfortable in her roomy knickers, chipped nail varnish and anachronistic beehive. It would have to be someone really special to knock her off her own hamster wheel.

It was getting towards Christmas again and the odd Santa had sprouted up in shop windows. One weekend on from their phone call, Dave and Pat arrived in Hastings with their suitcases feeling full of anticipation (Dave) and trepidation (Pat).

Dick, who had pulled himself together slightly over that week and was promising himself he would have a grown-up meeting with Helen in which he would not cry or threaten to kill himself, suddenly regretted allowing Rachel's boyfriend to move in and bring his father, for Christ's sake. He couldn't remember what had happened to Dave's mum and didn't want to ask in case he offended him or Pat.

Rachel had worked really hard to make things ready, pushing Alan and Clive back into a room together with a huge amount of protest from them.

'Oh, come on, please,' she said. 'For fuck's sake, it's not going to be for ever, I promise. Just till Mum and Dad are sorted out.'

'All right,' said Alan grudgingly. He had left school and was working part-time for a dodgy music promoter in Brighton, who had a sideline in selling drugs. All manner of jobs – flyposting, taking money from here to there, a bit of security – were all technically within his remit. He loved this job because each day was exciting, unpredictable and distinct from the day before. He'd turned into a gruff but friendly young man with a sardonic line in humour and a propensity to pour ten to fifteen pints a night into himself with no short-term ill-effects. One day, Alan had simply stopped going to school. The Headmaster had written several notes which were used to line bins on his way home, and there did seem to be more pressing social problems than a boy who was just about to leave school not turning up there very often.

Alan and Clive seemed remarkably sanguine about their mother running off with her lover and getting pregnant by him, but Rachel wondered whether they were burying their pain somewhere down deep, at the risk of it catapulting out sometime in later life.

Helen had arranged to meet Dick to tell him about the baby. She decided on a public venue where, if his behaviour got out of control, the police could be called. They sat in the restaurant at Debenhams, he with a bun and a cup of tea, she with a Coke, staring at each other as if they were about to take twenty paces back and then turn and shoot.

'So,' said Dick, 'you have something to tell me then?'

Shall I sugar the pill and talk rubbish for five minutes or shall I come straight out with it? thought Helen. She decided on the latter. 'I'm pregnant,' she said.

Dick coughed his bun all over the table. He realised that this really narrowed his chances of Helen coming back, and that all these years had been wasted thinking he was in love with some secretary he'd met in the pub when he was eighteen, when all along he had been in love with the brilliant, beautiful, unpredictable Helen. He wanted to say this but just wasn't able to articulate the words and ended up staring intently, a look which appeared full of hatred.

'I'm sorry, Dick, really I am,' she said. 'But somehow I've felt our relationship's never been really right for you.

I loved you so much at the beginning, I didn't think that it would matter, but I'm afraid it did. And now it's too late. I know that's a cliché but I don't think I could possibly get those feelings back.'

Now was Dick's chance to spit it out but he still didn't. Instead, he said, 'I can't believe you're doing this,' and, 'I don't know what to do.'

'Well, I just wanted to tell you and I will work out some way we can see each other and talk about the details,' said Helen.

She got up and left and Dick threw the rest of his bun on the carpet.

'Pick that up, please,' said a waitress in her mid-fifties with a stern expression. So he did.

When Dick got home, he found Dave in the kitchen preparing a meal, Pat in the front room watching the racing and Rachel hoovering. The flat looked nice and smelled better and lifted his spirits a little.

'Cup of tea?' shouted Dave.

'Yes, please,' said he and Pat together and laughed.

'We won't impose on you too long, mate,' said Pat. 'Once Dave and Rachel are settled, I'll move on.'

'Oh, stay as long as you like,' said Dick.

They all had tea together that night. Rachel was very impressed. Dave had knocked up a big pasta thing. Very studenty, but it tasted nice so she opened a bottle of wine and she, Dave, Pat, Dick, Clive and Alan raised their glasses.

'Here's to a better future for all of us,' said Pat.

'Cheers,' said everyone.

Dave stood up. 'I don't really know whether this is the correct etiquette or not,' he said, 'so sorry if I do anything wrong, but I just wanted to say this in front of you all.' And he turned to Rachel and said, 'Will you marry me?'

Rachel's face went pink and she nodded. Everyone clapped and chinked their glasses. Dave turned towards her dad and said, 'Assuming I have your permission, Dick?'

Dick shook his head. 'I'm sorry, mate.'

The atmosphere changed to dark.

'Only kidding,' said Dick.

Uproar returned.

That night, Susan and Mark were out at a wine bar.

'Now just have the seven bevvies,' said Mark. 'I don't want you dribbling all over your desk.'

They were celebrating the fact that Susan had avoided getting the sack from work and had put on such a good performance of contrite employeeness that they had welcomed her back and almost promoted her into the bargain. She saw it as a wobble that would never happen again, knew that she was happy, and shook her head sadly when she read in the paper that her erstwhile hero Sid Vicious was sinking lower and lower into addiction, fuelled by his equally disturbed girlfriend Nancy Spungen.

'I'm glad we're not Sid and Nancy,' she said to Mark.

'Who's Sid and Nancy?' said Mark, who liked the Eagles.

'Never mind.'

'Look,' said Mark, 'I don't want to make a song and dance about this, but will you marry me?'

'Bloody hell,' said Susan, thinking to herself that he'd

said it almost as if he was choosing a flavour of crisps from the bar. But it was a proposal and it was from the bloke she wanted to marry.

'I accept,' she said, grinning, 'and I think we'll have a fucking lovely time together.'

'Sorry,' said Mark, 'I really don't like you using that word. Do you mind? It's just that it doesn't fit with how pretty you are.'

Chapter 25

The next day, Susan phoned Rachel at exactly the same time as Rachel phoned Susan. 8.32 a.m. Then they phoned each other a couple more times because they got the engaged tone. Rachel didn't want to miss Susan before she went to work. It was the same for Susan, who didn't want to wake Rachel either.

'Dave's asked me to marry him,' said Rachel at the same time as Susan said, 'Mark's asked me to marry him.'

Both heard the other perfectly clearly and set up strangled screaming that, had it been any louder, might have encouraged the neighbours to phone the police.

'God, I can't believe it!' said Susan.

'Amazing! What would Germaine Greer say?' said Rachel.

Susan made a snorting noise. Rachel had introduced her to Germaine Greer and she wasn't impressed. *The Female Eunuch* with its outspoken, prejudiced attacks on men was in her eyes a book for women who couldn't get a bloke and needed an excuse to explain it.

They discovered that neither had set a date for their wedding but Susan's would be in the summer whereas Rachel wanted to get married in the winter. Maybe February.

'You could do Valentine's Day,' said Susan.

'Not really me,' said Rachel. 'We'll see.'

'Shall we have a party?' said Susan. 'And invite everyone we know?'

'What a fucking brilliant idea,' said Rachel. 'Where?'

They both said, 'The Pier,' at exactly the same time.

When they phoned Derek, the manager of the pier, he said they didn't normally let it out for private parties, so Susan went down there to see him and within five minutes he had agreed. However, even with a substantial discount, also negotiated by Susan, it was still going to cost a grand to hire. The girls sat together in the coffee bar feeling dejected and discussing some of the other places that would have to do – a church hall, a room above a pub, even the Crypt – but given the incident in which Grumpy the barman had grassed Rachel up to her parents, they immediately dismissed it.

'I don't want to give up hope,' said Susan, 'because it's my dream to have my own party at the pier. We deserve it – we grew up in that place, all the times we've padded down there for a night of life-changing drunkenness. They owe it to us.'

'I agree,' said Rachel. 'Who do we know who's rich?'

'We don't know anyone who's rich,' said Susan. 'Let's think about it, shall we, and see if we can come up with anything.'

Rachel told Dave later that evening about their grand scheme.

'What a bloody brilliant idea,' he said. 'God, you could have the party to end all parties on that pier.'

'But we just don't have any money to pay for it,' said Rachel, 'so we're thinking of having it somewhere much cheaper.'

'Don't do that,' said Dave. 'I'll cough up the money.'

'You haven't got a thousand pounds,' Rachel said sadly.

'Well actually,' said Dave, 'a few years ago I won a prize for a piece of art, and to be honest with you I was a bit embarrassed about it so I kept quiet, put the cheque in a savings account and thought I'd keep it to spend on something I really wanted. There's nothing better that I'd like to do with it than blow it on a massive party.'

'Are you sure?' said Rachel, reaching for the phone.

They had six weeks to organise the party, and as soon as Derek the pier manager had OK'd the deal and extracted a hefty deposit, Susan and Rachel set about working on it.

'Who are we going to invite?' said Susan.

'Everyone we know,' Rachel told her, 'and a few more, or the place'll be empty.'

'Anyone we shouldn't invite?' Susan enquired.

'Mad Mick Mason,' said Rachel, and Susan made the sign of the cross and they giggled.

'Music?' asked Susan.

'I think we need a band,' said Rachel. 'How about Dave's band, Dogmeat?'

'What – a punk band? What about the old 'uns?'

'Well, can't we get a crappy rock band as well, for the old 'uns to jig along to?' said Rachel. 'There's always Lee Greenwood. His band was pretty shit but the over-thirties would bloody love all that "Hi Ho Silver Lining" bollocks. Shall I get Jen to ask him?'

'I suppose so,' said Susan. 'Do we have to pay them?'

'Dunno. Some bands are so pleased to be in front of more than twelve people they'll do it for free.'

'And we need a disco too,' said Susan, 'to play some good stuff to dance to, just in case both bands really are shite.'

'Is there anyone from school who could do it,' Rachel wondered, 'a bit cheap?'

'How about Marie's brother?' said Susan.

'Are you still talking to her?' said Rachel.

'No, but he won't give a toss about that.'

'What do we do about decorating the place?' Rachel asked. 'Who do we know with a flamboyant and uncontrolled imagination who can work on something on a big scale?'

'No idea,' said Susan.

'I reckon I could ask Pauline to do it,' said Rachel. 'His bedroom looks like a fluffy torture chamber.'

'My nan wouldn't like that,' said Susan.

'She bloody well would,' said Rachel.

'And what about your mum and dad?'

'Oh, they wouldn't notice it, I don't suppose,' said Rachel.

'No, I mean are they both going to come?' said Susan.

'Sure,' said Rachel. 'Someone can pull them apart if necessary.'

Dogmeat and Lee Greenwood's new band which had risen from the ashes of his old band and was unsurprisingly called Phoenix, agreed a deal. Lee had originally asked for five hundred quid and when Susan had laughed, he dropped the price to free beer. Dogmeat just wanted a floor to kip on.

Rachel phoned Pauline in a state of excitement and happiness verging on hysteria. 'How are you?' she asked.

Pauline was still at Woolies and struggling to have a laugh without Rachel. 'Oh, not bad,' he lied. 'You?'

'I need you to come down and help,' said Rachel.

This was all the asking Pauline needed. He came down on the train the following day, having phoned in sick at work, and he and Susan and Rachel sat huddled together in Susan's house while Vince marvelled at Pauline as if he were a butterfly displayed on some felt.

'Look,' said Rachel, 'we haven't got that much money, but do you think you could decorate the main ballroom in a Christmassy yet fairly unconventional way?'

'Just make it look fucking brilliant,' said Susan, and caught herself thinking, Glad Mark didn't hear that.

That weekend, Dogmeat came down for a rehearsal and they all piled into the flat as well. Dick, Alan and Clive found themselves sleeping in the same room.

'Sorry,' said Rachel. 'It's only for two days.'

Dave was pleased to see Dogmeat too. He'd missed torturing the ears of the good burghers of Swindon with them. Part of him was also missing the familiarities of Swindon of which he was so fond, and Pat admitted to being a bit homesick, too, but neither felt they wanted to go back, especially Pat who, slowly coming free of the shackles of the grieving process, wanted some new experiences.

Terry had agreed to do some of the catering which was a nightmare because two hundred and fifty people were expected. These were made up of Rachel, Susan, Dave and Mark's family members, their friends, work colleagues and anyone in Hastings whom they thought was vaguely interesting. This meant that the group of people on the pier on that night would be as diverse as Susan's nan, Dave's art-school friends, some fishermen that Mark knew from school, Matron and some of the more sturdy patients from the TB hospital, and some drug dealers with whom Alan and Clive were friendly. It was the sort of occasion that promised so much and had the potential to go very badly wrong.

Rachel wrote to Sid Vicious and Nancy Spungen, Siouxsie Sioux, Poly Styrene, the Damned, Elvis Costello, Malcolm McClaren and the Ramones, in the vain hope they might think, Oh fuck it, I'll go to Hastings and cause trouble. Susan wrote to Donny Osmond. A week before the party, there had been no RSVP from any of them.

Every night Rachel and Dave lay in bed thinking about the party and seeing it as a launchpad to the rest of their lives. It would bring everyone they knew and loved together and then fling them all out into the world again with an unforgettable night etched into their grey matter.

Susan was worried that Mark would hate it. She was so looking forward to it herself that she tried to block out the occasional negative comment he made about the preparations and said to herself, If it all goes wrong and he doesn't like it, I'll just get pissed.

Helen and Barry were unsure about whether to go.

'I don't know,' Helen dithered. 'Dick'll be there obviously and we'll only upset him.'

'I know,' said Barry, 'but come on, this is our chance to finally be together in public and show everyone that we're a couple. It's the perfect opportunity, surely?'

Helen was having a grim early pregnancy full of nausea and spotting incidents, and she was worried that she was going to miscarry. She felt sure a disaster of some sort would occur if they went, but Barry was absolutely determined to go.

Dick had decided he would put on a brave face and turn up. It seemed obvious to him that Helen was not coming back so he might as well try to put all that behind him and find a new direction in his life. He had just started to build up a solid portfolio of clients for his quantity-surveying business before Helen left, and although he had pissed a few of them off, he was sure he could pick up where he had left off.

Two days before the party and five days before Christmas, it was bitterly cold and a small amount of snow fell.

Brilliant, thought Rachel, who was tucked up in bed with Dave, still in the Sex-All-Night-And-All-Day zone.

Shit, thought Susan, who had visions of all the old 'uns slipping over and her female family members having to revise their plans to wear virtually no clothes.

Over in Bromley, Siouxsie Sioux rolled up their invitation, stuck it in the gas fire and lit her fag with it.

As these things inevitably do, the night finally arrived and everyone took a deep breath, some to tackle rising panic like Pauline whose fears ranged from everything falling down to being beaten up because his final Christmas tableau was so awful, others to breathe in as much cannabis smoke as possible, like some friends of Dave's who were so stoned they went back to bed and didn't wake up until the party was over.

Vince was buried under his usual pile of female beauty products and clothes while Terry, Jen, Kim and Susan prepared for the night. Mark came round, took one look at what he called, 'the Prozzies' Parlour' and went upstairs to read a rallying magazine.

Pauline had enlisted the help of a couple of local lads he had met in Hastings's only slightly gay pub to sort the decorations out with him. They had headed to the pier with yards of glittery material, crepe paper and paper chains stuffed in the back of an old white van, and began feverishly pushing in drawing pins, winding the decorations round columns, and balancing stuff along the tops of windows – anything to disguise the drabness and peeling paint. Unfortunately there was so much pier and so little decorative material that they had to concentrate most of it in the ballroom, so as one wandered along the pier to get into the party there was only the odd sorry plastic reindeer or a droopy bit of mistletoe Sellotaped to the handrail or wound round the cast-iron structure.

'Like I feel, dear,' said Pauline to his two acolytes, eyeing the forlorn mistletoe.

Susan's nanna had left out her teatime Mogadon in celebration of staying up for a bit and was also round at Terry's, trowelling on some very thick make-up which transformed her into a crimplene-covered Widow Twankey.

The party was due to start at eight o'clock and at six thirty Susan and Rachel met at the pier to ensure that everything was ready to go.

Dogmeat and Phoenix had both sound-checked in the afternoon, rather too close to each other, and now left by separate entrances, all muttering 'wankers' about one another.

The toilets had been cleaned and flushed with a disinfectant that could take off the top two layers of skin with no difficulty. The bar area had been swilled with dirty water and only smelt a bit of beery ashtrays as compared to smelling a lot of beery ashtrays. Some security men, courtesy of Alan and Clive, were in place, the DJ was having a long, enjoyable shit backstage, and two hundred and fifty people were preparing to progress towards the pier on this night of nights.

Susan and Rachel thought the venue looked brilliant.

Pauline had done his best with the funds available and there was holly and mistletoe everywhere, which Rachel suspected he had got a few people to nick off a local farm, but she wasn't going to investigate. The ballroom was full of gold, glittering drapes and twinkling silver lights with an enormous Christmas tree next to the stage.

Susan and Rachel laughed with glee and hugged each other.

'Our own party on the pier, fuck me,' said Susan portentously.

Rachel produced a small bottle of brandy from her coat pocket. 'Here's to us,' she said. 'Don't be nervous or worried. Let's have a bloody good night, shall we?'

'Yeah,' said Susan, swigging a big gulp from the bottle. 'Well done you and well done me.'

'Let's go and finish our make-up and wait for everyone to come.'

The first to arrive were a few girls from Rachel and Susan's school, the ones who had clung on for dear life when all around them were drowning in drugs, useless boyfriends or hormonal overdrive with the result that they were ejected from home by their parents. These clever clogs were all set to go to college.

There were a couple of Susan's old best friends there, both of whom had accepted that the triumvirate was smashed and their D'Artagnan gone forever. Bev had found a new best friend, Lesley Keerman, amateur bully, and they were a match for each other in competition and unreliability. Poor Marie, however, remained kind, loyal and dull and consequently friendless.

Nanna had brought the district nurse with her and the old guy called Sid who lived next door, for moral support. It was so long since Nanna had been to a party, let alone this sort of party, that her blood pressure was rising fast and the nurse had to keep telling her to sit down and take it easy.

A compilation Christmas tape of camply performed carols was playing as people arrived and handed over their coats in the manky cloakroom next to the toilets. Some immediately went and got them back as it wasn't too warm. Guests began to gather in the bar and in the ballroom, but once the number had passed the seventy-five mark, which happened very quickly, it didn't feel quite so much as if they were a few frozen peas rattling around in a great big saucepan.

The arrival of Mad Mick Mason also heated the blood of those present. He'd heard about the party in the pub and made his way grumpily to the pier, somewhat miffed at not being asked as he usually was to most parties just to stop him coming round and smashing down the door. Clive and Alan's bouncer friends took one look at him and moved back to let him pass. As he went into the bar, a hushed murmur ran round the place. In fact, the only people who didn't feel their bowels move with fear at the sight of him were Matron and the old 'uns, who welcomed him into their circle and began chatting amicably to him – an approach which cheered him up and moved him to behave like a civilised party guest.

Dave's money had stretched to a glass of pomagne for

each guest to kick-start the good will, and although everyone straggled in too disorganised a fashion for a formal toast, most people were so pleased to get a free drink, they toasted Susan and Rachel as they took their glasses.

Dogmeat, after a few 'technical' problems – that is, they couldn't find the drummer, who was shagging posh Amanda in the toilets backstage – appeared to bemused applause onstage and were about 80 per cent energy and 20 per cent talent, with ear-bursting loudness being the major factor in their performance. The inevitable feedback sent Nan's friend Sid scuttling to the toilet to have a look at his hearing aid, and took everyone of Rachel and Susan's age back to lots of gigs in pubs and the early days of the pier. Rachel was captivated to see Dave singing again but no one else was, not even Pat, who mouthed to Dick, 'What a racket.'

Dogmeat kicked off with 'New Rose' by the Damned, and immediately the able-bodied under-twenties started pogo-ing. Instinctively, the middle-aged moved back and shook their heads at what they considered to be the beauty and elegance of the jiving they used to do compared to this frantic and intimidating animal behaviour involving a lot of spit flying around.

Pat and Dick were at the bar trying out the Guinness when Dick spotted Helen and Barry Nesbitt arriving. Dick and Pat had become quite good friends, and when Pat noticed Dick starting to bristle, he bought him another pint.

Posh Amanda's mum and dad, who had been responsible for bringing Rachel and Dave together in the first place, were also in the bar, looking round them at what they pooh-poohed as riffraff, having absolutely no idea what their daughter was up to about twenty yards away with Dogmeat's drummer.

Dave's art-school friends, rather fish out of water-ish, having been removed from the safety of London's fashionable enclaves, were huddled together in a group like urban refugees drinking vodka martini cocktails and turning their noses up at the décor which just wasn't avant-garde enough. Pauline, who had at one time fancied himself as an art student and wondered if he had artistic leanings, was put off by their enclosed and cliquey air, although there were a couple of normal art students who had broken away and were getting pissed at the bar.

Three-quarters of the assembled company couldn't wait for Dogmeat to finish, but the rest were ecstatic, and the noise could be heard at the White Rock Pavilion just over the road from the pier, where people were being treated to a panto with a couple of vaguely recognisable minor celebrities off the telly.

The Old Town fishermen, friends of Mark's, were at two tables playing drinking games and were out of their heads before eight thirty. They only normally went to places where there was a huge amount of alcohol and the opportunity to start fights with other groups of people they didn't like. At the moment they were eyeing up the art students and wondering if it wasn't just a little bit too easy. They also thought that as a group they could perhaps all take on Mad Mick and then rather sensibly decided against it.

Almost everyone under the age of twenty-five had had some chemical assistance to get them through the evening. A fisherman called Stuart had brought along enough speed for pretty much everyone at the party and as some of the slightly older ones such as Sid and Nanna were likely to refuse, some people were having seconds, which did not bode well for the general mental health of the party.

After Dogmeat had finished their final song, 'Smash It Up' by the Damned again, they filed off and Dave, who was carried away by the moment and by a bottle of red wine, shouted, 'I love you, Rachel, and I'm glad I'm marrying you.'

Only two people heard it, one of them being Rachel, despite the fact she was saying to Susan, 'Has Mad Mick hit anyone yet?' She stopped in her tracks and glowed. The other person who heard Dave's words was Sally, Dave's one-time lover who Rachel had met in the Anchor on the Claudio night. She had sneaked in with a fisherman who was very keen on her. Before Dave had even left the stage she flew at him like a rabid cat, nails out, and managed to get him on the floor.

'Oh look,' joked Vince, 'Dave's got an eager fan,' and he and Terry laughed until they realised about six blokes were trying to drag her off without much success.

Rachel was about to join in when Dick grabbed her arm. 'Don't get involved, love,' he said. 'They'll sort it.'

By 'they' she realised he meant Clive and Alan who, along with some of their bouncer mates from Brighton, had hauled Sally off and were transporting her above their heads like a coffin, out through the door where she was dumped on the boards at the end of the pier. As soon as they had disappeared, she vaulted over the locked gate and got in through a door further up.

For a brief period while Phoenix prepared to do their set, the DJ played a selection of Christmassy songs. At last Nanna and Sid got a chance to move in and sway a bit, as did Terry and Vince, and Barry and Helen. Helen was dubious and felt that dancing in front of Dick was rubbing it in too much.

'Come on,' said Barry, 'he looks very relaxed,' as he led her into the middle of the floor.

At this point Dick was saying to Pat, 'If he dances with her in front of me, I'm going to give him such a punch in the face.'

'Come on,' said Pat. 'It's your daughter and my son's engagement party, don't spoil it for them.'

'All right,' said Dick. 'I'll punch him tomorrow,' and had another Guinness.

Terry had not seen Helen for ages and found that whatever she had been drinking had made her extraordinarily bitter when she thought about the antics of 'the patronising bag' as she called her. Then she found herself badmouthing Helen to Vince in a very unexpected way.

'Look at the silly fucking cow,' she said. 'Who does she think she is, parading her new man in front of us all like a prize bull?'

'Mm,' nodded Vince. He was thinking about how much the cleaners would have to do in the morning.

Finally, Phoenix arrived onstage to play the standards that most people actually hate but tolerate because they think everyone else likes them. They struck up with 'Hotel California' and Mark immediately joined in with, 'Mirrors on the ceiling and pink champagne on ice' as loudly as he could manage.

'Fuck me, listen to him,' said Pauline to Rachel. 'She's got to put up with that for the rest of her life.' Pauline seemed on edge. He looked up at the ceiling a couple of times.

'Are you OK?' said Rachel.

'Yeah, fine,' said Pauline. 'Having a sooper-dooper time, dahling,' and waltzed off to the bar in his huge white boiler-suit with many bells sewn on.

'Ding dong poof,' said Mark as he disappeared.

The end of the evening was fast approaching for some, earlier than others, as Matron gathered together her charges ready for a wheel down the pier in their chairs. Mad Mick had parted company with them some two hours earlier and had got well and truly stuck into numerous Bloody Marys, his favourite drink. Rachel hugged and kissed them all, and apologised that no one had sung something they might like. Over someone's shoulder she saw the face of Stefan, who had definitely not been invited since the spiking incident, and he caught her eye and started to run.

Oh fuck it, she thought. I'm not going to chase him.

After Phoenix had trampled a few more middle-of-the-road tunes and finished their set by assassinating Slade's 'Merry Christmas', Dick, who had swallowed six pints of Guinness, stepped onto the stage.

'Quiet everyone,' he said and the DJ turned down 'I Saw Mummy Kissing Santa Claus'.

Oh dear, thought Rachel in a panic. What's he going to do?

'I just want to say very quickly how glad I am that my daughter has found a very nice bloke to marry, and to welcome him into the family. You're all right, Dave mate,' he said, thumb-upping at Dave, who smiled back. Terry was pushing Vince forward and he climbed rather clumsily onto the stage. Susan looked around for Mark.

'And *we're* really pleased too for Susan and Mark,' he said. 'Let's all raise our glasses to . . .'

'Just one more thing,' interrupted Dick. 'I'm sure you all know my wife Helen and what's been going on since she left me for that fucking—'

At that point he was rugby-tackled by Pat and they both fell backwards through the curtains, where Sally had been hiding drinking a bottle of red wine. Dick fumbled the curtains closed.

Suddenly, 'I Saw Mummy Kissing Santa Claus' was whacked up to full volume. Pauline ran on to the stage.

'Happy Christmas, everyone!' he screamed. 'Long live punk rock.' He made a sign to the DJ and a deluge of glittery snow plunged from the ceiling, accompanied by a huge inflatable Father Christmas who landed on the stage and sat bolt upright, allowing everyone to see that he had an enormous erection.

A shocked squeak ran across the crowd. Some laughed, some tutted, pretty much according to age, but the general feeling was that it was in very bad taste. Mad Mick, whose three happy childhood memories included two concerning Father Christmas, was most upset and roared as he made straight for Pauline who, seeing him coming, headed out of the door onto the walkway as fast as his little fat legs would carry him.

Helen and Barry Nesbitt got in a cab, Barry unscathed for once. Nanna caught Sid's teeth as they dropped into his Guinness and Dave and Rachel looked at each other and laughed.

The night seemed to be at an end and people began to leave as the loud Christmas music continued. The fishermen happily trailed the art students as they left. Terry tried to pour a few more drinks down her throat and Vince tried to stop her.

Outside, there were some loud bangs and everyone ran to see that Pauline, who had disappeared by now, had saved a bit of money for a couple of rockets which, launched by one of his lieutenants, climbed and exploded in the wintry sky, saluting another shift in Rachel and Susan's lives.

The next morning, well after noon, Rachel opened her eyes with the terrible realisation that she was going to be sick. She made it, naked, to the bathroom and positioned her pounding head at the right angle.

Dave came in behind her. 'I'm not sure I want to marry you now,' he said.

'I don't blame you,' said Rachel. 'What a fucking brilliant night though, eh?'

'Amazing,' said Dave. 'Where's that Pauline with our breakfast? He promised.'

'I'll call him,' said Rachel. She looked into the front room where he should have been snoring on the sofa. There was no sign of him.

'He's not here,' she said, feeling worried. 'I'll just ask Dad if he saw him at the end of the party.'

She knocked on her dad's door and opened it. Clive and Alan weren't there but she could see her dad's shape in the bed and then another head popped up beside him.

'Hello,' said the head. It was Sally. Not quite the romantic rehabilitation Rachel had hoped for her father.

Unable to say anything positive, she shut the door again and said to Dave, 'My dad's in bed with fucking Sally.'

'But is your dad fucking fucking Sally?' said Dave.

Rachel laughed and then returned to Pauline's absence. 'Where could he be? He doesn't really know anyone except those two young guys. Do you think he's with them?'

'Oh, I expect so,' said Dave. 'Don't worry, he'll roll up soon enough.'

They were just getting in the bath together when the doorbell rang. Dave put a towel round his torso and opened the door. Dick and Sally were busy. A policewoman stood on the doorstep, the same one who had accompanied Rachel to the station some years ago.

'Yep?' said Dave in a rather surly manner, since he was not a great fan of Her Majesty's police force.

'I'm PC Elaine Beckett. Can I come in, please?' said the

WPC betraying no emotion, not because she was professional but because that was her nature.

'All right,' said Dave, showing her into the empty front room where Pauline should have been.

Rachel appeared in a dressing-gown. 'What is it?' she said, immediately fearing the worst because that was what she was like. She thought someone was dead. Dave assumed Dogmeat had committed some drug offence and given Rachel's address.

'We've found a man's body under the pier and we understand you had a party there last night,' said WPC Beckett.

'Who is it? Oh Christ, it's Pauline,' said Rachel, clutching Dave's arm.

'I said, "a man",' said the policewoman.

'Pauline *is* a man,' said Rachel. 'It's a joke name.'

'Is Pauline a homosexual?' the officer asked.

'Yes,' said Rachel and wanted to add, 'Are you?'

It seemed WPC Beckett had forgotten about their encounter in the van after Rachel had hit the detective at the T. Rex gig, or perhaps she would have suspected Rachel of foul play.

'Is your friend Pauline' (she said it with distaste) 'a big fellow?'

'Oh dear, yes,' said Rachel and reached for Dave's hand.

'We may have to ask you to come and identify the body,' said the policewoman.

Rachel started to cry and Dave put his arm round her. The doorbell rang.

'I'll go,' said Dave.

Outside in the street stood Susan with a very bedraggled-looking Pauline. Dave led them through to the front room. When Rachel saw Pauline, she flung herself at him, weeping.

'Bloody hell,' said Pauline, 'the Christmas deccos weren't that bad.'

'You're alive,' Rachel managed to say.

'Barely,' shivered Pauline. 'I've spent all bleeding night on that pier under a tarpaulin, too fucking terrified to move.'

Susan said, 'He got chased by Mad Mick. He doesn't like gays.'

'Doesn't like is the understatement of the year,' said Pauline. 'I thought he was going to kill me. I was running round outside in the dark with him after me like King Kong shouting and screeching. Didn't you hear?'

'No,' said Dave, Rachel and Susan.

'Thank God he gave up eventually,' said Pauline, 'but I thought he might be waiting to ambush me so I just stayed where I was. You were all so pissed you obviously didn't even notice I'd gone.'

They all nodded, even WPC Beckett.

'So who is the body in the sea then?' asked Rachel.

Epilogue

The body in the sea turned out to be that of Mad Mick Mason. Fuelled by Special Brew and amphetamines, he had decided after being unable to find Pauline that he would go back to the party. Finding that the door he'd come out of had banged shut and couldn't be opened, he'd walked round looking for a way in, only to come up against a blank wall. The one way round this was to gingerly step along the outside of the handrail, with the sea directly below him, and then swing back over, onto the main walkway. Halfway along, given his level of inebriation, he stumbled and plunged headlong towards the freezing water, observing to himself on the way that this was quite a laugh.

A collective sigh of relief was expelled by the bullied of Hastings, whose lives had just got a little bit easier now Mad Mick was no longer around. Even his mum thought Christmas would be less frightening.

Rachel felt ever so slightly sorry for Mad Mick Mason. 'He didn't deserve it,' she said to Dave.

'Bullshit,' said Dave. 'If anyone deserved it, he did.'

'Why don't you ask *me*?' said Pauline, coming into the room with a plate of crumpets. 'The fucking twat had it coming to him with knobs on. All the Hastings poofs'll tell you that.'

Rachel and Dave got married on 13 February 1980 with Pauline as best man. Helen and Barry had a little boy they called Matthew. Dick and Sally went off travelling together and Mark and Susan split up in the summer, a month before their wedding. Susan was relieved.

'Good fucking riddance,' she'd said to Rachel, relishing the swearing as they sat drinking coffee and eating Aztec bars in Rachel's front room. It was her front room now because they'd they'd taken over the flat from Dick and Helen.

'Will you be OK?' asked Rachel.

'Oh yes,' said Susan. 'I've just had a letter from Italy. I'm off to see Luca tomorrow.'

'I'll miss you,' said Rachel.

'Bollocks,' said Susan.

'Can I tempt you to one last dance, madam?' Rachel enquired.

'Go on then,' said Susan. Rachel put on 'Smash It Up Part 2' by the Damned and the girls went fucking mad pogo-ing and kicking the furniture. For exactly two minutes and fifty-nine seconds, they threw themselves into a joyous frenzy of sweat and mayhem. Then suddenly it was quiet and the madness was gone. Through the almost eerie silence came a thump above them and a fleck of plaster floated down from the ceiling as a voice upstairs bellowed, 'Shut that bleeding noise up, you silly tarts.' Susan and Rachel laughed for a long time.

Sorting Out Billy

JO BRAND

Sarah is besotted with the unpredictable Billy. But after another 'accident' involving his temper, Sarah's face and a night in A&E, Sarah's friends Martha and Flower decide that it's time to take action. What should they do?

- Reason with him?
- Send him to Anger Management classes?
- Shoot him?

Martha and Flower have issues of their own: Martha is seven months' pregnant by one of three possible blokes; and hippy Flower's career as a stand-up comic is more sit-down and weep after some nasty encounters with south London's finest hecklers. Will Martha survive single-motherhood on a council estate in need of a peace-keeping force? Will Flower find the perfect put-down? And will they sort out Billy before he gets to them first . . . ?

SORTING OUT BILLY is an hilarious novel about the things we do for love and the elaborate combat strategies we devise when it all goes wrong. Jo Brand gives as good as she gets in a novel as sharply observed as it is eye-wateringly funny.

'A smart stylist with a confident narrative voice. An accomplished comedy of bad manners' *Observer*

0 7553 2030 1

review

Driving Big Davie

Colin Bateman

Dan Starkey – journalist of ill repute, international man of inaction – is happily reunited with his wife Patricia and determined to keep out of trouble.

But the sudden death of punk icon Joe Strummer and the impending nuptials of his old friend Davie Kincaid combine to send him off on an American Odyssey.

Or extended stag night.

But Dan, with fantasies of Florida sun, sea and girls who fancy a bit of freckle, is in for a rude awakening which involves a massive deception, mayhem, violence, robbery, Al Capone's gold and a very severe case of sunburn.

IF YOU HAVEN'T READ A COLIN BATEMAN NOVEL BEFORE, THIS IS WHAT YOU'RE MISSING

'Fast and furious . . . Laugh-a-minute lad lit' *Daily Mirror*

'A fast-paced, violent tale of law-breaking brilliance' *Zoo* magazine

'Extremely funny, brilliantly dark, addictively readable and possibly Colin Bateman's best book to date' *Loaded*

0 7553 0921 9

headline

If you have enjoyed **It's Different For Girls**, you may enjoy the following titles also available from your bookshop or *direct from the publisher*.

FREE P&P AND UK DELIVERY
(Overseas and Ireland £3.50 per book)

The Haven Home for Delinquent Girls	Louise Tondeur	£7.99
The Mysteries of Glass	Sue Gee	£7.99
Secrets of a Family Album	Isla Dewar	£6.99
Atlantic Shift	Emily Barr	£6.99
The Distance Between Us	Maggie O'Farrell	£7.99
Green Grass	Raffaella Barker	£6.99
Jaded	Lucy Hawking	£6.99
Amazing Grace	Clare Dowling	£6.99
The Woman on the Bus	Pauline McLynn	£6.99
Play it Again?	Julie Highmore	£6.99
Two of Us	Brendan Halpin	£7.99
Fame and Honour	Jincy Willett	£6.99
Spit Against the Wind	Anna Smith	£6.99
Sorting Out Billy	Jo Brand	£6.99
The Bad News Bible	Anna Blundy	£6.99
The Secret Life of Bees	Sue Monk Kidd	£7.99

TO ORDER SIMPLY CALL THIS NUMBER

01235 400 414

or visit our website: www.madaboutbooks.com

Prices and availability subject to change without notice.